The Avestan Prophecy

by

E. Cooper Ostresh

 www.trafford.com

North America & international
toll-free: 1 888 232 4444 (USA & Canada)
phone: 250 383 6864 ♦ fax: 250 383 6804 ♦ email: info@trafford.com

The United Kingdom & Europe
phone: +44 (0)1865 487 395 ♦ local rate: 0845 230 9601
facsimile: +44 (0)1865 481 507 ♦ email: info.uk@trafford.com

10 9 8 7 6 5 4 3 2 1

Acknowledgements

I wish to thank Laura Cave and Cornia van Rensberg for helping with editing. Cornia has also been especially helpful in encouragement and constructive criticism. Thanks, Cornia!

Thanks also goes to my Dad, Dr. Lawrence M. Ostresh, Jr., and my Stepmom, Wendye Ware for their input and encouragement and all the help they've given me.

Also thanks to my mom who helped with editing and encouragement.

Finally, my thanks go to Sam, the German Short Haired Pointer who was my mom's dearest companion, for being the inspiration for one of my favorite characters.

PROLOGUE

VAFA BURIED IT deep. Finally, after twenty years, he felt safe enough to bury it. He'd been at this site now for over two months and not a soul had passed by or even come close, so he felt this was the safest place to leave it. He knew he would never leave this place alive and when he was gone, well, he could only hope that no one would ever find it. This would be its final resting place: deep inside a cave, high in the mountains near the most eastern shore of this land. This country was primitive. The few people he had seen had been farmers, but there would be no farming on this mountain top and no one to enter this cave.

After he buried it, he piled rocks on top and then more dirt to make it look natural. He couldn't chance an animal finding it either. He sat down exhausted and began to reminisce about his life. For more than twenty years this thing had been his life. He'd been a warrior for his king in the most beautiful, civilized land in the world, Persia. He had a wife and son and life was good. And then Alexander happened. This power mad young man couldn't be satisfied with taking over his father's place and ruling Macedonia. He had designs on the whole world. All of Persia knew he was planning to expand his empire to the entire known world. His ambition was endless.

Just after Alexander defeated the Persian army at Granicus, King Darius III summoned Vafa. Vafa had never met the King privately before. He was a loyal soldier and would lay down his life for his King, but he was unsure why he was summoned when his commanding officer was not. He was ushered into the King's personal chambers and quickly prostrated himself before the King.

"Rise, rise, my son." The King was sitting at a small writing table with his Chancellor Mahdad standing near him. Vafa stood but kept his eyes lowered wondering what error he had committed, something he had done or something he should have done.

"Vafa," the King said. "Son of Hami, the Protector. Your name means 'loyalty and faithfulness.' You know this?"

"Yes, Sire." Vafa was still unsure where this was going.

"And are you loyal to your king, Vafa?" The King had leaned forward as if to pierce Vafa's soul with his eyes.

"Yes, Sire."

"Yes, yes," the King now looked at Mahdad. "My general tells me you are most loyal." The King stood and walked over to Vafa, lifting Vafa's face to look directly into his eyes. Vafa kept his eyes downcast as looking directly into the eyes of royalty was not allowed, but the King protested.

"Look at me, Vafa. Look into my eyes."

Vafa looked directly at the King and the King studied his eyes carefully. Vafa felt he must have committed some great evil for the King to be speaking with him like this.

"I see fear here, Vafa. Are you afraid?"

"Sire, my fear is that in some way my Lord is displeased with me. To displease you, my Lord, would be my greatest sin."

The King released Vafa's face and turned back to Mahdad. "Vafa, it is not I you must fear. I would have your loyalty and your courage for a task that must be fulfilled."

Vafa almost sighed out loud as the realization hit him that the King was not displeased with him but merely testing him to see if he would perform some special job.

"My Lord has only to ask and I will lay down my life." Vafa bowed as he said this.

"It may require that, my son. It may require that." The King sat at the table again as Mahdad went to a large chest near the wall.

"You know that this Alexander is attempting to conquer the world," said the King.

"I know he is near, my Lord, but I also know that King Darius III leads the world's greatest army. We shall show Alexander that we are not to be taken lightly," Vafa said proudly.

"Yes, yes, and I hope you are right. But there is something here that Alexander desires perhaps more than anything else. Something that has been guarded by my father and his father before him and his before that. Something that no one else in the world should ever have." As the King spoke, Mahdad had taken a wooden box from an ornate chest sitting near the king's chair and placed it on the table before the King. He opened it and pulled out something wrapped in a dark cloth. He set it down and opened the cloth and Vafa saw the largest pearl he had ever seen in his life. It was a black pearl, rare enough but the size of it was huge. It was at least as big as Vafa's fist and it sat in a metal holder of some sort.

"My Lord! I've never seen anything like this." Vafa came close and thought he saw a light coming from within the pearl.

"This is not an ordinary stone," Mahdad said. "This stone contains the spirit of an evil that could take over the world. In the hands of someone like Alexander, it would not stop its evil until no living soul was left."

"But, my Lord, it has been safe here for these generations. Why should we now risk taking it away?" Vafa could still not take his eyes off the huge pearl.

"Alexander's forces are mighty and he grows stronger. He has defeated us at Granicus. We cannot risk that he will defeat us again. If that should happen, there would be no stopping him from getting this." The King had actually pulled away from the stone as he spoke. "If your predictions are correct and we should be able to turn him back, you may return to our country and I will once again secure and guard the orb, but for now, we must get this as far from Alexander as possible. Do you understand, Vafa?"

"Yes, my Lord. What would you have me do?"

"You must take it far from here. You must go to the ends of the earth and you must not let anyone know what you carry."

"Yes, my Lord."

"And Vafa," Mahdad was wrapping the orb and placing it back in its box. "You must not even tell your wife your mission. You must also know that if Alexander is able to continue his conquests, you may not have a home to come back to."

The King and Mahdad both looked at Vafa now to make sure he understood the seriousness of his task.

"You need to leave right away, Vafa." The king handed him the box. "I have had provisions and horses made ready for you. You have only time to say goodbye to your wife and son. It may be best to go east as far as you can."

And with that Vafa had taken leave of the King. He held this box with its strange orb inside and after being given the horses the King had prepared, he stopped by his house just long enough to say goodbye.

He remembered now how his wife had wept. He told her that if he did not return in five years time she should think of him as dead and to tell his son that he had died a warrior serving his king and country. She wept and promised to do as she was told but begged him to return to her. He remembered holding her for the last time and telling her "If I do not return, you must find a new husband. Find a man who will not beat you and who will be good to our son."

He wondered now if she had done so. Did she ever think of him? Was his son a good man? Did he know of his father? When he left, he traveled east through the Hindu lands, hoping all the time that he would receive news that Alexander had been defeated. Instead, he learned that Alexander had conquered Persia and had gone on to India as well. Vafa kept moving east, seeing other humans only when necessary for tools or weapons and sometimes food. He'd lived off the land and his horses had been his best and only friends. Even after he heard about Alexander's death, it seemed the world was in such chaos he dared not try to return.

Now as he sat thinking over his life, he felt the sadness again. Loneliness had always been a companion for him but it had been much worse this last year since both of his noble friends had succumbed to old age. He also knew he felt loneliness more now because he too was nearing the end of his life. It was only natural that he would look back and wonder what his life might have been. He had no regrets about having served his King. Even after Darius' fall to Alexander and his disgraceful retreat after the battle at Issus, Vafa comforted himself with the knowledge that even if his King had ultimately disgraced himself, Vafa had not. Vafa had been given a task by his sovereign and he kept faith with his promise. He knew that he would have an honored place in the afterlife and he was content with that.

But now, he needed to eat. He had worked hard all morning burying the orb and felt satisfied that this was the right place to keep it safe through eternity. He had also buried the scroll on which he'd written of his journey since he left Persia. He lifted his tired bones and aching muscles, took his fishing spear and went outside into the warm afternoon air. The sun was late in the sky and with the coming of evening, the fish would be eagerly snapping up the insects that played on the water. Vafa walked the half mile to the mountain stream, taking care to always use a different route so as not to wear a noticeable path in the landscape.

He heard the stream before he saw it, gurgling and bubbling over the rocks and cascading its way down the mountain to the sea. The water was clear and fresh and cold and the fish were fat and tasty. He sat by the stream, poised motionless, waiting for just the right moment to send his spear into the fish that would do him the honor of becoming his dinner. He was concentrating so hard on the fish that he didn't hear the crunch of the leaves behind him until it was too late. Before he even turned his head, the tiger was upon him, snapping Vafa's neck as it hit him. Vafa was dead before he even hit the ground.

Chapter 1

The most merciful thing in the world, I think, is the inability of the human mind to correlate all its contents. – H.P. Lovecraft

THERE ARE CERTAIN moments in a person's life that no amount of mental or physical training can prepare you for. Soldiers spend months, even years training to kill and avoid being killed in a battle. Extreme skiers train to quickly locate and rescue a friend captured in an avalanche. But, until that first bullet flies past your head, or you watch in horror as a friend gets buried under a ton of snow, you will never know if you are up to the challenge. F.E.M.A. had no idea how truly bad it was at its job until Katrina hit. And now Hugh Luminaire and his boss, Jack Dorn, found themselves in a similarly critical moment in their lives. What made this a particularly horrific moment for them was the fact that they were monster hunters and at the present time they were staring at a monster.

The two stood frozen in fear. A good twenty feet from their truck on a dark moonless Arizona night, they had come across a recently killed cow. Panning across the body with the narrow beam of a mini-mag flashlight, their eyes and brains began to process the easily identifiable features first; the glazed eyes of the lifeless cow, the bell collar that had been ripped from the cow's neck, and finally, the three distinct quarter sized wounds on the cow's neck. The blood still flowed freely from the wound and Hugh was about to comment that they must have just missed the attack when he became aware of another pair of eyes staring at them. Hugh realized those eyes had always been there, hovering just above the dead cow, but it took some ten seconds before his brain registered that fact.

Slowly, Hugh's brain processed more of the scene. Most predatory eyes appeared green or yellow when illuminated in the night, but these glowed red. They protruded from a grayish, almost reptilian skin that covered a doglike head. Two large fangs plunged down from the mouth while one smaller fang pointed up. Though the rest of its teeth looked like a dog's, these three teeth gave the monster a viper like appearance. The rest of the hairless body was shaped like a dog but the size of a lion. A series of boney protrusions running from the base of its skull along the spine to the end of the tail made it look part dragon. Hugh Luminaire and Jack Dorn had come to the Sonoran Desert of southern Arizona to find the legendary Chupacabra and to their shock and horror they had found it.

The monster stood motionless until it realized it had been spotted. Then it reacted. It stood from its hunched position, opened its mouth and gave out a dull hiss. At that moment, horror replaced the shock that Hugh and Jack had been experiencing. Hugh's fight or flight reflex kicked in, giving him a powerful urge to run, but he forced himself back to a rational state of mind. He knew this animal could overtake him in seconds. In his short career as a film cameraman, he had mostly done wildlife shows, several of them about large predators. His training in dealing with these animals had taught him some safety tips. He tried to ignore the glaring red eyes, the three inch fangs and the unearthly grayish skin and see the creature as just a wild animal and not a demonic monster.

"Jack," he said in a calm, quiet voice.

"Huh?" Jack squeaked out.

"*Don't* run!"

"Ahh. . . .okay," Jack said feebly.

The creature hissed again and took a step forward. This could be the beginning of an attack and if Hugh didn't get this right, one or even both of them could be dead in an instant. With his camera hanging by the strap from his shoulder, he dared not move to get it in place until he could deflect the beast, so he simply stood taller and held his arms and flashlight as high and wide in the air as he could.

"Whoa! Whoa! MONSTER! I'M RIGHT HERE!" He said it as loudly as he could and still remain calm. "Easy, boy!" He then countered the monster's move by making one small step forward. Outwardly, he made every attempt to look large, powerful, and ready to fight. He hoped the monster couldn't smell fear.

It seemed to work. The Chupacabra and Hugh stood in a stalemate, "Jack, I want you to slowly, very slowly, sidestep towards me with your arms as high as you can make them. Look big!"

"Okay," Jack wasn't sure this was a good idea, but Jack's expertise had been covering the war in Iraq. Since he had never done nature shows, he bowed to Hugh's experience and hoped it was right. Jack was no coward but this took more courage than he knew he had. Somewhere the thought flashed through his mind that if this didn't work, he'd be just as dead as if a bullet went through his brain but the bullet sounded better than being ripped to shreds by a monster.

Once the two stood side by side showing a united front, the Chupacabra slunk its shoulders and took one step back. Hugh wasn't sure what this meant. If a wolf dropped its shoulders, it usually meant submission but if a bear dropped its shoulders, it meant it was preparing to charge. Since prevailing science didn't even acknowledge the Chupacabra existed, there wasn't exactly good information available. Hugh waited a second and then backed up ever so slightly and inwardly sighed when the animal didn't advance.

Hugh then very gently began to lift his camera to capture the animal before it was out of sight but once he lowered his arms, the animal turned and ran.

"Shit!" said Hugh.

"Let's go!" Jack was already running for the truck to chase after the creature before he got too far away.

The sun was beginning to peak on the horizon and they could see the dust trail heading south. They jumped into the truck and Jack had it started and moving before Hugh even got the door closed.

"Get the camera rolling, Hugh! We're just going to have to shoot and hope we get him in frame somewhere." Jack was a pretty good off road driver and Hugh knew they were just seconds behind the beast but, filming while driving under these conditions was not going to be easy. Jack's truck, a Toyota off road 4x4 pickup with a three inch lift kit and upsized tires was good but maybe not the best for driving this terrain.

Jack had peeled off the gravel road onto the shallow arroyo where the cow lay. As the truck leaped up on the opposite side of the arroyo, it caught some air and Hugh banged his head on the roof.

Hugh was trying to watch through his camera lens but the field of vision was greatly reduced. In order to keep up with his prey, he looked up several times.

"Right! Go Right! I see his dust trail going off that way!" Hugh tucked the camera to his eye again to follow the dust trail. Jack had to swerve to avoid a Saguaro cactus. Driving off road in the Sonoran Desert was no small task. While the ground was caliche and mostly devoid of grass, the desert was rife with many forms of cacti and bushes, many which could ruin a tire with a single puncture. Some of the creosote bushes were ten feet high and almost as wide and the Saguaro, the king of all cacti, stood between 10 and 20 feet high. They were thick and heavy with water and could weigh more than a pine tree of the same size. The most difficult area was the arroyos. These were drainages that filled with water in the monsoon season but were barren gravel pits the rest of the year. They ranged in sizes and could be wide and shallow, narrow and deep and anything in between. Worst of all, at the speed they were now traveling, Jack couldn't see them coming until they were diving down into it or soaring above.

The truck crashed through some smaller bushes and was airborne into the center of a wide arroyo. Jack quickly checked for the best exit and the truck lifted up and after the prey. Hugh caught sight of an animal out of the corner of his eye.

"There it is!" he yelled as he panned the camera onto the blurry image of a running animal. Jack matched speed with the creature allowing Hugh to get a clearer focus. "Shit! It's just a coyote." Hugh looked away from the camera to search again for the dust trail.

"There! To the right!" said Jack.

Hugh glanced off quickly and put his camera up again. He could see glimpses of the dust trail through his view finder but there were always too many bushes in the way to see the Chupacabra. Just then the truck was airborne again and Hugh felt himself being tossed upwards. The slam down on the other side of the arroyo jammed the camera into Hugh's eye and he was momentarily blinded. Just then, Jack put the brakes on and slowed to a stop.

"What?" asked Hugh as he looked at his boss with a very red and watery eye.

"Look," said Jack as he pointed behind them. Hugh saw that they had just sailed over a large wide arroyo that they might easily have gotten stuck in. "This is not happening today, my friend. One more like that and if we don't kill ourselves we'll probably be taking a very long walk home."

Hugh couldn't respond to his boss. He knew Jack was right but it was heartbreaking to watch the Chupacabra's dust cloud slowly disappear into the sunrise.

Chapter 2

THE DAY WAS warm, the air clean and the view of the Mediterranean from his balcony, captivating. Lee Bondurant was enjoying his espresso with a pastry and the newspaper. The scene was reminiscent of a Cary Grant movie of the sixties, with Lee every bit the handsome sophisticated international man of mystery that Cary Grant always played so well. At forty-one, Lee was just over 6 feet tall with a slender but muscular build. His short cropped black hair was peppered with gray. He had on beige Armani slacks and a short sleeved white silk shirt that looked stunning on his mocha colored skin.

Ever faithful Sam was lying at his feet, enjoying the warmth of the sun warmed tile on the floor. Sam was a German Short-Haired Pointer, completely liver colored, or as Lee preferred "chocolate velvet". Sam was comfortable in any of Lee's homes, whether it was the "cabin" in the Colorado Rockies, the cottage at Cahirciveen, County Kerry, Ireland, or the villa here in Manarola, Italy.

The villa was not huge, certainly not by American standards, but nothing in Manarola was exactly huge; there simply wasn't enough land for it. But the view and the weather made up for any inconvenience in size. His home was built into the cliff side and his balconies overlooked the Mediterranean Sea. He had three bedrooms on the upper floor, each of which had balconies on either side, one overlooking the sea and one overlooking the courtyard that seperated the living room from the kitchen. The living area on the lower floor walked out onto a larger patio that also overlooked the sea. The house was very comfortable for Lee and Sam and big enough to have Lee's son, Jim, and friends visit. He loved that after the renovations, the house looked as if it had lived in this hillside for nine hundred years. It was classic Italian down to the tile.

Even though Lee could afford a household staff, he didn't really like having people around all the time. His only concession was to have a housekeeper who came in twice a week for cleaning. She also took care of the place while he was away.

Lee did much of his own cooking but preferred eating out for dinner. Manarola was such a haven for tourists, foreign and domestic, that it had many wonderful little restaurants sprinkled around the hills. Of course, he could bring Sam to any of them which is what he also loved about Europe.

While in Manarola, the daily routine was up at 6:00 a.m. for a two mile walk up and down the hills, which were pretty steep and made for a good work out. They finished their walk with a quick swim in the little inlet at the base of the cliff which Lee's villa crowned. Back home by 8:30, they would fix breakfast and sit out in the courtyard or on the balcony to eat and relax. Today had been the very same kind of routine and the comfort and peace this place and this routine gave them was priceless. Well, maybe not priceless since it had cost a minor fortune to buy and renovate the old villa but Lee always knew it was well worth the money spent.

He finished with the local paper and had just picked up his *Wall Street Journal* when the phone rang. Lee had to step back into the bedroom to get the phone and as he picked it up he looked at the number out of habit. It gave some odd numbers which told him it was probably an international call. He thought maybe it was Jim who was at Oxford attending school.

"Pronto," answered Lee

"Lee? Is it you?" came a familiar voice.

"Yes, who is this?"

"It is Sam Da Soo from Korea."

"Oh, Jonesy! It didn't sound like you. How are you?" Da Soo and Lee had been roommates and colleagues back at University College, London, where Lee did his graduate studies after his Bachelor's degree from Howard University in the States. Since Sam Da Soo and Lee were working on doctorates in archeology when the Indiana Jones movies came out, Da Soo had been nicknamed "Jonesy" by his fellow students because he was the adventurous one of the group. He didn't mind the nickname since it was a sign he'd been accepted into this small group of very brilliant and energetic young scientists.

"It's been too long since I've talked with you!" Lee took the phone back to the balcony and sat down in his chair. Sam looked up but was content to go back to sleep.

"I know, I know, my old friend. I am very bad at sending email or calling. I keep very busy." Jonesy and Lee had kept their friendship alive long after college days and had even worked a few digs together. The other members of their little group had gone on to other things and occasionally would see each other at conferences and such but Jonesy and Lee clearly had a special bond that continued. They both shared a passion for antiquities, especially those surrounding the myths of ancient folk magic.

"Well, I understand. So what have you been up to these days? I think the last time we talked you were working a dig near Busan?"

"Yes, but recently I've been working a site near Sokcho on the East Sea. I just unearthed something I think you would be interested in seeing."

"Really? Well, you've got my attention. What is it?"

"Lee, I can't really explain over the phone. It's quite unique and I really would like you to come to Korea to meet with me and I can then show you and discuss it with you." Jonesy sounded very nervous but then he was a bit of a "kook" and obsessive compulsive about many things. Still, he was someone that Lee had always found trustworthy and a good friend.

"Sounds very cloak and dagger, Jonesy, but you know I'll come. When do you want to see me?

"The sooner, the better. I can call and book a flight for you tomorrow if you can leave then?"

"No, don't worry. I'll have my pilot bring us in my plane. Should we fly into Incheon?

"Oh, I forgot. Yes, my rich American friend has his own plane now." Da Soo had always regretted not going into business with Lee right after college. Lee had made several million dollars on an internet company and sold out before prices dropped. Lee and his wife had cleared a cool 40 million which got divided during the divorce, but Lee was still wealthy enough for all he needed.

"Come to Incheon. Right now I'm in Seoul doing research at the university so I will just wait until you arrive. Can you call me when you know what time you will be landing? If you can make it tomorrow evening, perhaps we can just leave from Incheon."

"Well, my pilots will need to sleep. It's a long flight."

"Of course, I forgot. I'm sorry."

"No, no—we'll just plan to stay at the hotel at the airport. There's a Marriot there, yes?"

"I think so."

"I'll call and book rooms for us for tomorrow night. We should be able to leave here this afternoon and arrive sometime tomorrow. Does that sound okay?"

"That is wonderful, my friend. I look forward to seeing you again."

"It will be good to work on a project together again. I've been much too lazy of late so this will be great."

"I don't think you'll be disappointed," said Jonesy.

"I'm sorry I'm not stateside. I could stock up on some Cheezit's for you." Lee laughed remembering his friend's one weakness for American junk food.

"Oh, that would be nice but I have been getting them from time to time."

"Really?" Lee remembered his trips to Korea and while it was now a very modern country and one could get a lot of things, Western foods were still strange and a bit difficult to come by.

"We'll talk about it when I see you."

"Okay, see you soon, buddy."

"Thanks, Lee. Thanks a lot." Da Soo hung up.

"Well, Sammy, looks as if we are off on another adventure. You up for that, Pal?" Sam perked his ears up and put his head in Lee's lap, letting him know he was ready for action. Lee scratched behind his ears and neck and then picked up his phone and dialed his pilot.

Chapter 3

SAM DA SOO clicked his phone off and sat back in his chair and breathed a huge sigh. He was about 5'8" and trim but with a muscular build. He was sitting in the library at Seoul University, so was dressed in his black suit with orchid shirt and dark purple tie. When working in the field, he wore jeans and T-shirts or sweatshirts with his leather jacket and Fedora as per his name sake but, once in the city he dressed properly for a scientist and University professor. Having lived in England for many years, his English was very good and he did his studies in both the ancient texts in Hangul as well as ancient English works. It made his study much more thorough but even at that, he knew he needed his friend to help him decipher just what he had to do now.

Sam Da Soo was obsessive about a lot of things; Cheezit's just being one of those things. He also refused to drink water unless it was bottled and when possible he preferred the bottled water from JeJu Island. He bought cases of the stuff and carried it with him on his travels. He was obsessive enough about his notes and his work that he had never had time to have a romantic relationship. His mother had lamented that until her dying day and Da Soo was not happy that he had let her down but he couldn't take the time to court a woman and then spend time with a family. At least he had a younger brother who had carried on the family name.

Now he found himself obsessing on his find. He closed his books and went back to his apartment where he quickly changed into more comfortable clothes. He had brought some take out food and put it out on the table in the living room but, he couldn't restrain himself any longer. He opened the wall safe behind the piano and carefully removed the wooden box. He set it on the table where he'd put his food and sat down cross legged on the floor. Gently, he opened the box and began moving the packing materials aside. He reached in and pulled out a round object covered in a dark blue velvet cloth. The object was heavy and he laid it carefully on the box lid and gently unwrapped it. The blue black of the orb was almost luminescent. It seemed alive to Da Soo and he wondered if he were infusing it with so many hopes and dreams that it was coming alive for him. He hoped it was what he thought. Certainly the age seemed right. His preliminary tests of the object showed it to be at least 8000 years old, however the site itself seemed to be more recent so there were many unanswered questions.

He began eating his food, kimchi, jap chai and rice and just kept looking at it. It was not perfectly round, but looked like a natural black pearl except it was the size of a softball. It rested in an intricate metal worked holder inscribed with glyphs he'd never before encountered. That was why he needed Lee to see it. He knew the value of this find was priceless. Even if it was nothing but an unnaturally large pearl given to some ancient queen, it was immensely valuable because of its age as well as the intrinsic value of a stone this big. But Da Soo believed this was much more than just a pearl. That, too, was why he had to have Lee come. If this was what he believed it to be, he needed someone with Lee's ability in Arcanum to help him unlock the secrets.

As he turned the orb over in his hands, he suddenly felt dizzy and decided he needed sleep. He had been at the library for twenty hours straight. He was exhausted. Carefully, he wrapped the orb and packed it once again in its wooden box and placed it back in the wall safe. When he replaced the wall tile, the safe was virtually invisible. He then moved the piano back in front of that. Da Soo had his apartment equipped with this special safe and a special alarm system when he bought the place five years ago. The nature of his work meant that sometimes he would be in possession of priceless artifacts and while he usually kept those at the university, he often felt uncomfortable leaving things so precious out of his control.

When he was sure all was secure, he finished his food, cleaned up his clutter and got into a warm shower to help him relax. Once he finally crawled into bed, he was asleep almost immediately.

Chapter 4

ERIK SCHANTZ PULLED trim up on the nose of his C-1 trader as he made final preparations for the landing at Wonju airport. A C-1 trader was a nice sturdy, if somewhat aged, airframe. It was a classic retired military aircraft that had somehow been overlooked by most collectors of old military planes. This was fortunate for Schantz since he couldn't afford a bidding war with a warplane collector.

There were a few reasons that a military surplus C-1 could still be found cheap. First, it was a cargo plane. Most collectors were looking for old fighter planes or bombers. The only cargo plane that had become popular was the C-47; most likely, because it was the plane that delivered the paratroopers at Normandy. The next most prolific buyers of retired military craft were firefighting units. Still, the C-1 had been overlooked primarily because fire aviation tended to look for airframes that already had a bomb door. Many WWII bombers had initially been acquired by the fire services but now those agencies more commonly used some form of anti-submarine warfare craft. Indeed, the S-1 Tracer was the ASW variant of the C-1 and most of the available airframes had been snatched up by the fire services. So the sturdy airframe of the duel engine turboprop C-1 was still available at a cheap price to someone who knew what the hell a C-1 was.

Erik knew exactly what a C-1 was. He had spent the last six years flying the C-1 Trader's successor, the C-2 Greyhound. The C-1 and C-2 respectively were the only planes in the history of aviation to be designed specifically for Carrier Onboard Delivery or C.O.D. The job of the C.O.D. pilot was to deliver needed supplies and personnel to the super carriers of the United States Navy. It was an essential job that garnered all too little credit to the aviators who flew them and the airframes in which they flew.

The C-2 had been designed not only to carry the cargo but also to survive the impact of over 5,000 carrier landings. The pilots who flew C.O.D. often had more carrier landings than the fighter pilots that Tom Cruise had immortalized in "Top Gun." Erik had been one of those C.O.D. pilots and because of that, he realized the old C-1 he saw parked in a plane graveyard in Greybull, Wyoming, was a gem. The company that owned it was going to strip it for spare parts as needed for their S-1 but when Erik offered twenty grand in cash, they saw it as a bit of a windfall and took the deal. With another ten thousand for modifications and renovations, a few months later, Schantz had himself an airplane that could start making him some money. He called her the Pegasus and had a caricature of the famed winged horse painted on the nose, a symbol reminiscent of his Navy squadron. For his intended purpose, it was a bonus the plane was tough enough to handle some of the roughest landing strips in the world.

While it was nice to know that his airplane had such capabilities, it was fortunate that the Wonju Airport was not a rough backwoods airport. In fact, it was the perfect place to deliver shipments into Korea. Korea is a hilly and sometimes mountainous country. While there are no mountains that rival the Rockies, there also are not many open plains as in the US Midwest. In short, land in Korea is at a premium. Any flatland in the country is usually highly populated. In aviation terms, this meant that remote airstrips were few and far between. Any that existed were heavily monitored by Korean military, American military or Interpol. Agents of these entities were constantly on the lookout for Chinese Snakeheads transporting refugees to the US or Taliban drug lords exporting their heroine to the Pacific North West.

Wonju Airport was not exactly remote. It handled over 80,000 passengers a year. Not a lot of people in the grand scheme of international airports, but enough to preclude too much attention by authorities. It was located 90 miles east of Seoul, South Korea's largest city. This meant that it was not so small as to attract the attention of the police and not so large as to incorporate state of the art security devices. In fact, for a smuggler like Erik, it was the perfect airport for shipments into South Korea.

After landing his Trader, Erik taxied to the oldest, and sleaziest section of hangars. The hangars and adjoining buildings were ½ cylinder aluminum style structures that the Army Corps of Engineers had built all throughout Korea during the war. Two of the hangars and three smaller office structures still remained on this section of the airport. It was home to one of the few private aviation clubs in Korea. Private pilots rarely flew at night and so the old buildings became something of a meeting place for nefarious peoples after the rich business men went home from a day at the tarmac. Of course, the place was guarded but the private security guards were easily bribed to look the other way so long as the planes and equipment they were paid to protect were left unmolested.

Park Bin Dong was a flunkey employee of the man who had hired Erik. Since Park had done his two year military duty in the Korean Air force, he was always picked to guide Erik in to his parking spot. Bin Dong's compulsory military service had been spent in janitorial duties at an administrative building so Erik never really paid attention to his flapping and waving of the

E. Cooper Ostresh

orange flashlight batons. Erik simply parked the plane where he thought best and began winding down the engines.

After the propellers had stopped and Bin Dong gave the thumbs up that the plane was chalked, Erik finished his post flight check and exited the aircraft. Erik had a stocky build with muscular arms that stretched the sleeves of his shirt. He had a ruddy complexion with blue eyes and a mop of disheveled dark blond hair. His body type and facial features were every bit characteristic of his Prussian heritage. The only characteristic that detracted from his otherwise good looks and athletic build was the extra twenty pounds he carried around his mid section.

He wore the trappings befitting his current profession. After six years in the stuffy regulation uniforms of the U.S. Navy, he had let go more than just his gut. He had tossed out his old flight suits in favor of more comfortable cargo pants like those worn by the carrier deck crews. The pants he wore today were actually cutoff just above the knee. After years in an environment where the only shoes allowed were the aviator brown dress shoes and combat boots, he had promptly purchased his first pair of outdoor sandals. He was now wearing his Chaco hiking sandals that he had hardly taken off in his nine months of civilian life. He even wore them in cold weather with a pair of wool socks. His shirt was a short sleeved green plaid button down shirt manufactured by an outdoor clothing company. Casual was the key word for Erik these days. He hadn't worn a belt, a dress shoe, or tucked in his shirt in the last 9 months. The only article of clothing that he still had from his Navy days was his full brim khaki dress hat. He had pulled the innards out of it so it had the floppy look of McHale's Navy. Stepping from the airplane in the humid summer air of the Korean peninsula, Erik Schantz had modernized the stereotypical cliché that was the smuggler pilot.

"Elique! Dung Head!" cried Bin Dong the moment Erik stepped from the plane. Erik snapped his gaze to Bin Dong. He really didn't like this guy. Bin Dong was trying to be a snappy dresser as was the current norm for well dressed Korean businessmen. However, Bin Dong was doing it on the cheap. He wore a cheap looking gray silk business suit and a baby blue shirt with a white collar topped off with a pink necktie. It was fashionable for Korean men to wear lots of color in shirts and ties but somehow Bin Dong's attire just didn't make the grade.

"Shit head!" Erik replied to him.

"Buayo?"

"It's pronounced 'shit head' not 'dung head'. Dung isn't a curse word. Shit is," Erik said laughing. He loved it when Bin Dong tried to curse in English. In the last few months of trading with Koreans, he had realized that most were incapable of properly swearing in English. Erik hadn't decided if that was a good thing or not.

Bin Dong responded by swearing in Korean and while Erik's grasp of Korean was not great, he could tell he was being trashed.

"Here paawk!" Bin Dong said pointing in front of his feet. "There, no! Here!" It was the same argument they had each time Erik flew in. Bin Dong wanted Erik to park where Bin Dong said, not where Erik decided even though the distance between the two spots was barely ten feet. Erik decided it was a matter of "saving face" for Bin Dong but Erik didn't much care about Bin Dong's face. He'd met him through an old friend of Erik's from Montana and while Erik didn't like Bin Dong personally, Bin Dong had introduced Erik to Hallil Naziff who was the man that now hired Erik on a regular basis. So like it or not, Bin Dong was a fact in his present world.

"Get over it, Bean. Where's your boss?"

Just then, he saw Nariff's shadow emerge from the closest hangar. He saw a light flicker from a cigarette before Nariff emerged from the shadows into the dim light of the evening street lamps.

"Right here, Mr. Estrada."

Erik knew Nariff pictured himself as some sleazy gangster from an old Humphrey Bogart movie, but it amused him to try to picture it. Nariff was a short wiry Pakistani about 5'6" tall. His dress was subdued by Bin Dong's standards, since he wore nice brown slacks with a button up light brown shirt and no tie. He had on a green nylon pilot's jacket that was hemmed at the waste. The angular features of his face were highlighted as he pulled a drag of the thin cigarette in his mouth.

"*Thank God for international trade*," thought Erik. "*Without it Phillip Morris would be starved of one of its last great markets: Asia.*"

"Smoking will kill you, Hallil," Erik said as he spit a wad of chewing tobacco on the tarmac.

"In thirty years, my friend," Hallil smiled. "Tell me, Mr. Estrada, what gangster lives to see thirty years of business?"

"You." It wasn't a compliment to Nariff's brilliance as a criminal mastermind but more of a reality check Erik liked to toss in his face. Erik simply couldn't imagine this guy being important enough to ever get himself "rubbed out." Despite the sparring they always engaged in, Erik and Nariff liked each other.

"Fuck you, Erik," mumbled Nariff.

"Got to pay me first," smiled Erik.

Nariff stood quietly pulling a drag from his cigarette. He nodded to Bin Dong from across the tarmac. Bin Dong retreated to his Hyundai parked close by and returned with a briefcase. He walked forward and set it at Erik's feet.

Once Bin Dong backed away, Erik knelt to inspect the contents. Several nice bundles of worn and unmarked Euros: five thousand of them to be exact. Erik insisted on Euros and not American dollars. Since the Iraqi war, it had been more stable to do business in Euros and was certainly more portable than the won or the yen.

"Looks good to me. Want to see what you bought?"

"Of course," replied Nariff.

Erik set the money bag back on the ground. It was customary in smuggling circles for each side to inspect the goods before taking possession. He walked to the back of Pegasus and opened her rear hatch ramp. Nariff and Bin Dong moved in to see the contents. Erik unloaded sample boxes of each of the products: a box of Marlborough cigarettes, a box full of Copenhagen snuff chewing tobacco, and a box of Bicycle playing cards. Erik didn't have big ambitions in his new career. If he wanted to make millions, he would have gone into smuggling guns, drugs, or people, but making those millions also meant you had to deal with real gangsters and potentially with real hard time should you get caught. Erik preferred dealing with a small time hood, this time a Pakistani businessman who owned several of the few foreign food stores in Korea. Tariff smuggling wouldn't make you rich but it could keep you flying. His biggest worry about getting caught wasn't jail time, it was having to lose his plane.

Each of the items Erik had on display would fetch a hefty price in Nariff's stores, one of which was in the Itaewon neighborhood of Seoul. It was an area rife with Western expats who would pay a healthy price for a taste of home. A can of Copenhagen chewing tobacco that would sell for $5.00 in the US would bring in $14.00 in Itaewon, a can of refried beans that would cost less than one dollar US sold for close to five here.

The fact that each of the parties involved was guilty of nothing more than tax evasion didn't stop them from their own delusions of grandeur. Nariff got to think of himself as a tough street gangster and Erik fancied himself as a Han Solo action hero.

"Okay, Mr. Estrada. Where is the real shit?" asked Nariff.

"Help me unload the rest of the tobacco and I'll show you."

The three men worked quickly to unload the first group of pallets. There were two large cartons of miniature marshmallows, three cartons of Licorice Nibs, two cartons of grated Parmesan cheese and box after box of cards, cigarettes and tobacco. But then came the real prize of the trip. The tobacco products were an item sought after by many US G.I.'s stationed in Seoul, but the mother-lode of the expedition appealed to all the salt-starved foreign nationals in Korea; Canadian and American English teachers, U.S. soldiers, and Western diplomats alike all yearned for one thing above all else in a land where garlic bread and potato chips were generously doused with sugar: Cheez-its! There at the back of the cargo hold, were cartons upon cartons of the little gold treasures.

"You have done well, my friend. Can I buy you a beer?" asked Nariff. After the long flight, that was exactly what Erik wanted to hear.

"You bet. Let's get this crap unloaded and hit the town," smiled Erik. Then he cocked his eyebrow at Nariff, who was not only his employer but a decent drinking buddy as well. "Uh, does Been Dicked have to come, too?"

"BIN DONG! My name is BIN DONG! You dog son sex mother!" cried Bin Dong.

Nariff and Erik quietly chuckled together. Erik slowly turned to face his nemesis, "I think you mean 'son-of-a-bitch, mother fucker!'"

Chapter 5

L EE'S PILOT, HANK Miller had said they would be ready to take off by 2:00 p.m. that afternoon. Hank and Janice, his wife, were a team and they were each other's co-pilots as well as a great married couple. On long flights like this, one of them would nap in the back for at least four hours so they could relieve each other. Lee's plane was small but luxurious and efficient. The main cabin had 4 of the sleeping suites now common on Singapore and Korean airlines. The galley was small but certainly large enough for the small plane. Lee had never had more than six people on board at a time; the two crew and four passengers. Usually, it was just Lee, Sam, Hank and Janice.

Hank and Janice, who were employed full time by Lee, kept the plane provisioned and mechanically sound and ready to go at a moment's notice. That's why he paid them a combined salary of $150,000 a year. He also liked them as people. They were both very smart, very capable and had more than once come to his aid in crisis situations. They also could be trusted with any information that Lee might not want made public. It was these qualities that caused Lee to have them assist him in many of his projects. Anytime Lee made a big discovery, he shared any profits with Hank and Janice. They were in every sense of the word 'family'.

Lee gave his housekeeper, Maria, a call to let her know they would be gone for a few days and then packed for the trip. He usually brought more books than clothes on trips like these although he knew Jonesy would have a lot of the research materials they needed. Still, he always had some books that he took on every trip. Some reference manuals he kept copies of in the plane at all times but when he had special reference materials he would bring it along. He also had equipment in the plane to do some types of field testing.

When they were packed, Lee and Sam walked the little distance to the train. There were no cars allowed in or out of Manarola and while there were a few local vans to transport tourists to and from the train, Lee and Sam enjoyed the short walk. Once on the train, it was a twenty minute ride to get to La Spezia where Lee housed his plane at a small airport.

Janice was waiting with the car at the station and opened the door for Sam to get in the back while Lee put his bag in the trunk.

"Everything ready?" asked Lee

"Of course. We'll have steak tonight with a fresh salad. Hope that is okay."

"Sure, sounds good. We haven't had steak in a while."

"It's too expensive this side of the Atlantic, even for you, boss!" Janice was laughing as they drove through the crazy Italian traffic.

"Well, probably good. We're eating healthier here."

It took a half hour driving through traffic to get to the airport, longer than the ride from Manarola to La Spezia by train. Once there, Janice parked the car in the hangar that was owned by Lee's corporation and they all boarded the small jet.

"Hey, Boss." Hank was under the plane doing last minute checks.

"Afternoon, Hank."

"Hey, there, Sammy." said Hank as Sam eagerly greeted Hank. "Your coach awaits, sir." He was talking to Sam, of course, and stepped aside giving Sam the grand entry to the plane.

"Gee, wish I could get the red carpet treatment like that." laughed Lee as he followed Sam onto the plane.

"Yeah, well some of us are just more special than others." said Janice as she followed them on board.

"At least someone recognizes my true worth," said Sam. Sam was Lee's familiar, an animal shaped spirit used to help the wizard perform magical feats. Among other things, Sam had the gift of speech and wasn't shy about using it. Lee said Sam also had the gift of sarcasm but Sam insisted that was a well developed skill learned from years of study at the master's feet.

Sam jumped up in his seat and Janice attached his harness and got him secured in the chair for take off. He gave her a big lick once she clipped him in and she scratched his ears and smiled.

"A special steak for you tonight, sir." She said.

"Woof" said Sam in anticipation of a special dinner.

" 'Woof', my ass," chuckled Lee. "It's a long flight, Sam, so we might as well get comfy."

Chapter 6

LEE HAD CALLED Jonesy from the plane as they were nearing the Incheon airport. He gave him the landing gate and so was not surprised to see Jonesy waiting as they passed through customs. He was surprised to see how he looked, though. His friend of twenty years had always been a neat freak, compulsive about his appearance as well as his work and food. Now, he looked disheveled and probably had not shaved for a couple of days. He was in a sweatshirt and sweat pants which was extremely unusual for Jonesy who was always neatly attired as a proper Korean business man should be.

"Jonesy?" Lee said as he walked forward and took his friend's hand. "Are you okay?" Lee noticed Jonesy's hands felt clammy and the look in his eyes was not the same.

"I'm okay, Lee. I think I caught a virus or something. Just not feeling very well."

"Well, maybe you need to go to the doctor and we'll hang around til you are okay." Lee was genuinely concerned because even when sick, Jonesy never let his appearance go like this. Besides that, Lee was astounded at how much his friend had aged. It had only been about 3 years since they'd been together but Jonesy seemed to have aged ten years. Lee put his hand on Jonesy's shoulder to lead him through the terminal.

Sam was uncharacteristically quiet around Jonesy and did not do his usual happy greeting but Lee thought it was because he was a bit miffed at having to be on a leash. They went outside the terminal and found Jonesy's car and climbed in.

"Lee, I had planned on taking you out to dinner but I'm not really feeling up to it." Jonesy started the car.

"No, that's okay, Jonesy. Do you want me to drive? I mean you really don't look well."

"I said I'M FINE!" Jonesy snapped.

Sam growled and Lee was startled at his friend's sudden anger.

"Okay, okay" he said as he reached back to pat Sam on the head and let him know it was okay.

"I'm sorry, Lee. I'm sorry, Sam." Jonesy wiped his forehead which was suddenly wet with perspiration. "Let's just go back to my place where I can show you the orb and if you want food, we can call up and have it delivered."

"An orb?" asked Lee. "It's an orb you found?"

"Yes."

"Where did you find it?"

"In a site in Seorak, near Sokcho on the East Sea. Lee, I think this thing may be 8000 years old."

"What does it look like?"

"It looks very much like a black pearl but it is huge." Jonesy was getting very animated now. "It has a metal holder of some kind that certainly can't be that old so must have been added later but. . .well, you just need to see it."

"So what was the condition of the site? Had it been disturbed that you could tell?"

"No, I think it was a clean site and everything I've pulled from it gives me dates of about 2000 years ago, probably 2 or 300 BC but I'm sure the orb is much older." Jonesy kept wiping his forehead and swerving in traffic as he sped along the highway.

"Okay, well we can . . . .WHOA!" Lee said as he reacted to a near miss on the highway. "Hey, Jonesy, are you sure you should be driving right now?" Lee didn't mind speed and in fact he loved driving fast on the Riviera roads that clung to the sea cliff but Jonesy was making him very nervous.

"I'm sorry, Lee. I'll slow down–yes, we must get home safely." As he said it, he exited the freeway and turned left under the overpass. "My apartment is just there." He pointed to a complex of tall apartment buildings and once through the gate, drove into the underground parking garage.

They took the elevator to the 23rd floor and Jonesy let them in to the apartment on the left. He kicked his shoes off as he entered and Lee did the same. He took Lee's bag and led Lee and Sam down the hallway to the room that was obviously set up as a guest room/study. He switched on the light and put Lee's bag on the bed.

"I know this isn't much but you and Sam are welcome to stay here rather than a hotel if you want." Jonesy still looked nervous and seemed anxious.

"Thanks, Jonesy. Let's see how you are feeling in a bit. Might be better for Sam and I to go to the hotel and let you get a good night's sleep."

"Come, come and see this." Jonesy was heading back into the main living room that was open to the kitchen. On the wall opposite the entry door was a solid wall of glass overlooking the city. A narrow balcony extended the length of the glass and a sliding door gave access to the balcony area. There was a fireplace on the right side and on the opposite wall sat an upright piano and a large uncomfortable looking sofa. In front of the sofa was a very sturdy coffee table.

Lee watched as Jonesy pulled the piano out from the wall and pressed a wall tile behind it. The tile popped open to reveal a safe. Jonesy spun the combination lock a few times and finally clicked the handle to open the safe door. He pulled out a wooden box about 8" deep and 10" square. He then put the box on the coffee table and sat on the floor cross legged.

"Here, sit," Jonesy said excitedly still sweating. Lee sat on the opposite side of the table on the floor with Sam next to him. They both watched intently as Jonesy began to unwrap his find. When Jonesy had placed the orb in the lid of the box, he took the blue velvet covering off and sat back to observe Lee's astonishment.

"My God, Jonesy. What the hell have you found?" Lee was overwhelmed with a thousand questions all popping into his head at once and yet he heard that little warning bell in his head that usually told him something wasn't right.

"That's what I wanted you to come help me find out," said Jonesy. Jonesy's sweating had stopped now and he suddenly seemed quite calm and in control again. He lovingly caressed the orb as he stared at its beauty.

"When you said 'huge pearl' I was envisioning something marble sized. I never imagined anything could get this big . . .I mean a stone or a pearl. This is amazing. Is it a pearl?" Something kept Lee from even wanting to touch it. He felt as if he would get lost in it if he actually touched the orb.

"I think so, but can you imagine the size of an oyster that would produce this?" Jonesy was continuing to caress and fondle the thing as he would a loved one.

"I know this sounds crazy, Lee, but I think . . .I think this is a dragon orb. I mean a real dragon orb."

"Whoa! Jonesy," Lee looked at his friend in disbelief. "That is crazy! We've never been able to prove these things ever existed. What makes you think that? I mean it's probably just a very expensive trinket for an ancient lady of nobility. Why jump to the conclusion that it's a dragon orb?"

"I don't know, Lee. It's just instinct but the size of it, the markings–look, look at this metal work on the holder. It is beautiful." He was holding the orb in both hands, now holding it so Lee could see the metal working that served as a holder for the orb.

"But, wait, Jonesy. I thought you said this thing might be 8000 years old. This metal work can't be that old. That's not possible. At least not according to what we know of human development." The earliest metal working that Lee was aware of dated to 5000 BCE. This would change the age estimate quite a bit.

"I know, but the tests I've run on the pearl itself seem to suggest it was here much earlier than the metal holder. I'm thinking the pearl had been around and when it finally came to rest in the hands of a culture that knew metal work, the holder was made."

"So they might be two different ages." Lee was thinking out loud.

"Maybe three." Jonesy said. "My initial estimate of the site was that it was maybe 200 or 300 BC."

"So we're talking about two or more different cultures. I mean maybe the pearl was not original to the Korean peninsula. Maybe it was traded here or something." Lee wanted to hold the thing but something told him not to touch it.

"I suppose that's possible but I think it probably was discovered here and through the old magic was imbued with the power to bring the Imoogi to her full potential–a dragon.

"I know that dragons in the West were always seen as evil and malevolent creatures," Jonesy continued. "But in the east, the dragon has always brought good fortune and prosperity. To bring forth the dragon from her rest or from her lesser forms, that of an Imoogi, you needed a magical orb. Nothing in what I've read ever describes the orb but many of our ancient art work shows a dragon holding a pearl in one claw. So this seems to fit into that legend."

"So what are you saying? That if the orb is held by the creature it becomes a dragon?"

"Something like that."

"So are you thinking of holding on to it and turning into a dragon?" Lee wasn't sure how Jonesy was envisioning this thing.

"Not me. I'm not an Imoogi but I think if we can summon the Imoogi and give her the pearl, she could become the Dragon. I need you to help me do that, Lee."

"Bark! Bark! Bark!" said Sam. "What the hell are we trying to raise a dragon for?"

"Yeah, and correct me if I'm wrong here, Jonesy, and I know I'm from the West with the tradition of the evil dragon, but how do we know that 'bringing forth' your dragon would be a good thing? I mean we're talking about tremendous destructive potential, you know." Secretly, of course, Lee was excited about the possibility. No one in modern times had ever seen a dragon. We had finally convinced ourselves they never existed at all except as fictitious creatures, used to scare the populace into giving over power and resources to the lord of the land: protection games circa the middle ages.

But if he *could* summon an Imoogi and *if* she did turn into a dragon–well, WOW! What a find! What an experience! From the corner of his eye, he caught Sam staring at him. He looked at his faithful friend and Sam gave him a look as if to say *"are you totally nuts?"* Sam always seemed to know what he was thinking before he even thought it.

"And they eat dogs, don't they?" Sam asked. "Like their cousins, the crocs?"

"Well, yes," said Jonesy, "but so did my mother and she was a pretty nice lady."

"Okay, let's not get sidetracked here, guys," Lee interrupted. "Just explain to me why we are even contemplating this?"

"We are contemplating it because we are seekers of truth and wisdom and we are contemplating it because if we can accomplish this, the Dragon can bring so much order, so much healing to a world broken into fragments by hate and poverty. Look at what North Korea is doing? The dragon could reunite my country under a President, not a dictator. Isn't it worth trying to do that?" Jonesy continued to stare into the pearl and seemed transfixed by his own words.

"Jonesy, I can't tell you that the thought of being able to resurrect a real dragon isn't intoxicating but I have this little voice in the back of my head saying 'danger!' I don't know that either of us have the ability to stop something this powerful if it goes awry."

"Dammit, Lee! This is the find of a lifetime. Imagine what we could do with this?"

"That's the problem I'm having, Jonesy. Imagining what *this* could do."

"Well, that's why you have to help me—so I can do it right and find a good Imoogi. Because here's the thing, Lee, whether you help me or not I am going to keep trying to find the Imoogi. I am going to try to bring out the Dragon."

Lee looked at his friend and saw someone other than the Jonesy he knew and trusted.

"Calm down, Jonesy. Calm down. I didn't say I wouldn't help you. I'm just uncomfortable with the whole notion of deliberately trying to bring a dragon to life." Lee now felt trapped. He knew he had to help because his friend seemed to be quickly losing control. If he wanted this to have a good outcome, he needed to try to steer the investigation in the right way.

"Okay, okay. It's just such an important discovery." Jonesy was holding the thing close to him now and his face was reflected in the light off the orb. "Look, it almost seems alive."

Sam was still giving low growls and seemed very uneasy. Lee put his arm around him and petted him, trying to reassure him. Lee was disturbed by his friend's actions but didn't want to make him angry.

"Yes, it seems to have power in its own right," said Lee, noticing that it appeared as if some of the light was actually coming from within the stone and not all of it from the outside. Still he did not want to take it into his hands for fear of its potential power. "Look, Jonesy. This is a stunning development and one that we will work on together, okay?" He wanted to divert Jonesy long enough to make a graceful exit so that he and Sam could go meet with Hank and Janice and talk this over without Jonesy around.

"Yes, yes," said Jonesy. "Thank you, Lee. I do not think you will be sorry."

"I hope you're right, pal. Look, I'm going to call a cab so Sam and I can go back to the hotel. I think you need to get a good night's rest and in the morning we'll hook up again and you can tell us what you think the first step should be for our research. Is that okay?"

"Yes, okay. Yes. I do need to rest. I have not been well. I need sleep and rest."

"Yes, Jonesy. I think you do."

"Let me call a cab for you, Lee."

Lee was grateful for that because he still did not know much Korean. He could say a few things but getting a cab and letting him know where to take you was not easy. Jonesy put in the call and Lee heard him say "Marriott." Hopefully they would not have any problem getting where they needed to go. He and Sam picked up their belongings from the guest bedroom, leaving Jonesy at the table still staring and caressing the orb.

"Do you want me to get you some dinner before we go?" Lee asked.

"I do not feel like eating, but thank you, my friend. I will get something in a minute."

"Then call me in the morning when you get up, okay?" Lee asked as he and Sam went to the door to leave.

"Yes, of course," Jonesy said absently while still sitting at the table looking at the orb. Jonesy would never have allowed them to leave without getting up and showing them to the door. It just was not polite and Jonesy was every bit a true Korean gentleman genetically engineered with politeness. But he remained seated as Sam and Lee let themselves out the door.

"Good bye, Jonesy. I'll talk to you tomorrow." Lee said as he closed the door behind them.

"Whoa, Sammy, what have we gotten ourselves into this time." Lee pushed the elevator button.

"There was a presence there that I did not like," Sam said.

"Was it from the orb or from Jonesy?" Lee asked his very special friend.

"It seemed to be from Jonesy but it definitely was stronger when he was holding the orb. I felt something when we first met him and it was stronger when we got in the car but then when he got the orb out, it was stronger still. It was not a positive force." The elevator arrived and Sam quit talking in case there were people in the car. The door opened and two little girls giggled when they saw him and reached out to pet him before looking at Lee. Lee smiled and nodded his approval and they petted Sam and gave him a hug and giggled and jabbered on in Korean before exiting the car.

"They really have the cutest kids." Lee chuckled as he and Sam got in the elevator and pushed the down button. A man got on at the next floor and they all rode down to the lobby in silence.

Chapter 7

B Y THE TIME Lee and Sam got to the hotel, Hank and Janice had checked in and left a message at the desk for Lee. Lee and Sam took the elevator to the 10th floor and found their room was a connecting suite to Hank and Janice's. Lee knocked on the connecting door and Janice opened it.

"Hi, boss. Honey, Lee and Sam are here," she called out to the other room in their suite. "Come on in. We were thinking about getting dinner. Have you eaten yet?"

"No, but I think I'd like us to get room service so we can talk about what just happened," said Lee as he came in and sat down on the sofa in the living room.

"So was it good or are we in for a wild ride?" Hank stepped into the living room looking as if he'd just showered and shaved. He was 38 years old, about 5'10" with a stocky build. After starting to go bald some years back, he finally just shaved his head. He was wearing a comfortable white cotton T-shirt and a pair of khaki cargo shorts with flip flops on his feet.

"Could be a wild ride." said Lee.

"So fill us in." Janice was an elegant looking woman, six years older than her husband. She was 6' tall with an athletic build, trim and muscular. Her close cropped hair was all gray and made her even more attractive. She was dressed in a beige T-shirt and khaki cargo pants with leather sandals. Her only jewelry was her simple gold band that was her wedding ring, a gold locket with a Celtic knot design and small gold stud earrings. She poured two cups of coffee from the in- room coffee service and brought one to Lee and the other to her husband.

"Thanks, babe," said Hank as he took the cup and sat in the easy chair.

"Thanks, Jan," said Lee accepting the cup and setting it on the table in front of him to cool. Lee leaned forward, elbows on his knees and then rested his face in his hands.

"Uh, oh," said Janice as she got her own cup of coffee and sat down on the other end of the couch. "This is the 'oh, shit we are really fucked now look'. I hate it when you get that look."

"Yeah, well, guess what? Oh, shit-we-are-really-fucked-now," said Lee, smiling at her but knowing she was right. Janice and Hank had known him so long they could read his expressions pretty well. He was usually able to keep things from other people but not from these two.

"So, what's the deal?" asked Hank.

"Okay, Jonesy has made a find that is extraordinary." said Lee

"And where's the 'but'?" asked Janice.

"The 'but' is he thinks it is a dragon orb and he wants me to summon an Imoogi to turn into the Dragon." Lee reached out and picked up his coffee

"What's an 'Imoogi'?" asked Hank.

"A mythical Korean serpent. Kind of a baby dragon, I think. When it's given a dragon orb, it becomes a full blown dragon."

"Oh, well, that doesn't sound so bad." Hank's sarcasm kept them all from taking themselves too seriously at any one time. "I mean, we'd all like to see a dragon, right? So why not? Course I'd advise stocking up on fire insurance but,"

"You mean he's serious about this?" asked Janice.

"I mean he's very serious about it." said Lee

"Lee, that's just nuts. I mean there really never were dragons were there? Isn't all that just a myth?" Janice tended to be very rational in thought and while she accepted some psychic phenomena as real, she was definitely in the skeptic category. She always said it was because she was born in Missouri–the "Show me" state.

"Well, I thought so but..." Lee started.

"But, if Lee can summon an Imoogi and we can actually turn it into a dragon, think how incredible that would be," said Sam with more than a little disdain in his voice.

"Okay, Okay, Sam. I admit the thought intrigues me. It would be a tremendous accomplishment but. . ."

"But you might be responsible for introducing yet one more evil, possibly-destroy- the- world- type- thing that might not look so good on your resume?" said Hank.

"Well, it can't be done anyway," said Janice, "so what's the problem?"

"Yeah, okay. Yes, Hank, it would be a real downer to do this and have it go bad–bad karma, bad resume–and all the rest. And I don't know, Janice. It might be possible."

"That's why it is something we shouldn't even try." said Sam.

"So that should end the discussion, yes?" said Hank.

"It should except that Jonesy is determined to do this with or without us." said Lee.

"But he can't, can he?" Hank asked. "I mean he's not a summoner, right? So how could he pull this off without you?"

"By finding someone else who would do it. Maybe someone not as honorable as our favorite boss man," said Sam.

"Yeah," said Lee. "I guess that's why I feel we're up the creek without a paddle. If I refuse to do it, he's so obsessed right now, he'll find someone and that could be even worse. I think we need to be there with him so that in case this is possible to do, at least maybe we can steer it in the right direction or even end it quickly if that is necessary."

"I hate to agree," said Sam, "but seeing the way Jonesy was obsessed with this thing, I think we do need to be there for protection and hopefully to add some rationality to the process."

"So what does this entail for us?" Janice had gotten up to refill her coffee and leaned back against the cabinet.

"Well, Jonesy is supposed to call in the morning. I'm going to suggest we meet him for breakfast to see if he's still bent on doing this and if so, then I think we need to go to the site where he found the orb. I'd like to check out the surroundings myself and see if there is anything else that gives us clues to this thing. I'm going to do my best to stall for time in the hope that he'll snap out of this delusion he's in right now. I don't know all the details yet, but we can work them out as we go."

"So what kind of equipment are we going to need for this little venture?" Hank was the man of action and it was often his quick reflexes that kept them from getting into perilous situations or getting out of them once there.

"Well, I think we need to all become familiar with the Imoogi legends. I'm sure Jonesy will have some reference materials. Beyond that, I suggest we take some fire power with us, Hank. You never know where this may take us."

"Okay, I think I can handle that.'

"Stock us up on food and water provisions, too, will you? And make sure we have medical supplies. Let's try to be prepared for all contingencies."

"I'll take care of that, Lee," said Janice.

"How about getting some food right now?" said Hank. "I'm starving!"

"Sounds good. If you guys can order in, I'll go get a shower." Lee stood up and headed back to his room.

"Will do," said Hank.

Sam jumped up on the couch to nap while the others bustled about.

Chapter 8

HUGH LUMINAIRE WAS back from the field and working in a quiet editing room in Hollywood, California. Hugh was about 6'1" and had a lean wiry appearance. He fit the bill of a hippy cameraman. He had shoulder length black hair that flopped on a few rows of beaded necklaces. He tended to wear hemp sweaters and ripped jeans but in hot weather the sweater was replaced with a ratty T-shirt that had some form of political slogan. In fact, Hugh had three different versions of the Che Gueverra T-shirt. His hobby since high school had been climbing and as such, he had developed the peculiar musculature that was common amongst climbers. He had strong shoulders and a heavily muscled back although his chest was relatively undeveloped. His forearms were almost the size of his biceps giving him a Popeye like appearance.

While at film school in U.C. Berkley, he took extended weekend trips to the big walls of the Yosemite Valley. He began filming his buddies climbing many of the difficult routes around the valley and by the time he was done with college, he already had lead camera credit on several low budget, climbing inspiration videos. He quickly moved from that into better paying jobs with various wildlife shows. Within two years, he had garnered a reputation in the documentary community as a guy who was willing to put in long hours in difficult weather conditions to get footage of some of the world's most elusive predatory animals.

The editing room Hugh and his bosses were sitting in was being rented out by the "Truth Seekers" syndicated documentary show. Truth Seekers had capitalized on a T.V. formula that had first been made famous by Leonard Nemoy's ground breaking "In Search Of" TV series. Truth Seekers tried to investigate unexplained phenomena throughout the world by using a blend of documentary reporting, scientific analysis, pseudo-scientific hypothesis, and even mythological explanations. Since "In Search Of" many TV series and TV documentaries had followed, but most of them differed in that they searched for only one aspect of unexplained phenomena.

Truth Seekers was an attempt to return to the original formula. For starters, Truth Seekers examined phenomena in many different areas of expertise. There were paranormal investigations, UFO investigations, and investigations into undiscovered species, such as the Loch Ness Monster, Big Foot, and the Chupacabra. The other key element of the formula was that Truth Seekers' editorial staff was keen on maintaining some journalistic objectivity in fields of study that were very divisive. The executive producer of the show made sure to give equal interview time to believers and non believers alike.

Jason Spurlock was that executive producer. He had great success on a cable show where a team of magicians set about debunking a lot of popular myths and it was then he realized that skeptics were just as interested in UFO investigations as believers, so he decided to make a show that would appeal to both. One of the keys to the success of the show was hiring its host, Jack Dorn. Dorn was respected amongst his peers for his unbiased reporting in both Afghanistan and Iraq. He was respected by the TV watching public because of his rugged good looks that made him look dashing either clean shaven and in a tuxedo or with a two day stubble in battle fatigues. Jack was the show's lynch pin that gave it credibility. Because of this, it was important to keep him from looking like a flake.

While all this made sense from a business standpoint, it was heartbreaking for Hugh to listen to the decisions being made in the editing room.

"Okay, look, guys," began Jason as he addressed Jack and Hugh. "You're going to need to reshoot Jack's first hand experience dialog. We can't have our host going out on a limb claiming that the Chupacabra is real without clear photographic evidence."

"But Jason," protested Hugh. "Just give us another week in the Sonora and maybe I can get some better footage."

"No can do. " Jason looked at the young cameraman with pity. "Look, kid, I know it's a raw deal but we don't have the time here in TV land. Jack has to catch a morning flight to Ireland for the Killarney Ghost episode. Then next week I need both of you in Scotland for our Loch Ness episode."

Jack took the news like the seasoned professional he was. The two journalists had been very close to the biggest discovery in Taxonomy since the confirmation of the Mountain Gorilla over 100 years ago. But he had been in this business long enough to know that it really was a business. There were sponsors to please and a schedule to keep.

On the other hand, Hugh was new to TV and its dollar and cents mentality. He was more interested in covering something ground breaking than rehashing stories that were unlikely to provide results, "Nessie? Gaddamnitt Jason! People have been covering Nessie for the last 80 years. If we haven't found her yet she probably doesn't exist!"

"Hey, Nessie sells. No self respecting spook show would be complete without devoting at least one episode to her."

Hugh rubbed his recently blackened eye in defeat, "Well, what the hell do you want me to do here for the next week? We missed getting film on that thing by seconds. We've got nothing to show."

Jason laughed out loud, "Bullshit, kid! You have a 'possible' Chupacabra in an exciting chase scene. That's better than I ever hoped for!"

"We have a dead cow and the 'exciting chase scene' is clearly nothing more than a coyote we stumbled on while searching for the real deal."

Jason smiled at his young cameraman's naiveté. "It's not clearly a coyote until it comes into focus. The first 10 seconds are too blurry to tell what it is. We just need to cut the footage a bit and change Jack's dialog so it's a little less descriptive. The sooner you two get that done, the sooner Jack can get some shuteye before his flight. Now beat it you two. I've got work to do in here."

The two left the editing room and headed down the hall to gather up equipment for the shoot. "How do you want to shoot this?" asked Jack.

"Just throw on a khaki shirt and meet me in the blue screen room. I've got some stills I shot in Arizona that we can use for a background." Hugh replied.

Jack could see his young colleague was taking it hard.

"Look, don't take it so hard, kid. I hate to say it, but Jason is right. We don't have the evidence to support my previous dialog. We have to tone it down."

Hugh shook his head slowly in agreement.

"Hey look. I'm not mad at you, Jack. I'm not even mad at Jason." He looked to the ground in a dejected way. "I should have got that fucker in the frame sooner. It's just maddening! Two seconds earlier and we would have shaken the world of science!"

"Whoa! Whoa! Don't blame yourself, kid. I know guys who have been around a long time who couldn't have got that shot. You're a hell of a videographer. Don't sell yourself short. You have to look at it from the big picture. A guy with skills like yours will get the action on film twice for every one you miss. This is just one of the ones you missed. Don't let it eat you up." Jack smiled in a big brotherly way hoping that he'd imparted some good advice. Jack really believed in the kid. When Jack had been hired, he stipulated minimal creative control in his contract. He had the right to cut scenes he did not like but couldn't overrule Jason's cutting room powers. Other than that he was given hiring power for one of the show's sound operators and one of the show's cameramen. He picked a sound operator from his Iraq days but took a gamble on Hugh without ever having met the kid. So far he had been impressed.

The pep talk didn't seem to help Hugh too much. He still looked dejected.

"I can't tell you how much I wished I hadn't missed that one."

"Hey, don't worry about it." Jack patted Hugh on the shoulder showing empathy. "Maybe you won't be the guy to prove the Chupacabra exists. But just think about the show you work for. You'll have plenty of opportunities just like we had in Arizona. The next time, I know you won't miss. Your next opportunity is one week away. You might be the first guy to prove Nessie exists!"

Hugh seemed to brighten a bit with the pep-talk but then his expression faded into a pondering look.

"What now?" asked Jack.

"Can I show you something?"

"Sure."

"You have to promise not to laugh until you hear me out."

Jack didn't like the sound of that, "Okay, but once I've heard you out I reserve the right to laugh."

"Fair enough. Follow me." Jack followed Hugh back to his cubicle in the office area. "Jack, I came across a still photographer who seems to get that magical shot."

"A competitor?"

"No, not really," Hugh said uncomfortably. "He covers some of the same phenomena that we cover on this show but…I don't think he's quite as professional."

"I don't like where this is going." Jack raised an eyebrow.

"Trust me," said Hugh as the two rounded the corner and came to a stop at his workstation. Hugh picked up a copy of the *Weekly World Investigator* and handed it to Jack. The headline on the front page read, "Aliens Probe George Bush's Brain Checking For Leaks."

Jack broke his promise and laughed out loud. Hugh raised his hand defensively. "Just listen, Just LISTEN!" He said, having to raise his voice over Jack's laughter.

"Hugh, get real. This photographer you want me to check out works for the Weekly World Investigator?"

"I know it's crazy but…"

"But what? I mean…I realize that I can't say too much. After all I'm doing spook journalism myself but…you know 'Truth Seekers' may be a spook show but it's the most respected spook show out there. We never doctor photos and we won't make definitive comments on anything without undeniable evidence to back it up. As a spook documentary we have more journalistic integrity than any of them. And you're showing me a copy of a spook magazine that is so out in left field that even the craziest UFO believers think it's full of shit!"

"Yeah, but…" Hugh said trying to butt in.

"Look, I know I promised I wouldn't laugh," continued Jack, "but I didn't expect this. These guys jump to the nuttiest conclusions in the world and I doubt there is a photo in the whole magazine that isn't doctored."

"Jack! Shut up and listen to me!" It was the first time Hugh had ever yelled at his boss and it had the desired effect.

"Sorry. It's just…" Jack had made a promise and realized he was in the wrong,

"Don't apologize!" Hugh insisted. "I realize your skepticism and you're not wrong. It is a trash magazine and they do pull shit out of their ass to make a buck but that's why I want you to look at this article."

Jack did as told and scanned the article. The front page was an obviously doctored picture. President Bush was wincing. It was probably taken as the flash of a paparazzi camera caught him off guard. The offending paparazzi had been edited out of the frame and replaced by a space alien zapping him with a "mind probe" that looked more like a flashlight. In the upper right corner was an inset picture of a flying saucer. The implication was that the alien came from that space ship.

"Okay, so what's so cool about it?" inquired Jack.

"The flying saucer in the photo," replied Hugh.

"I'm sure there are many more just like it in that rag."

"Not like this there isn't," Hugh countered. "The WWI loves this particular photo. It was first aired in a feature article about two years ago. They have since used it as a feature at least once more and they use it quite often as an inset image like it is here."

"Okay, I'm listening. Where is this going?"

"A buddy of mine has a job as a copy editor for *Bachelor Monthly Magazine*." Jack knew the magazine Hugh was referring to. It was a magazine aimed at men in their twenties. *BMM* was mostly dirty jokes, gadget reviews, and, of course, women in skimpy outfits. "*BMM* is the parent company for the *Weekly World Investigator*. I called him a few weeks back and asked if he could hook me up with a copy of the original photo. He did me one better. He let me stop by and look at the original slide."

"Go on." Jack's interest was getting peaked.

"Let's just look at the photo for starters. About 90% of all UFO photos are taken of an object very far away. By the time you blow the image up, it's just a blur. You can't tell if it's an airplane, lenticular cloud, or a real flying saucer. Of the ten percent that are taken close enough to show distinctive details, like this one, you can usually tell that it has been photo-shopped or faked in some way. The few that aren't obvious usually lack spatial reference so there is no way to know if it was taken of a model ten feet away, or a real spacecraft a half a mile away."

Jack studied the picture carefully.

"Okay, so what makes this different from that ten percent?"

"First of all, it wasn't shot digitally. It was shot on F100 slide film, very high quality resolution. I got to see the original print first hand and I guarantee you the image you see on this page is the same as the original."

"Okay, so it isn't altered in the photo-shop. What about a model?" asked Jack.

"Spatial reference!" said Hugh with a grin. "Most photos in the 'model hoax' category are shot at the UFO with the sky as a background. This one is shot from above looking down. It was obviously taken by a pilot," Hugh added. "You can even see the plane's engine in the upper left of the picture. If my Wiki-search was correct, I believe this shot was taken from a Navy cargo plane."

"I knew a lot of pilots in Iraq." Jack scoffed. "These guys pride themselves on playing pranks."

Hugh paused considering that possibility.

"Well, there's more. This photo actually shows a shadow of the UFO being cast on the ground below."

Jack examined the picture looking at the shadow Hugh pointed out.

"Okay. How does that help us out."

"Well there are also a few roads that can be seen down below. I used the width of those to get a rough estimate of the height the plane was flying at, the height the UFO is flying at, and the size of the UFO."

Jack was now thoroughly impressed by the depth of investigating Hugh had done. He smiled at his young protégé.

"I know you got a kicker. What is it?"

Hugh smiled back almost pompous in victory.

"If this is a prankster pilot dangling a model off his wing then the model is twice the size of the airplane he's flying."

Jack smiled broadly knowing that they potentially had an Emmy winning episode on their hands.

"Okay. When you're not stuck being Jason's bitch this week, your side job is to find a photo forensic specialist to corroborate your analysis. I'll get Jason to buy the original from *BMM*. And finally I want you to find out who took the photo and get us an interview."

"Got it."

"Let me know what you got when we meet up in Scotland."

Chapter 9

I T WAS ABOUT 1:00 AM and the mood at the bar was slowly winding down. Erik felt half dead. His run to Korea was a solid ten hours of flying, not including the time on the ground for one refueling stop. To follow that with five straight hours of heavy drinking had pretty much wiped him out. He was tired enough to think that sleeping on the floor of the dingy bar would be acceptable accommodations and he was drunk enough not to care what anyone thought. He felt a light slap on his cheek just as he was about to doze off.

"Oh, piss off, Hallil! I'm going to sleep."

"Erik, you ass! I'm telling a story."

"Yeah, yeah, some Korean dude found an orb."

"Not just any orb. He thinks it's a Dragon Orb."

The word dragon woke Erik up a bit. Any word like dragon, monster, ghost or UFO had a tendency to do that to him lately. His hobby since high school had been journalism. He worked for both his high school and college papers and would usually make contributions to the paper of whatever aircraft carrier he was assigned to in the Navy. After the Navy, he had been trying to turn his hobby into a more steady income. He had a few legitimate publications but the magazine that bought most of his work really didn't expect him to do any hard hitting investigating. Instead, they counted on his unique ability to spin an outlandish tale of bullshit and make it sound almost believable.

The Weekly World Investigator thrived on any form of supernatural story so when Erik heard certain key words, it gave him hope that he might meet some nutcase who would go on record. Sometimes a quote could make the whole story. He once met an Alaskan fisherman who claimed that he caught his wife in bed with the three hundred year old spirit of a circus midget. If there was a Pulitzer for best yellow journalism, he would have won it for that piece.

Erik slapped his own face, shook himself awake, smiled at Hallil and asked, "Exactly what is a 'Dragon Orb'."

"I don't know but I asked my wife. She likes to read about such things."

"What did she say?"

"I guess it's like a crystal ball, or maybe a big gem. Not so sure really, but she says it gives a dragon great strength and power."

Erik cocked an eyebrow and smirked.

"Aren't dragons supposed to have great strength and power anyway?"

"I guess not. She says that lizards and snakes are the descendants of dragons and that with a dragon orb, they can grow to become a full dragon."

Erik laughed at the suggestion.

"Yeah and humans are descendants of space aliens. I've heard all of them. Hallil, I've met your wife. She's a kook!"

"You should be nice! She reads your magazine." Hallil Nariff returned Erik's comment with a sharp angry stare.

Erik pondered this with a confused stare.

"That's my point."

The two sat silent for a moment. Hallil was almost pouting and Erik was beginning to feel a little bad. Telling a colleague/ drinking buddy that his wife was a nutter was pretty rude, even if it was the truth. Before Erik could begin to apologize he felt the cell phone in his pocket vibrate. He looked at the clock in the bar, 1:30 am. What the hell was someone doing calling at this hour. Then he looked at his watch still set on US time. Geez! That meant he'd been awake for over 24 hours.

"Hello?"

"Hello, may I speak to Erik. . .ahh. . is it Severide?"

Erik had to stop and think about that one. He liked pseudonyms. He gave himself a new one for just about every nefarious or sleazy job he had ever done, just in case he one day became a famous writer or owned his own airline. "Oh, Yeah, that's me."

"Any. . .?"

"No. No relation. Who's this?"

"Oh, my name is Hugh Luminaire. I work for Truth Seekers television program."

"Never heard of it. Don't watch much TV."

Hugh paused momentarily. "Oh. Well, we are an investigative show."

"Oh, fuck!" thought Erik. Some muck raking journalist discovered he's providing the Korean Peninsula with its main supply of Cheez-its! "What's this about?" he asked concerned.

"I want to get a comment on a picture you took a few years back."

"*Oh, thank God!*" thought Erik. "Anything you need," he said.

"Great. Well, I was looking at a photo of a flying saucer you submitted about two years ago to the *Weekly World Investigator*."

"Oh, that one?" Erik knew the one Hugh was referring to since it was the only article he had submitted to *WWI* prior to leaving the Navy. "What do you want to know?"

"Well, first of all, I was wondering what you estimated the size of the craft to be? I have been analyzing your photo and wanted to know how your eyewitness account lines up with the numbers I've run."

"It was the size of an F-15." Erik laughed.

Hugh paused at this response. Most eyewitnesses tended to over exaggerate the size of a craft. . .not under estimate it.

"Excuse me?" he asked.

Erik was really gloating now. He loved shattering the dreams of the believers when they confronted him first hand. Now, he had obviously fooled some Hollywood schmuck with his picture and that made him feel even better.

"It was about the size of an F-15 because that's what it was. I just caught the light right and made it kinda look like a flying saucer."

Hugh could not respond. His calculations put the object at about four times that size. Had he run the numbers wrong?

"Hey, look, bud," Erik finally broke the silence. "I'm paying for international roaming right now so if you don't mind I gotta go."

"Ahh. .okay. . . thanks for your time," Hugh replied still stunned.

Erik turned off his phone and turned his attention to Hallil.

"Look, I'm sorry I said that about your wife. She's a wonderful lady and a damn fine cook. I shouldn't have said that."

Erik looked sincere so Hallil nodded.

"Apology accepted." Hallil finally acquiesced.

"So tell me about this Dragon Orb."

"Well, the archeologist who found it also happens to be the guy that buys most of my Cheez-its."

"No shit! I want to meet him." As Erik said this, his mind started writing the next headline, *'Man finds ancient sex orb and turns wife into Cheez-it eating Dragon.'*

Chapter 10

"YAMASEHYO," CAME THE voice on the other end of the phone.

Erik gingerly proceeded with what little Korean he knew.

"Anyong-haseyo. Ahhh ..speaky English?"

"English...yes I speak English. May I ask who is calling?"

Erik thought on that for a moment.

"Ahh, my name is Erik Severide. I'm a freelance reporter and I'm trying to do a piece on," Erik paused considering just how direct he should be. "I'm interested in Dragon Pearls."

He could tell by the lack of reaction on the other end that he had either stunned the man or he had called someone who knew nothing about 'Dragon Pearls.' "Is this Dr. Sam Da Soo?" Erik asked.

"Yes, this is he. I'm sorry who did you say you are?"

This was always the trickiest part for Erik. He made it a point to use a pseudonym while flying illicit cargo or writing an article for the *Weekly World Investigator*. Partly, he did this because he took glee in being a pathological bullshitter, but also because he figured it would come in handy if he ever decided to get a legitimate journalism or flying job. Commercial cargo carriers didn't want pilots who logged most of their hours smuggling and respectable newspapers were not interested in journalists who did most of their work for trashy tabloids. This rarely proved to be an issue in smuggling since most people paying for that service don't ask too many questions. When he was digging for a good story to send to the *WWI*, things were a bit more tricky. If you were a person in a respectable profession and you knew what the *WWI* was, you certainly knew you didn't want to be quoted in that trash rag. Erik knew that the best way around that was to simply call yourself freelance.

"Well, I'm a freelance journalist. I have an interest in a piece from *Archeology Week*, but naturally if my investigation proves fruitful enough I am hoping *National Geographic* will be interested." It was all total bullshit. Erik didn't even know if there was such a magazine as *Archeology Week* but knowing that there were at least three magazines devoted to every sport, hobby, or job in the world, he figured the lie would sound good enough.

"Ahhh, I see. What brought you to Korea?"

"Well, I've been traveling through Asia for the last two months," *bullshit*, "doing research for the piece," *bullshit*, "and I got your name from a source of mine," *partial bullshit*. "I know that Korea doesn't have as rich a history with dragon legends as China or Japan but I thought I might as well give you a call to exhaust all leads," *manipulative bullshit designed to bate the ever prideful Korean male ego.*

"Who told you we didn't have a 'rich tradition!'" Jonesy exclaimed. "Korea's history with dragon myths and folklore predate both Japan and China! Our understanding of the complexity of dragon culture goes far beyond what our neighbors to the east and west could ever understand!"

Hook, line, and sinker! Erik gleefully thought.

"Oh, Dear!" Erik said faking concern. "I certainly didn't mean to offend. Perhaps I was misinformed. Would I be able to meet with you to set the record straight?"

"Certainly. I would be glad to give you a more accurate scope for your article. Indeed, I can provide evidence that the myths of dragons and their magical pearls may have originated right here in Korea," replied Dr. Sam Da Soo excitedly.

"Really?" Erik said faking interest.

The evidence Dr. Sam spoke of was exactly what Erik was looking for. A picture of the good doctor with this large pearl, a few misquotes from the good doctor, and a little photo-shop work was all he needed to make college boys laugh and old ladies quake in their boots. And that would get him a few hundred bucks from the *WWI*. The two exchanged information and set up a time to meet. Erik hung up his phone with a satisfied grin. Getting your foot in the door was half the battle for a respectable journalist, it was the whole battle for a *WWI* correspondent.

Chapter 11

LEE AND HIS familiar, Sam, had just arrived at Jonesy's apartment to continue their work with his newly discovered orb. Lee should have known from the get go that something was up. Jonesy arrived at the door dressed in a fine suit topped with a shiny orange tie. The tie would have seemed gaudy on almost anyone else but Jonesy could pull it off with his complexion and refined tastes in businessmen's fashions. Jonesy ushered the two inside and told them to make themselves comfortable and then ran back into the bathroom to finish getting ready.

"Why are you all dolled up?" asked Sam.

"A reporter is due here any minute," replied Jonesy from his bathroom.

"A reporter? You think that's a good idea?" Lee cocked an eyebrow and glanced at his familiar who was cocking an eyebrow back at him.

Ding Dong! Came the door bell before Lee had a chance to protest further.

"Could you get that, Lee? I'll be right out!"

Lee shrugged in disappointment and did as he was asked.

"Hello?" Lee was met by a man of slightly below average height with a stocky build. He had crystal blue eyes and a mop of dirty blond hair. The man was wearing a photographer's vest over a Hawaiian shirt and an expensive looking 35 mm camera slung over one shoulder. His khaki pants were full of zippered pockets and looked like the bottom half of an aviator's flight suit. He looked more like a war correspondent. That didn't necessarily mean he looked like a reporter. Reporters had a tendency to dress like whoever they were interviewing. White house reporters wore suits and ties, war reporters wore khaki's, and science reporters wore something a professor might wear, like casual slacks and a nice blazer. In short, he had the right costume for the wrong interview.

"Dr. Sam Da Soo?" Erik asked with a confused look.

"No, I'm Dr. Bondurant. One of his colleagues. You are?"

"I'm a reporter. Erik Severide."

Lee looked queerly at him, "You mean like...?"

"Oh, no. Not that one. No relation."

"Well, come on in. He should be out in a moment. Please take a seat," Lee said gesturing to the couch.

Erik took one look at the German Short-hair Pointer and his eyes lit up. He loved dogs, especially hunting dogs. Erik bent down and held his hand out for Sam to sniff.

"Hey there, Sparky! What a beautiful dog!"

Sam looked at Erik with a contempt that only Lee could detect. "*Sparky?*" thought Sam. "*What makes this oaf think I look like a 'Sparky'?*" Sam growled slightly and gave a little bark.

"Easy boy," replied Erik. "Just trying to be friendly."

"Sam, settle down!" Said Lee.

"Oh, he's a Sam," said Erik. "Well you're a good looking dog there, Sam."

Just then, Jonesy entered the living room and extended his hand to Erik, "You must be the reporter."

"Yes. I'm Erik. You must be Dr. Sam Da Soo?"

"Correct."

"Sam the dog and Sam the professor," Erik quipped.

"Actually Sam is my family name. In Korea the family name comes first. My English name is Jonesy."

The two shook hands while Sam and Lee exchanged glances.

"Well, Dr. Sam, you have a beautiful home and a beautiful dog as well."

"Actually, Sam is Dr. Bondurant's dog."

"Oh, my apologies...You have a nice dog, Dr. Bondurant." Erik was looking around at all the beautiful artifacts decorating Jonesy's apartment. It would be a great backdrop for a picture for his piece. His only regret was that Dr. Sam Da Soo looked more like a businessman than a mad scientist.

"Thank you," Lee politely replied. He couldn't believe Jonesy had invited a reporter in so soon. Anthropologists and archaeologists usually preferred to keep the press out of their discoveries until after they had published in an academic journal.

"Sam's more than just a nice dog," interrupted Jonesy. "He is a very special dog," he continued enthusiastically.

Erik cocked an eyebrow and Lee slightly gasped. Lee couldn't fathom why Jonesy had invited a reporter and now it seemed he was about to spill the beans about the fact that Sam could speak. Sam was also taken aback by the direction Jonesy was going with this. Lee and Sam had long ago decided to limit the number of people who were brought in on that secret. Nevertheless, it would have spoiled the secret had Sam decided to tell Jonesy to stuff it.

"Yes. Unlike any other dog Sam has the ability to..."Jonesy continued on, oblivious to the 'be quiet' looks Lee was sending his way out of Erik's view.

"Play Chess!" interrupted Lee.

Jonesy and Erik snapped their attention towards Lee. Jonesy then realized that Lee didn't want the reporter to know that Sam was a familiar. Erik added a cocked smirk to his cocked eyebrow. A chess playing dog was a better story than a nutty professor with a big pearl any day.

"He can play chess?" blurted Erik.

"Yes," replied Lee sheepishly.

Sam liked that recovery. He hadn't played chess in a while.

"How the hell did you teach a dog to play chess?" Erik asked with a chuckle of excitement.

"Long story."

"Well, I'd be interested in that story as well but perhaps we should begin with your interview, Dr. Sam?"

"That's a good idea. Why don't you follow me into..."

"Actually we'd love to have a story done on him," interrupted Lee. "Why don't we set up the board and you can play a game with him. Jonesy and I will go make some coffee and get the room ready for the interview."

Sam's tail wagged with excitement but Jonesy looked confused.

"Well, actually I'm ready to..." Jonesy started to speak.

Cutting him off and taking him by the elbow, Lee finished the sentence for him.

"Give the interview after we make some coffee." He gave Jonesy a stern look until he finally understood.

"Oh...Yes...we should make some coffee first."

The whole scene was a bit suspicious, but Erik was willing to roll with it. He may never have a chance to play a game of chess with a dog again.

"Sounds good to me. Ahh, do you mind If I take some pictures of him playing?"

"Of course not. Sam's very photogenic." replied Lee. "We will just be a few minutes," he said whisking his Korean friend off to the kitchen.

Erik went over to a fine marble chess table that was ornamentation for one of the living room coffee tables. He reset the pieces as he eyed the dog suspiciously.

"Okay, boy....black or white?" He asked, not thinking the dog would understand. Sam stood up and walked over to the table and sat next to the white pieces. Erik still wasn't sure if the dog understood or had arbitrarily chosen a side. It had probably been five years since Erik had played chess, but he remembered that the white pieces got the first move, and thus the initiative of attack.

It was a slight advantage in a game but he figured what the hell. It was a dog after all.

As Jonesy and Lee entered the kitchen, Lee whispered to him.

"Jonesy, are you nuts!"

"Why?" Jonesy looked hurt.

"Don't you think it is a little soon to be bringing the press in on this?"

"Well...?" thought Jonesy out loud.

"I assume he is here to see the Orb?"

"I guess I had thought about showing it to him..."

"Why did you invite him here?"

Jonesy pushed Lee back slightly and took on a defensive posture.

"He is doing a story on Asian dragons. He seemed to get the impression that Koreans didn't have much to offer. I thought I could set the record straight."

"By showing him that Orb!" Lee looked astonished. He was becoming increasingly worried about his friend. Ever since finding that Orb, the once rational professor had been acting more on impulse.

"Well, he has the impression that Asian dragon myths stem from China and Japan. Lee, if this Orb dates as far back as I think it does then I can prove that Asian dragons, perhaps all dragons, originated in Korea."

"You mean you invited this interview out of Korean pride!"

"Well, curse you, Lee! There is much to be proud of."

"Agreed." Lee softened his posture and tried to reason with his friend. "But you need to understand where I am coming from. First, from an archaeological perspective; we have a lot of digging and research to do before we can support this theory of yours. If news of this leaks out before we can write a peer reviewed paper, then a whole host of problems can arise. You could be dismissed as a media loving quack before anyone ever bothers to read your true hypothesis. Interest groups might sue to shut the site down, even treasure hunters and grave robbers might destroy the site before our work is finished!"

Jonesy's expression saddened as he digested the logic.

"Second," Lee said considering how to best phrase this. "You believe that this object has more than just Archaeological significance. You believe it has magical powers. We have studied magic since graduate school, so for us that possibility is very real. The rest of the world has been blissfully unaware of the true power of the supernatural world since the Renaissance. Do you think it is wise to let a reporter study what could very well be a magical talisman before we have had the chance to understand it?

"My friend. You simply can't allow your pride and ego to interfere with the decisions you make on this matter. We must both follow oaths of secrecy that we swore twenty years ago. God knows the consequences if we do not."

Looking at the floor, Jonesy slowly nodded in agreement.

"Okay." he said. "You're right. I'll still give the interview but I won't mention my discovery. I'll give him a good run down on Korean dragon mythology and leave it at that. How would that be?"

"Thank you," Lee said with relief. "That is a great idea."

Erik was transfixed in amazement as Sam carefully picked up a pawn with his mouth and placed it exactly two squares in front of his king. It was stunning to see a dog that had enough dexterity in his snout to move an individual piece on a chessboard without knocking about the other pieces. Erik was preoccupied snapping away with his camera as he realized the dog was staring at him with big brown eyes. It was as if the dog knew it was Erik's turn and was waiting patiently.

Erik looked down at the board. Pawn to E-4 was the most common opening move for white in all of chess. Erik countered with the next most common move in a chess opener; black pawn to E-5. Two pawns stood facing each other on the table.

The dog then carefully picked up the king's side bishop. The bishop could only move diagonally and thus the white king's side bishop would always remain on a white square and the queen's side bishop would always remain on a black square. Sam moved the bishop diagonally to C-4, a white square.

Erik was amazed as he snapped away at the chess playing dog. Realizing it was again his turn, he decided to use one of his knights. In chess, pawns moved straight ahead and attacked diagonally. Bishops moved and attacked diagonally. Rooks, or castles, could move forward and back, left and right. Kings and queens could move in any linear direction, left, right, forward, aft, and diagonal, with the queens moving as far as they wanted and the kings being limited to one square. This was all well and good but, in truth all the pieces moved in a linear direction. Erik could see how a dog might be trained to move these linear pieces with Pavlovian techniques. That didn't mean the dog could play chess. It meant it was a trained dog....albeit, a very well trained dog. Erik chose to test his hypothesis by moving a knight, or horse. The knight is the only nonlinear piece on the chessboard. It moved in an L shape and could jump over other pieces. Erik decided that using a knight might confuse the dog's training. He picked up the knight that was on the left of the queen and her bishop and moved it forward two squares and to the left one. He placed it at C-6.

As expected, Sam responded like the well trained mutt that he was. He moved the queen, the most powerful piece, out into the open. She moved diagonally to the left two squares. She came to rest at F-3.

Erik was pretty thrilled as he snapped away but he was sure he'd figured out the gag. The dog had not reacted to the knight and had not noticed the dangerous position he had put his queen in. Erik used his wiley knight again. He moved it one square to the left and two forward. It sat at D-4. He had put the queen in a classic knight fork. In a fork, a player has put his knight in a position that forces his opponent to choose between one piece or another. If Sam retreated the queen, then Eric could take a pawn without retribution. If Sam instead moved the pawn, then Erik could trade his knight for the queen. A very good trade in chess parlance. Three moves and Erik had already exploited the well trained dog's weakness.

Still impressed with the dog's performance but slightly smug in his own success, Erik snapped away as Sam made his last move. Sam picked up his queen. Erik was impressed. The dog must have been trained to retreat in this situation. But then, Sam moved the queen forward four squares to sit on F-7. He took a pawn that he carefully picked up with his dexterous snout and set it aside. The dog then went "woof." Erik wasn't sure what that meant as he analyzed what had just happened.

Sam had grown tired of acting like a dumb dog around their new visitor. Whopping the ass of the guy who had called him "Sparky" wasn't good enough. Lee's cautious nature be damned, Sam was going to speak! And as the word *'Checkmate!'* formed in his mind he let it fly out of his mouth. More than being beaten by a dog, this Erik guy was going to get the surprise of his life when he heard a dog talk! But Erik didn't respond. He just looked at the chessboard. Sam said it again, *'Checkmate!'* but the word that came out of his mouth was, "Woof!"

"What the hell?" he said. But all that came out was, "Bark, Bark, Woof?" Sam couldn't talk! He wanted to talk, but he couldn't. He wanted to say, "Checkmate!" He wanted to say, "In your face, smart guy! Call me 'Sparky' again and I'll piss on your tires!" but all that came out were barks and woofs. Just like a normal, everyday, boring mutt. He had to wait for the guy to figure it out all on his own. That could take a while, thought Sam.

Erik looked at the surprising move. The queen was sitting diagonally to the left of the king in the position previously held by one of his pawns. At first, he thought it was a really stupid move. All he had to do was kill the queen with his king and he was still up a queen. Then he realized that if he did that, the bishop could freely slide across the table and kill his king. Oops! Now he realized he was in a predicament. He had to protect his king. As he looked around, he realized that his own pieces were in the way of his king's escape! Furthermore there were no pieces that could sacrifice themselves for his king. As he examined the board with Sam giving out an occasional bark, he realized that the mutt had just put him in checkmate!

"I don't fuckin' believe it!" exclaimed Erik. "I just lost to a dog!"

Chapter 12

ERIK WAS IN a rental car driving up and down the eastern coast of South Korea. He had already gotten a good little story done on the chess playing dog, albeit, acquiring it came at a small cost to his ego. But when it came time to interview Dr. Sam Da Soo, the Korean archaeologist seemed evasive. Nothing he could say would convince the professor to bring out this Dragon Orb Nariff claimed to know about. Erik was in a bit of a fix. He couldn't come right out and admit that he'd heard through the grapevine that the good Dr. had found such an object without sounding like a treasure hunter in disguise. In truth, he was a treasure hunter of sorts.

Erik could have just given up and flown home. He did have one story already and he didn't really need two, but there was something about the quest that appealed to him. Just to lay eyes on what this Korean archaeologist had discovered, appealed to him. Erik didn't believe for a second it was truly a magical Dragon Pearl, but unlike Erik, Nariff wasn't the kind of guy who made up stories. He had heard something significant. And if it was as big as a softball, as he claimed, it had to be the biggest pearl ever found.

Erik wasn't due to fly another shipment for Nariff for another month and he figured kicking around Korea and hopefully talking that doctor into showing him this pearl would be a lot more fun than getting drunk with fishermen and squandering his cash at the Alaskan Bush Company. Anchorage Alaska, Erik's port of call these days, didn't offer a lot of excitement for him when moose season was closed and when the salmon weren't running.

Satisfied with those reasons, Erik rented a car and decided to take a road trip from Seoul to the beautiful mountains of Soraksan and then down the coast to Busan. Most said that it was about the best road trip you could take in Korea. Already, Erik had been impressed with the mountains of Korea. They were quite different from the Rockies with more vegetation and much more development near by, but they were still quite beautiful. The eastern coast was also quite beautiful. Rocky islands dotted the sea. The coastline was rocky with cliffs plunging directly into the surf. Here and there a beach would emerge but most of them were crowded with tourists.

After several hours of driving, Erik finally found a quiet beach that looked like a good picnic spot. He pulled the rental onto a small stretch of dirt road that led to the beach. The beach was about 100 meters long and twenty meters wide. Sandwiched on each end were two ten meter high bands of cliffs that continued north and south from the small beach. He was shocked that no one was here. It seemed like a great place to enjoy the ocean. He realized that because the cliffs created a little canyon, high tide probably flooded the area. For all he knew the beach was totally under water at those time. It mattered little to him now however, for at this time of day it was nice enough and best of all, no one else was here. He grabbed his camera bag and lunch box and followed a small trail down to the beach.

After taking a few pictures of his surroundings, he sat on the sand and pulled out his lunch. As he sat eating his lunch and listening to the waves gently crash onto the beach and the cliffs beyond, he caught sight of something out of the corner of his eye. At first he thought it was a large piece of debris washing up on the beach. But as he turned to look directly at it, he realized it was swimming purposefully through the surf. It was an animal of some kind. He attached a telephoto lens to his camera to get a better look.

It appeared to be a lizard of some sort. It definitely had scaly skin like a crocodile. It's body seemed leaner than a crocodile but much of what he could see from the surface looked similar. He was no taxonomy specialist but it seemed as if it might be a Komodo Dragon. He was sure that Komodos were not supposed to be anywhere close to Korea, but he was definitely looking at something similar. This could be a good story by itself if he could get photographic evidence that one had somehow migrated to Korea, but then a frightening thought struck him.

In his six months of flying goods under the radar of the tariff police, Erik had learned a lot about the nature of smuggling. Almost anything in the world can be smuggled from one location to the next. Items were smuggled in planes, trains, ships, automobiles, and sometimes in the intestines of people they called mules. Tariff smugglers, like Erik, accounted for the highest volume of traffic but the least return in profit. The big money makers smuggled people, drugs, guns, and much less known about, exotic animals. It was common for smugglers to dump their cargo if it looked as if the customs agents were on to them. If you were going to be a successful smuggler, you needed to be willing to dump your cargo no matter what it contained. The thought of dumping a load of Cheezits and Marlboroughs never weighed much on Erik's conscience, but you had to be pretty cold blooded to drop exotic animals or, worse yet, people off the side of your boat or out the door of your airplane. Nevertheless, there were people in this world willing to take those sorts of actions.

Erik was clearly looking at an exotic animal of some sort. He was doubtful it had come to Korea on its own. Had there been a zoo escape, he probably would have heard about it. Chances were this thing had been dropped off the side of a boat before the Korean Coast Guard had boarded and searched. If Erik took a bunch of pictures and published them, there was no telling the sort of retribution that was in store for him. Especially once the offending parties realized that he too was a smuggler. It was better to just look at it through the lens and marvel about what a wondrous creature he had happened upon.

Suddenly a new thought came to his head. Dr. Sam, the Korean Archaeologist, mentioned something about an Imoogi. It was some sort of baby dragon. It would never become a full dragon without a Dragon Orb. Maybe if the good Dr. thought there was a real living Imoogi on the East coast of Korea, he might be more willing to show Erik that pearl he was hiding.

Erik pulled up his camera and began snapping away. He was careful to blur out any images that would reveal exactly what he was photographing. If he took shot in focus, he made sure he was zoomed so close you couldn't get a perspective on what the creature was. After about ten carefully framed pictures his phone rang.

"Hello?"

"Hi! Is this Erik?"

"Yes. Who is this?"

"This is Hugh Luminaire. I called you a few days back."

"Oh! You were the guy who called me at 2:00 AM."

"Oh, yeah. Sorry about that."

"No big deal. I was out late getting drunk at the time. Hope I wasn't too rude."

"No more than I would have been."

"Well, if I recall, you were asking about a picture of mine... my story hasn't changed."

"Yeah. That's what I'm calling about. Are you sure about that? 'Cause I have done some pretty serious photographic analysis on that thing and it sure seems legit."

"Look. Who did you say you work for again?"

"*Truth Seekers* television show."

Suddenly, Erik felt he had another angle to play to convince Dr. Sam Da Soo to let him see that pearl. An Imoogi and a TV show.

"Look, bud. Forget about that photo. If you want something new, you need to get to Korea right now."

"Why is that?"

"I just took a picture of an Imoogi."

There was a pause. "What's that?"

Erik began to explain.

Chapter 13

C HO JOO-EUN SLIPPED back into the surf. She was confused by the reaction of the man at the beach. She had lived near that beach for over five hundred years. The beach was close to a wonderful cave that she had made her home. The erratic tide made it a less popular beach than some and yet it's beauty meant that occasionally she would see visitors.

Cho Joo-Eun was an Imoogi. Imoogi's were reclusive creatures and yet very generous and friendly. The mere sighting of an Imoogi would bring good fortune to one's family for a year. Cho Joo-Eun realized that good fortune could be a self fulfilling prophecy for one fortunate enough to lay eyes on her, but she liked to believe that she had the magic within her to parcel out that good luck. So when the small beach wasn't inundated with surf, and a lone person, or perhaps a family decided to picnic on the beach, it was her great pleasure to come out from her hidden cave. She would swim on the beach long enough for her visitor to witness her glorious beauty; her eel like grace, the rainbow mane of feathers that framed her beautiful face. To know that one look at her was enough to bring joy and good fortune to those lucky enough to visit this place was all she needed to sustain her otherwise lonely existence. She needed those moments because, for all she knew, she was the last Imoogi left on this dying world.

As she looked at her latest visitor, she was struck by his lack of enthusiasm. When he first saw her, he didn't jump with excitement. He cautiously looked at her but displayed no joy, only confusion. It was as if he was deciding what to do. Finally, he pulled out a camera and began taking pictures without emotion. She happily danced in the surf for him, knowing that few humans believed what they saw in a photograph these days.

As she played in the surf, a cold thought hit her. She stopped and let her body settle in the sand as the waves gently caressed her shoulders. She stared at the man and realized he was no longer taking pictures. He had put his camera down and had answered a phone of some sort. He no longer seemed to notice her at all. It was different than other humans who had used those little hand held phones they had. Usually, they screamed with excitement at whoever spoke on the other end. But this man seemed to be speaking of other things. Things that did not concern her. It was as if her grace and beauty made no effect on this man. She looked down into the water at her reflection. She saw her rainbow mane and her crystal blue eyes. Perhaps she had lost the beauty that humans had once revered. Or perhaps fickle humans could no longer see her beauty. A tear came from her eye and trickled down her cherub cheek. If she could no longer bring joy and luck to the few visitors she had, what was the use of this lonely existence. She dove back into the murky waters and gracefully swam back to her quiet lair.

Chapter 14

"Jack, this is Hugh!" The voice on the other end of the line was hurried and excited. Jack was not. It was five o'clock in the morning Dublin time and the call had just awoken him and his overnight guest.

"And who the fock would be callin' at this hour of the mornin'," whined his beautiful red haired guest.

"Go back to sleep, Niamh," Jack softly spoke to his new friend. "I'll take care of this in the other room." In a grumpy mood, Jack put on a robe and took his cell phone into the living room of his hotel suite. "What the hell is it, Hugh! You know what time it is here?"

"It's 5 AM."

"If you knew that then why the hell are you calling me! I didn't quit my network job just because of the bullets you know!"

Hugh was undeterred.

"I'm calling you at 5:00 because by noon I'm supposed to be on a flight to Edinburgh."

"If it's a problem with tickets then deal with the producer. That's not my job."

"There is no problem with the ticket. The problem is that I need the ticket changed to Seoul, South Korea. For that I need your approval."

"Hang on a sec," Jack set the phone down and guzzled a bottle of water hoping to clear his head from a night of Guinness and Jameson's. "Okay, why the hell would I want to authorize that change? Did you get a lead on the guy who took that photo?"

"Turn on your laptop and check your E-mail," said Hugh.

Jack grumbled and walked to the desk to turn on his computer.

"So, how did the Killarny Ghost episode go?" asked Hugh while the two waited for Jack's computer to boot up.

"Total crap! Mostly night vision camera work with a couple of kooky locals that hammed it up every time the water heater turned on."

"Sorry to hear that."

"Okay, I'm pulling up your e-mail now," Jack paused as he opened the pictures Hugh had sent. Most of them were slightly out of focus or the telephoto was so tight that it was hard to distinguish exactly what he was looking at. It looked like a large lizard of some sort. The anomaly was the blue eyes visible in some of the close up shots. "What the hell am I looking at?"

"That guy who took the photo's of the UFO? Well, he also took these off the coast of Korea."

"What the hell is it?"

"He says it's an Imoogi. Some sort of Asian dragon."

"Can't really tell that from the photos."

"True. But you can tell it's some sort of large lizard and there aren't a lot of those with blue eyes."

"Good point. Photo-shopped perhaps?"

"It was a digital file so I can't say for sure, but my trained eye says no."

"Hmm..." Jack mused out loud. "Problem is, I really need you here for the Loch Ness piece."

"Why do you need me there?" Hugh knew that wasn't true. "You have two other cameramen with you right now who can do that job."

"Damnit, Hugh!" Jack gruffed. He didn't like being questioned by his staff. "I need someone with your skills at capturing unexpected action. What if we see the thing?"

Hugh sighed in frustration.

"If you need my camera for that, then you really need me in Korea!"

"Why not here?" Jack said exasperated.

Hugh had anticipated Jack's displeasure so he had practiced his argument before he called.

"Because there won't be a need for an experienced nature photographer in Scotland. There won't be a need for me because the Loch Ness Monster doesn't exist! I told you this last week. Scientists and laymen have been up one side of that lake and down the other for the last 80 years! They have flown on top and dived underneath! They've used radar and sonar and all the other "ar's" available! All they have to show for it is fuzzy photos, most of which are proven hoaxes, and eye witness reports from locals who have an interest in keeping the myth alive.

"A week ago you gave me a nice pep talk saying that the next time I saw a new species I wouldn't miss the shot. If you believe that, you need to send me to a place where I have a chance to photograph a totally new species. In Scotland, we'll be rehashing a story that's almost a hundred years old. This Imoogi thing is fresh."

Jack paused considering his protégé's argument.

"Ahh, why do you have to pull this shit at 5 in the morning!"

"I got you within spitting distance of a Chupacabra. My same research methods have led me to Korea. At worst, we are investigating something new...at best, I can give you a show that will put us on top of the Sunday night lineup and guarantee a third season."

Jack had to admit the kid had a point. Even amongst cryptozologists, the people who dedicated their lives to discovering living remnants of mythic beasts, the Loch Ness seemed to be a lost cause. If his show at least investigated new sightings of unexplained things, it was better than rehashing stories that Leonard Nemoy had explored thirty years ago. He wasn't the budget Guru for the show but he quickly calculated what *Truth Seekers* would have to eat and then spend to redirect his young cameraman to Korea. He then thought about the Chupacabra episode. He had seen the thing with his own eyes. He knew it lived out there in the southern deserts of Arizona. Jack regretted not fighting to go back and look again. If he had, he and Hugh might have been in store for more than an Emmy, more than a Pulitzer, perhaps even the Nobel prize for biology. Grandiose thoughts aside, he owed it to the kid.

"Alright you sold me," Jack began. "But you can't go alone. I need one of our reporters there with you. Someone who can spice up the story if things fall flat." Jack thought about who he had on staff that he could use for cheap. He thought of Summer Dawn. She was the *Truth Seekers* resident psychic and one of the on camera reporters. She was paid a full monthly stipend when she worked even though she generally worked less than that. She had just finished a week of work on the Killarny Ghost episode so he could use her for three more weeks for just expenses. Best yet, Summer was a good sport.

"I'll arrange to get Summer out there to help you out."

There were times in everyone's life when you get exactly what you ask for and then regret it. "You mean that kooky hippie psychic!"

Chapter 15

"**Y**OU WHAT?" SHOUTED Lee on the phone.

"Lee, just listen!" Jonesy was saying. "This guy Erik has connections with a TV show and so I told him to bring the videographer and the reporter along with us when we go find the Imoogi he photographed."

"Ah, Jonesy. Why the hell are you giving all this stuff to the press before we even know what we're doing?" Lee was totally exasperated with his friend's very uncharacteristic behavior. Jonesy had always played things close to the vest, never revealing important information outside of a need to know basis but with this Dragon Orb, he seemed to have gone completely off the deep end.

"Because this is vital stuff, Lee! The world needs to see this!"

"Jonesy, you've put us in a box. If we now refuse to let them come, they'll get even more curious and make something bigger and probably worse than what it really is." Lee was frustrated but saw no way around his friend's blunder except to try to minimize the damages. "Okay, look, let's invite them to dinner. Your house. I'll cook. We'll say it is just to get to know each other before we head out."

"Okay, that's great! Tonight, then?"

"Yes, make it tonight. Then we can still leave tomorrow for Seoraksan."

"Great! You don't want me to cook?" Jonesy considered himself an excellent Korean chef.

"No, I'll cook Italian. I've got some good Chianti with me. I'm bringing Jan and Hank, too." Lee could get their input on these newbie's and Janice was great at researching backgrounds. He'd have her do some checking up on folks.

"I'll call them right now!"

Chapter 16

LEE AND JONESY waited for the others in the quiet parking garage of Jonesy's building. Lee didn't really like the idea of having the journalists tag along for a potential summoning. But after meeting the group at dinner, Lee realized that he knew Summer Dawn. He had met her about ten years ago at a seminar she gave on psychic intuitions. She didn't seem to have aged much and was still a beautiful woman probably in her fifties. She looked a bit like an aging "hippy" with her long grey streaked hair done in a thick braid hanging down her back. She wore a yellow gauze tunic and an orange broom skirt, belted at the waist with a turquoise and silver belt and her turquoise earrings hung to her shoulders. Her wrists were both covered in silver and turquoise bangle bracelets and she had big turquoise rings on her thumbs and two fingers of each hand. Her reputation as a psychic was solid even though her Santa Fe uniform screamed "flake." Lee remembered her speech as being well thought out and well received and he was somewhat comforted that she was the on camera reporter chosen for this gig.

The young cameraman, Hugh, seemed pretty straight forward and was very likeable but Lee would reserve judgment until he knew him better.

Erik was still a mystery to Lee. Sam had told him about the chess incident when he couldn't speak when he'd wanted to. Lee filed that away for future reference after scolding Sam for breaking the rule of silence around strangers. Sam had broken that rule again, however, when Erik had left last night's dinner before Summer and Hugh. Sam was watching Korean baseball on TV while the others cleaned up dinner. After watching the home team's left fielder duck a fly ball instead of catching it, he had screamed out.

"Catch it you, jerk!" When the fielder then fell on the ground and rolled around as if he'd been hit (which he had not been) and looked as if he would cry, Sam added "There is no crying in baseball, you twit!"

Needless to say, Hugh was stunned and thought maybe he'd had too much Chianti and Summer was delighted feeling at last her powers were working. She considered herself a dog psychic and had been trying to communicate with animals for real. Now she felt she'd accomplished it.

Lee was totally exasperated and just threw up his hands and returned to washing dishes. Obviously he had no control over anything anymore.

Lee had been happy to use journalists in the past to publicize his archaeological finds, but he had been careful to keep his summoning powers secret from the media. He had definitely tried to keep Sam's abilities private. Jonesy, on the other hand, seemed to freely embrace the idea of media coverage and even though Lee would do the summoning it was still Jonesy's show.

So now they sat here waiting for this group to show up and take a road trip to hell. Sam perked up his ears and looked at the two Magi.

"They're coming," he told them. It wasn't long before the humans could hear it as well. The car came closer until it rounded a corner and stopped next to the three. The vehicle was a simple black sedan and other than the lighted blue dome on the roof that said, "Best Driver Taxi," it was indistinguishable from any other Hyundai sedan on the road.

Lee looked at his watch as the three exited the vehicle, "Must have been difficult getting a taxi at this hour."

"I know the driver." Erik said stepping from the cab. He turned back to Nariff's henchman, Bin Dong, and passed over some money. "Thanks Bean."

Bin looked at the money and complained, mostly because it was their usual form of communication.

"You said more money!"

Erik looked at the cab meter, "I paid you twice the fair already!"

"Kiss, Ass!" was all Bin Dong could reply.

"That's kiss *my* ass! And while we're on the English lesson why don't you do just that."

Bin Dong sighed in frustration, spun his finger around his ear and then pointed it at Erik.

"You head Bing Bing." Just before putting the car back in gear, he extended his middle finger and stuck it in Erik's face. Erik replied in kind as Bin Dong sped off.

Erik turned back to the small expedition waiting to pile into Jonesy's van. Even the dog was looking at him with a curious expression.

"Old friend of mine."

Lee was still suspicious of Erik; mostly because Sam seemed as useless as a real dog when Erik came too close but also because Summer always had a puzzled look on her face when she talked to him. Though Lee was no psychic himself, he could still read body language. In short, Summer just seemed out of her element when Erik was around.

"Exactly what is the nature of your business here in Korea?" Lee asked.

Erik looked back at Lee with a smirk on his face and then shifted his focus to Jonesy.

"Ask your buddy. He knows."

Jonesy's face flushed with a momentary embarrassment and then shifted the subject back to the task at hand.

"Come on. It's a five hour drive to the cave. Let's load our gear and get going."

They all grabbed their respective equipment: Erik's and Hugh's cameras, Lee's books, Summer's herbs and art supplies, and Jonesy's two heavy black crates. They climbed into the minivan with Erik and Hugh in the back seat, Summer and Sam in the middle, Jonesy driving and Lee riding shotgun. It would be a long drive, so Jonesy tuned the radio to the English language station. It wasn't long before he heard people dozing.

After about an hour, Hugh gathered the nerve to nudge Erik awake.

"What?" grumbled Erik opening only one eye and casting it evilly towards Hugh.

"Look, I brought a print of your UFO photo." Hugh said holding up the picture.

Erik couldn't believe Hugh wouldn't let it lie.

"Oh my god, kid! You're more in love with me than me."

"Just look at it again," Hugh said pointing to the photo. "There is no way this is an F-15."

"Hugh, give it up. It's in a banking turn. Planes look like flying saucers from that angle. Everyone thought that Area 51 was full of flying saucers until the Air force revealed stealth bombers. I know what I saw. It was an F-15."

Hugh sighed and threw his hands up.

"Okay, I get that you don't believe. Just let me ask a different question."

"Shoot," resigned Erik.

"Do you know if anyone else saw a UFO around the time you took this picture?"

"Sure," replied Erik honestly. He then started grinning. "A whole flight of F-14 pilots saw one just days after."

"Ahh Ha!" exclaimed Hugh.

Erik laughed out loud.

"They didn't see theirs until a day after I had posted a print on the bulletin board. It was the best prank I ever pulled. They came to me and told me they had seen my UFO. When I told them what my photo really was they were the laughing stock of the ship for a month." Erik smiled to himself remembering the moment. "It was really great. The flight leader was such a prima donna anyway."

With Erik and Hugh chatting it up in the back of the van, Lee motioned Summer to lean forward.

"You seem uneasy around Erik. Do you sense something dangerous about him?" he asked in a hushed tone.

Summer looked at Lee, considering his question.

"No, I don't."

Lee sighed.

"Well, then does that mean he can be trusted?" he asked in frustration.

"I can't say that either. I'm sure he means us no harm. Feelings of malice are generally easier to detect for a psychic and I feel none of that."

"But you still don't think he's a friend?"

"I didn't say that either. He very well could be a friend," she said pondering. "Altruistic feelings are often the hardest emotions to clarify since even the most altruistic actions are often carried out by a person's own selfish desire to feel good about himself. But that's not it either" Summer said trailing off.

"What is it, Summer?"

"Dr. Bondurant, I feel no malice, no altruism, no selfishness. Nothing. I feel nothing good, bad or indifferent when he's around. I see no aura around him. I'm even having difficulty reading his body language."

"Seems mysterious," Lee looked at Jonesy who had been listening in. "Erik seemed to imply that you knew something about him, Jonesy. Spit it out old friend. What do you know about him?"

Jonesy squirmed as if trapped in a corner. "The man who drove the taxi. . . "he trailed off. "I believe Erik is the pilot Nariff uses to deliver my Cheezits."

Lee raised a knowing eyebrow and then started laughing but Summer simply shrugged.

"So he's a cargo pilot?" she said.

Lee was more fluent in international law and drew the connections. "No, Summer. He's a smuggler."

The van traveled on for another few hours winding its way through the Korean mountains until it reached the Sea of Japan. Bondurant was keen not to call it that in front of his friend. Koreans took some offense at that name. After all, most of it was international waters and the Koreans had just as much right to fish it as the Japanese. So to all Koreans, it was the East Sea.

As they drew close, Erik directed them to the specific spot from which he had taken the photograph. Even with Lee's suspicions being roused, he wasn't really worried about Erik attempting a hoax. First of all, even if Lee's eyes could be fooled by a hoax, Sam's couldn't. Secondly, even if Erik had led them to a location where he placed a fake Imoogi, it shouldn't matter. Lee had studied the ancient arts of the Magi but just like a modern day academic, the "post graduate" education of a Magi was very specialized.

In Lee's case, he was a summoner. Summoning focused on the calling of supernatural creatures. It was the magical equivalent of a hunter who uses various calls and scents to bring his prey to him. The second major field of summoning theory was to "convince" a supernatural being to cooperate with the summoner once it arrived. This was referred to as the "binding" phase. The biggest drawback with summoning was matching the desired creature or spirit with its desired habitat and insuring it could be "bound" once it arrived.

In this case that didn't matter. The team was on the coast with caves near by, so even if Erik was pulling a fast one on them, Lee was sure that he was in the right area to call the Imoogi. Bondurant's biggest concern was relying on Jonesy's assurances that Imoogis were benevolent. In the last two weeks, he had delved deeply into the literature and had yet to find a binding spell that was specifically made for these creatures.

"I think this is the one," said Erik as the van drew close to a turnoff that led down to the beach. Just as Jonesy had pulled off the main highway Erik called a halt, "Oh! Wait! I don't think this is it."

"Have you forgotten where you saw it!" Jonesy looked back with panic in his eyes.

Lee was becoming more and more concerned about his friend. In both of their shared professions, archeology and arcane magic, patience was less of a virtue and more of a job requirement. Many archeologists spent a career without uncovering anything more significant than a few pot shards in an already over worked dig site. In the same vein, a Magi could study for a lifetime without mastering any spells more powerful than moving a glass across a table. So for a colleague in both fields, Jonesy's urgency and panic were quite disturbing.

"Easy there. I know it's on the highway between these two villages. I just can't remember the exact turnoff. Hell, you seen one rocky coastline you've seen 'em all, right?" Erik was checking his GPS to get his bearings.

Jonesy placed the van into park and turned around to face Erik. Jonesy had followed a very different path in magic than Lee had. He was an enchanter. Where the summoner could call upon magical creatures for assistance, the enchanter could impart inanimate objects with certain magical spells. Jonesy pulled out a Zippo lighter he had used to frighten away many adversaries in the past.

Though not Darth Vadar powerful, Jonesy could be a force to be reckoned with when angered. He decided to give Erik a glimpse of his power. With a flick of the flint from his magical Zippo, his face transformed into that of a devil's. With glowing red eyes and horns, he blew from his lips a small blue flame that hovered in the van for a moment before extinguishing. The temperature in the van instantly increased by ten degrees.

"Don't play games with me! You won't like the consequences!" Jonesy hissed.

Hugh and Summer turned white, Sam growled, and Lee looked appalled. Erik had no reaction other than to the harsh words.

"You might want to back down there, chief." Erik said with a smirk. "I probably outweigh you by fifty pounds…and thirty of that is muscle. Besides, I'm pretty sure I've been in a few more bar brawls in my time." Erik started to chuckle and turned to Hugh still white faced. "Can you believe this runt? Thinks he's gonna kick my ass!"

Lee grabbed his friend's arm and pulled him closer. He whispered a harsh warning in his ear.

"You need to cool down NOW or I'm gone."

Jonesy almost immediately let go of his "devil" and looked into Lee's eyes. Lee could tell he realized what he'd done.

"You're right. I don't know what's come over me." Slowly he turned back to the rest with a heartfelt apology. "I'm sorry, my friends. This has been the find of a lifetime. We are so close and yet so much can go wrong. I'm just very anxious. I hope you can forgive me."

Erik realized he was in a very different place with some very strange people. These were believers: the people who actually believed in the bullshit he wrote and photographed. He had met believers before. He had interviewed them and had great skill in embellishing their stories beyond their own fucked up imaginations had allowed. What was different now was that he was outnumbered. But what was also different was that he found himself gaining some respect for them, at least for Dr. Bondurant. And now he was responsible for leading them to a cove that contained nothing more than some form of large reptile.

He felt prone to accept Jonesy's apology. He began to realize that the stories he wrote as a joke and to make some quick cash had a profound effect on people like this. He helped fuel their belief in something that didn't exist. Erik began to feel he was the guilty party,

"Dr. Sam, you don't need to apologize to me. I'm the one who owes you an apology."

A look of shock fell over Jonesy's face. The others turned to look at Erik as well.

"What...What do you mean?" asked Jonesy with his lower lip trembling.

"I didn't see the Imoogi." Erik felt awful. "At least I didn't see what you described."

"But you had a picture!" protested Jonesy.

"Yes," Erik began solemnly. "But the real critter didn't look like this Imoogi character. I purposely took the photo out of focus and made sure there was nothing in the background to indicate size." Everyone looked stunned. Erik felt like a turncoat even though he hadn't known any of these people more than a week.

"But why would you do this?" asked Jonesy with a tear of defeat in his eye.

Erik looked at all of them ashamed. It was one thing to pull a fast one on people you never met in person. Pulling a fast one on Top Gun graduates who thought they were God's gift to the sky was also justifiable. He was in the company of flakes, granted, but they were good hearted flakes. Summer and Hugh worked hard for their TV show trying to find scientific evidence of paranormal phenomenon. Jonesy and Bondurant were well respected archeologists who thought they had come across the find of a lifetime. Erik had lured them all out here in the hopes that he could get some pictures of them at the scene to use for the bullshit story he was writing. Every prankster at heart sooner or later pulls a gag that crosses the line between funny and cruel. What separates the fun loving from the asshole is when he recognizes that line. Erik couldn't have felt worse.

"I'm not a reporter like Summer and Hugh. They work hard to bring respectability and scientific reality to the study of the paranormal. Me, the editors I work for, and every other journalist I've met on the staff....we just make shit up. None of the guys I work for believe in this stuff."

"Then why do you write about it?" begged Jonesy.

"To sell copy. We cater to old ladies who'll believe anything they read and to college boys looking for a laugh. We make it all up. The crazier the better."

There was dead silence in the van. The most effected was Jonesy who sat in a catatonic state staring at the floor. Summer thought she now understood Bondurant's interrogation. This guy had duped them all into a wild goose chase. Everyone looked at Erik as if he was the asshole he felt he was. All, except Lee. Hearing a confession like that had confirmed some of his suspicions but dispelled others. Certainly Erik had an ulterior motive but his admission of guilt showed that he also had a conscience. Lee was beginning to formulate a hypothesis about some of the other peculiar traits this smuggler seemed to possess. Erik's proximity made Lee's familiar mute and a world famous clairvoyant deaf and blind. More curiously, Jonesy's magical display had made no impression. Erik had acted as if he hadn't seen the glowing eyes or a blue flame floating out of Jonesy's mouth. Lee finally had enough raw information about the man to get a gut feeling.

"Jonesy," said Lee in a reassuring tone. "Don't give up yet. Let's just go to the cove he described and find out what he really did see."

"But he just said that..." Jonesy trailed off despondently.

"Jonesy, he can't even verify what he saw," Lee said attempting to interject some hope. "I have one question. Do Imoogis live in sea caves?"

"Yes," he replied not sure where Lee was taking this.

Lee gave a confident smile and slapped his chest in a show of bravado.

"Well, then that's why you brought me." Lee looked back at Erik, "So you think it's the next turn off down the road?

Chapter 17

HEARING THAT THEY were going to go ahead with the search, took some of the edge off Erik's guilty conscious. After all, he'd done the right thing and confessed to the truth. If these people were still dumb enough to believe they should keep looking for an Imoogi, who was he to question?

"Yeah. Let's try the next one down."

Jonesy pulled back onto the road and drove a little further. He pulled into another access road and down to the beach. It was a small strip of sand beach, less than 100 yards in length. It was book ended on each side by rocky cliff bands that dropped sharply into the surf. On the southern cliff band was the cove from which Erik had first seen the critter.

"This is the place." Erik said. "That's the cove he came out of."

Parking the van about 30 yards from the cove, the passengers piled out and began assembling gear. Sam was amused at the way each one had dressed for the occasion. Depending on what social class, hobbies, and occupation they had, people had a way of carrying their own fashion style into the field. Lee wore khaki Ex-Officio convertible pants with a white Sahara style button down shirt, and a full brimmed Patagonia safari hat. Erik was the most unchanged. He had on his Chaco sandals and a Hawaiian shirt. He wore a pair of khaki flight pants that looked as if they had been the lower half of a standard nomex flight suit. Summer was still dressed much as they had always seen her; in a white gauze embroidered tunic and a multicolored broom skirt, with her turquoise squash-blossom necklace, long dangling turquoise and silver earrings and the 4 inches of silver loop bracelets on her wrists. The only change she had made was to replace her Birkenstock sandals with Teva Sport sandals. Hugh, the true outdoor fashonista of the group, wore casual outdoor slacks by Cloud Veil and a pullover top by Ark'teryx. But not to be outdone by any of them, Jonesy took his nickname to heart wearing his Filson Fedora, a brown leather jacket and khaki shirt and pants. Watching the five of them step from the van was like watching token representatives from every imaginable subculture of the outdoor community arriving at a summit event.

As soon as he was free of the van, Sam started pacing back and forth. To a casual observer he was just a dog anxiously awaiting the imminent walk, but Sam was actually testing the waters.

"The rain in Spain falls mainly in the plain," he said to himself. He repeated it until he finally heard a response from Lee.

"What's that, Sammy?"

"Just checking the depth," replied the old pointer.

"All the same, I'm glad to hear your voice."

`Sam judged his distance from Erik to be about 10 feet.

"If you need me just be sure 'he' keeps this distance."

Lee looked between the two and gathered the range for himself. "Understood."

Jonesy was used to their banter and paid no heed, focusing more on readying his gear. Summer noted the conversation's content but Hugh was still stunned every time he heard the dog talk. Erik was the only one who carried on as if nothing had happened. He simply busied himself with selecting the right lenses to take down to the beach.

Hugh and Summer were the first to get down to business. They walked off to the side to get some exposition shots with Summer acting as announcer for the piece. Lee grabbed some quick reference cards of magical spells and incantations he felt he might need. He placed them in a shoulder slung satchel and was ready to head down to the beach.

Erik was busy taking some landscape shots of the beach when Jonesy caught his eye. Jonesy had opened one of the trunks he'd brought and pulled out a belt that held both a holstered revolver and a whip. Just as Erik was ready to make a snide comment about how Jonesy took his nickname too seriously, he spied the rest of the contents of the trunk. The trunk was full of an assortment of weapons. Two swords, one with a blue scabbard and one with a red, a high powered rifle and scope, and an HK-MP-5 sub machine gun. The rest of the trunk was filled with extra clips and ammunition.

"Jesus Christ, Jonesy! You take yourself way too seriously!" Erik snorted at the slightly built archeologist.

Lee glanced over at the exchange and noted the weapons chest. He understood Jonesy's precautions. Magi had a tendency of running into some pretty mean critters both natural and supernatural. It never hurt to carry a little self defense just in case you miscast a spell. Lee had a Glock hidden in the small of his back but a chest full of weapons did seem a little much.

"I thought you said these things were benevolent?" Lee asked.

Jonesy buckled his gun belt on and then closed the chest. "They are. I always bring the whole chest just in case," Jonesy replied sheepishly. "Let's head down to the cove and begin, shall we?"

All agreed and began following Erik down to the area where he had taken the photo. Lee and Sam hung back and seemed to mope their way forward until the others were out of earshot and briefly out of sight.

"What do you think, old friend?"

"I think we need to take some of our own precautions," the dog replied. "I think you may need to give me some extra time just in case I need to find a helper quickly."

"You know I hate to do that to you."

"Until you perfect the time incantation, the blood scribe is the only way to guarantee results. Just do it quick before Summer catches you. Korean animal shelters are worse for dogs than Turkish prisons are for hash smugglers."

"Okay," Lee pondered his options but knew Sam was right. He pulled an ornate knife from its sheath on his belt. "I'd rather see you bloodied than in soup." Lee kneeled down and grabbed his friend to help brace him for the coming pain. He carefully lowered the point of the knife to the old dog's neck. Blood inscriptions were a form of ritual scarification practiced by many African shamans. By using a ceremonial carving knife to cut into one's flesh, an incantation that would take much longer to perform could be activated with one key word. Because of Lee's African ancestry, blood inscriptions were one of his specialties but he used them sparingly because it was a painful ordeal and there was only so much room on a body for scars. Lee had performed several on himself, usually hiding them on his chest, but always tried to avoid giving them to Sam. It wasn't easy for Lee to cause his best friend pain.

Pulling hair out of the way Lee carefully carved a brief outline of an hourglass while chanting the full incantation. Sam winced and whined as quietly as he could so he wouldn't draw attention. When the cutting and the incantation was done, Lee placed both hands on the wound and said, "Shiga."

"Oh, god, that sucks!" growled Sam.

"I'm sorry, my friend, but it's not done."

"What! How can it not be done!" He barked.

"We are near the ocean. There is another incantation that will help you find a sea sprite should we need one," Lee replied apologetically.

"Oh, why do I always volunteer for these missions," Sam whined.

"Sorry, Sammy." Then Lee quickly braced his friend and began cutting him again. This time he carved a quick oval with ten painfully squiggly lines following. When he was done with the incantation he said "Calamari."

The Magi and the Familiar had finished just in the nick of time. Summer had noticed their disappearance and her clairvoyant senses had told her that Sam was in pain. She doubled back looking for the two until they came into view. She saw Lee hunched over Sam and shouted to them.

"Sam, are you okay? I sensed…Pain!"

"Oh, that's just great!" barked Sam. "She caught us."

"Sam, don't worry." Lee said with a wink. "I'm just pulling a thorn from your paw."

Sam looked to his beloved person with his sad brown eyes and raised an eyebrow. Summoner's who choose dogs as their familiars choose them for many of the same reasons that normal people choose dogs for pets. They have the undying loyalty and unconditional self sacrifice that is hard to find in any other creature on earth. But that doesn't mean they blindly accept their master's stupid comments.

"Lee, she's a psychic!" Sam said marveling at how a man of such intellectual competence could lack simple common sense from time to time.

"Trust me. She must sense that I didn't want to cause you harm."

"Easy for you to say. You get an animal cruelty ticket. I wind up on the local menu!" They both shut up as Summer came within earshot.

"Sam, is he hurting you?" she inquired, casting an evil eye towards Lee.

Lee stood up and spoke the truth. "Yes, I am Summer. And for a good reason."

"How dare you! There are ways to train dogs that don't require pain. Besides, Sam is special. He is more than just an ordinary dog. I can hear him talk, Dr. Bondurant. Not only am I a trained psychic but I am a trained dog whisperer as well."

"Look, Summer," Lee said. "I know this might look like animal cruelty but trust me when I say you don't understand what's going on here."

Sam rolled his eyes. Lee never took the direct approach to things. "Look Summer," Sam interrupted. "We don't have time for this interrogation and if you even think of turning us into animal control I'm going to bite you!" He barked.

Summer took note of Sam's sudden hostility towards her attempted intervention.

"Oh, this is so sad. My dog whispering mentor often warned that the codependency of an abused dog was often stronger than that of a battered woman. You should be ashamed of yourself, Dr. Bondurant. I thought you were a much different person." Summer then huffed off back towards the beach.

Sam and Lee stood in momentary silence before following.

"She certainly misread you. You sure she's as good a psychic as she claims to be?"

"I wouldn't worry about it too much, Sam. According to most research, psychics tend to be very emotional people. That emotional sensitivity gives them much of their power. But that same sensitivity can cloud their gifts when confronted with something close to the heart. Summer is a card carrying member of PETA and a strong advocate for animal rights. She knew I caused you pain but she couldn't dig deep enough to discover the reason why."

"Still…I'm not altogether confident in this motley crew. Summer's crusading is clouding her clairvoyance, Erik is a magical black hole, and Jonesy is falling off the deep end. Who can we trust?"

"Hugh seems reliable. He appears to be a good cameraman and he's taking great pains to remain unbiased in his reporting."

"Oh, that's just great," Sam said rolling his eyes. "What the hell good will he be to us if something goes wrong? We'll have excellent documentary evidence of the world's first recorded Imoogi attack!"

"Don't panic," sighed Lee. "Powerful rich men who employ magical familiars are supposed to be the conspiracy not the conspiracy theorists."

Sam finally quit his whining and as the two were heading down to the beach he asked, "are Imoogis related to alligators?"

"I don't know. Why?" said Lee.

"Because alligators love dog meat maybe more than Koreans do!" lamented Sam.

"Sam, for Pete's sake! I'm not going to let anyone eat you, okay?" Lee stopped and looked directly at Sam.

"Yeah, okay." Sam was not entirely convinced Lee would have much say about it if things went south.

Chapter 18

THE OTHERS WERE standing at the far side of the beach almost to the cliff band as Lee and Sam got to the beach. It was low tide and the party followed Erik to the shallow surf so they could actually see the cove.

The cove faced the sea and as such could only be accessed at low tide. Even in the low waters, the floor of the cave was submerged. It was about twenty feet wide and ten feet from the waterline to the top. It was too difficult to see how deep from the waterline the opening plunged but judging from the shape of the visible opening, Lee guessed another five feet at low tide. The darkness in the cave made it impossible to tell how deep into the cliff band the cave tunneled but the echoing surf indicated that it was more than just a shallow cove.

"This is where you took the picture?" asked Jonesy in an excited tone.

"Yeah. Actually a little over to the side," Erik said pointing to a spot more inland. "I didn't want the size of some of the inland features to tip the size of the critter."

"What do you think, Lee?" Jonesy said turning to his friend.

"We can post someone here in the surf to keep an eye out for it, but I'll need to be further inland. I want to do a few inscriptions and I don't want them to get washed out in the surf."

"Sounds good. I'll stay here and keep watch. You and Sam can head inland."

This was too good an opportunity for Hugh to pass up. "Jonesy, I mean, Dr. Sam, do you mind if I stay here and film."

"Not at all and it is okay for you to call me 'Jonesy'."

"Thank you. May we also get an interview with the cave as a backdrop while we wait?"

"That will be fine, too."

Hugh was happy to see that since arrival, Jonesy's mood had calmed considerably.

"Summer, you have those questions we wrote?"

"Yes, Hugh. You want to do the interview in the surf?" she asked smiling.

"Yes, please. The backdrop is too beautiful to pass up."

"I like your style."

As the three began preparing for the interview, Sam and Lee walked about 20 feet up from the surf's edge. Erik followed them, mostly to get his feet dry, when he noticed Lee hunching over and inscribing a large circle in the sand.

"What the hell are you doing there?" he asked Lee.

Lee looked up from his notes and his inscription. "Just some more mumbo jumbo that you don't believe in."

"No, really. I'm curious. It looks like one of those floor markings the Satanists use in all the spooky movies. You going to draw a pentagram in that circle?"

"First of all a pentagram is not a symbol of Satan worship. Secondly, I'm not planning on drawing a pentagram in the circle."

"Okay, so what's it for?"

"Mumbo Jumbo."

"Okay, look, I call a truce. Maybe I don't believe in some of the stuff you all do but that doesn't mean it doesn't interest me. Does this symbol have some historical significance?"

"Well, if you are genuinely interested…yes, it does. First of all, floor inscriptions are used by almost all religions that predate

Judeo/Christianity and Islam. The old priests believed that the circle could be used as a platform from which to call supernatural creatures."

"You mean like demons and shit?"

"Demons, spirits, or any creature that possesses more magic than we do. The thing that determines what you hope to call depends on the inscription inside the circle."

Erik looked at the inscription Lee was working on. On the edge of the twelve foot circle, Lee was drawing what appeared to be hieroglyphic snakes. "So is that the inscription for the Imoogi?"

"Not exactly. I couldn't find a specific inscription for the Imoogi in the literature. This one just generally calls for a serpent."

"Ahh, so that will be your excuse if a snake shows up."

Lee stood up and glared at Erik momentarily. "If you're asking these questions only to make fun…!"

"Sorry, sorry," Erik replied holding up his hands in surrender. "It's hard for me. I grew up in Montana. If we didn't see it with our own eyes we didn't believe it."

"That's funny. According to Hugh, you have seen it and you still don't believe it."

"Oh, that's just Hugh. He's not a pilot. Trust me, when you first start flying, you start to see UFO's everywhere. Then you realize that every time you come close enough to an unidentified flying object to identify it, it is something innocuous; a flight of fighter planes in an odd formation, a weather balloon blown off course, or a curious looking cloud. It becomes obvious that a UFO means just that: Unidentified Flying Object. It doesn't mean alien space craft."

"Well, Erik, if that's your idea of an apology, I guess I'll accept it. But please try to understand that I do believe in a number of things which you do not and because of that I need to finish up here. It will be easier for me to do so uninterrupted."

"Sure, sure. Sorry. Be my guest. Actually, I'd love to take a picture of the inscription when you're done. From a humanist perspective, it is a beautiful piece of sand art."

"Actually, no!" Lee looked at him slyly. "I don't want to see my work wind up on the pages of your magazine."

"Oh, look, Doctor," Erik shook his head. "I may not agree with your beliefs but I respect you enough not to cheapen them by placing them on the cover of that trash." Erik was very sincere in his statement. To be told by such a cynic that he was respected was quite a compliment to Lee.

"Thank you for that but I'm afraid I still can't allow it."

"What, is it copyrighted?" Erik chuckled and acquiesced.

"In a way...yes." Real Magi were much like performance magicians in that they closely guarded their spells. Lee was as protective of his spells as David Copperfield was about his tricks. "In fact, I would feel happier if you found a spot over there while I finish up. No offense."

"None taken," Erik really didn't care that much anyway other than the beach art was beginning to look pretty cool. He walked over to where Lee had pointed and found a rock to sit on that was not too far from the trail leading up to the van. He could see why Lee had picked it. From this angle, the ground looked flat enough that there was no way he could cheat and photograph the inscription even if he used a zoom lens. While that was part of the purpose of Lee's banishment, the bigger objective was to make sure that Erik was far from himself or Sam should they need to cast spells.

With Erik out of the way, Lee quickly set to work. He finished the inscription and then studied some spoken incantations he wanted crisp in his memory. He looked to his trusty companion.

"You ready, Sam?"

"As I'll ever be," Sam woofed. "What's in the inscription?"

"As I told Erik, it's not specific to the Imoogi. It's more an all purpose inscription used to call and bind any serpent or reptile."

"Do you think you can control it, or at least influence it if it arrives?"

"Doubtful it will have that much effect. Not specific enough. But the binding should at least act as a temporary trap. So if it does have hostile intentions we should have a few minutes to run away from it."

"So how do we make sure it gets in the circle?"

"Any serpent or reptile should be naturally drawn to the circle but probably not as much as it is towards Jonesy's orb. We must make sure that Jonesy lures it onto the inscription before he gives it the orb."

"How do you plan to convince Jonesy of that?"

"Not a matter of convincing him. I'm not going to begin the summoning until they are done with the interview and I can ensure that Jonesy is standing behind the inscription."

"Good plan. You're clever for a human."

"Thanks, buddy. A compliment from you and one from the cynic. This day is looking up," Lee knelt next to his familiar and started scratching him behind the ear and scratched all the way to the small of his back. Sam loved this treatment. His tongue fell out the side of his mouth as he panted and his stub of a tail wagged in the air. Sam had learned long ago that the quickest way to get the scratch massage was to first stroke Lee's ego. The person who said that ass kissing never got you anywhere never had a scratch massage from Lee! The two stood up and headed down to the surf to hurry up the trio.

Chapter 19

HUGH WAS A seasoned enough cameraman to endure almost any hardship to film a good scene. Summer and Jonesy were knee deep in the water conducting the interview. Hugh had framed the shot beautifully in the early morning light. Summer was on the right and Jonesy, in his Indiana Jones attire, was on the left. Bisecting the two was the edge of the cliff band as it cut back towards the more mellow slopes of the sandy beach. In the far right of the shot, the cave plunged into the dark rock of the cliff.

To capture this scene, Hugh had to go deeper in the ocean than the others. He was waste deep in the gentle low tide surf. He had to steady himself as much as he could with the gentle waves pushing him slightly forward and back. In the editing room, he could stabilize the image with computer assistance but that required cutting off the outer frame of the shot. Because he didn't have much leeway on either side of his frame, it meant doing everything he could to stabilize the twenty pound camera in the surf. It was a strenuous job even at low tide.

"We're here on the Eastern shore of South Korea not far from the border with North Korea and the demilitarized zone," began Summer. Just then Hugh interrupted.

"Cut! Cut! Cut!"

"I hardly began." Summer looked surprised, "What did I do wrong."

"Oh nothing," replied Hugh apologetically. "Sam and Lee just walked into the left end of the frame." It wasn't that Hugh didn't want to interview Dr. Bondurant as well, but this interview had been set up for Jonesy and it was so picturesque that Hugh didn't want any interference in his background. He yelled onto them at the beach, "Dr. Bondurant, you are getting in the frame. Would you step back while we finish this up?"

Lee looked around finally realizing what he had done.

"Well, I need to speak to Jonesy!"

"Can it wait five minutes? I just have one more take here and the tide is about to come up!"

Hugh could see Lee turn and exchange a few words with the talking dog. Lee then looked up and shouted back.

"Yeah, I guess so."

As soon as Lee and Sam exited the frame, Hugh set himself up again.

"Sorry about that, guys. Not anyone's fault. Dr. Sam Da Soo, Imoogi interview #3, take 2 is rolling."

"We are here at the eastern shore of South Korea not far from the North Korean border and the demilitarized zone. I'm standing here today with Dr. Sam Da Soo, Chief of Archeology for Seoul University. Behind us is a cave where some sighting suggests a mythical Imoogi exists. Dr. Sam, we have already interviewed you in regards to your 'Dragon Orb' discovery. Can you enlighten us as to how exactly the myth of the Dragon Orb and the Imoogi fit together?"

"Well, of course, Summer. Dragon Orbs are thought to be the power behind a dragon. Almost any serpent or reptile that acquires a Dragon Orb will then become a dragon."

"Couldn't that be dangerous," Summer joked in the same condescending way that all TV reporters joked. Even though she was a sensitive psychic at heart, she knew how to act superficial for the camera.

"Well, I suppose it could but that is why we are here hoping to find the Imoogi. Imoogis have always brought good fortune in

Korean folklore. They are benevolent and kindhearted creatures. So it is believed that an Imoogi that becomes a dragon will use its new powers for good."

Hugh was doing his best to listen to the interview but it was difficult. On a two person team, the cameraman was often the defacto director because he was the one with the image in site. He was also the person responsible for noticing when something said on tape comes out wrong or sounds stupid. But three feet in the surf, it was next to impossible to perform all his tasks. To keep his image as stable as possible, Hugh was constantly scanning his eyes to the edge of the frame to ensure that he wasn't drifting too far to the right, left, up, or down. And while scanning to the left, he noticed something bobbing in the surf of the cave.

At first, it appeared to be a large curvy tree sized piece of driftwood coming out of the cave. But he realized the tide was slowly coming in, so how could driftwood be coming out of the cave? He was scanning back to check the right edge of his frame when he saw it. From his peripheral vision he saw two very large eyes.

"What the...?" he said as he ditched his frame and centered his lens in the general location of the sighting.

Summer noticed Hugh's reaction.

"Oh! My God! I sense something," she said without skipping a beat.

Jonesy spun around to see what was happening. Could it be he was finally this close to a culmination of a life's work? Then all three of them saw it. Swimming towards them was a twenty foot long serpent. If it had been any further away it could have been mistaken for an anaconda or a python but at this range it was obviously much different. It was easily twice the girth of a large snake and its face was totally different. Being much larger than it should have been, the head seemed totally disproportional to the body. Unlike the creepy yellow slits of a snake's eyes, the Imoogi had large round blue eyes. Compared to the rest of the face, the eyes were ridiculously large. It had a mane of large beautiful feathers in a brilliant bouquet of colors surrounding its almost cherub like facial features. As it approached, they could see a pair of small arms attached to the upper body, close to the creature's head.

Although its movements were dictated by its snakelike body, it did not slither through the water. Instead it seemed to bounce almost like a dolphin frolicking in the water, coming for a round of the "touch the red dot and get a fish" game. Hugh kept his camera fixed on the creature as it approached. Summer and Jonesy were speaking in audible excitement in the background, but Hugh wasn't paying attention. He was transfixed on this beautiful creature. He mentally searched his criptozoological database for answers to this curious morphology. What was the mane for, was it for mating like a peacock's tail? Why were the eyes so large and so bright blue? Why would it have such tiny arms? Why would a snakelike body need arms at all? No answers came to mind.

He was glad he had opted out of the Loch Ness expedition. Nessie had nothing on this. Nessie, like most creatures studied in cryptozoology, were theorized to be creatures created from the process of natural selection. They were generally thought to have long been extinct like Bigfoot, or products of recent evolution like the Chupacabra. The Imoogi had features and characteristics that were not bound by Darwin's model. In its form, movement, and regal behavior, this was a creature that seemed truly magical.

When the creature was within ten feet of Jonesy and Summer, it raised its head and little arms out of the water. It had a large friendly smile and slowly blinked its beautiful blue eyes. It then quickly clapped its little hands together like a child flush with excitement at a birthday party. Hugh couldn't believe his luck. Not only was this thing real but he was standing only ten feet away capturing it on hi-definition digital. It was big, it seemed friendly, it looked magical in every way imaginable, and most of all it was cute.

Trembling with excitement, Jonesy was the first to try to speak to it. He gave a traditional Korean bow and greeted it.

"Anyong Haseo."

"Anyong Haseo." The Imoogi replied and bowed in return.

Hugh hurriedly sidestepped, adjusting his frame so he had the image of Jonesy and Summer making contact with the Imoogi in the middle.

"Oh, my God, Summer! It even speaks." Hugh was thrilled.

"I know, I know. Are you getting this?"

"Hell, yes!"

"I'm going to see if it speaks English." Summer stepped slightly forward and bowed. "Hello."

The Imoogi blinked its big blue eyes at Summer.

"Herro," it replied. It giggled hysterically as it clapped its tiny hands over its mouth hiding its face like a shy child playing peek-a-boo.

"Do you speak English?" continued Summer.

"Ohhh! Englishy no!" The Imoogi giggled again and shook its head. "Aww," said Summer. "Your English is better than my Korean. You're very beautiful…and cute!"

"Ohh, me no cute!" The Imoogi obviously understood the compliment and shyly hid its face behind its hands and giggled some more.

"Oh, yes you are!" said Summer in a soothing tone. "You're the cutest, most beautiful creature I've ever seen." Summer then turned back to the camera, "I sense that this is a friendly animal."

Hugh was glad Erik was back on the beach with the others. He really didn't want to have to edit out, "No shit, Sherlock," or perhaps, "Thank you, Captain Obvious," from the background audio.

"Do you have a name?" Jonesy asked.

"My name is Cho Joo-Eun," the Imoogi replied covering her mouth with her hands and giggling again.

"Beautiful silver pearl," said Jonesy. "What a perfect name."

The Imoogi then focused its attention towards Jonesy's satchel. It was obvious that she must have known that the orb was within. It dropped its shy act and gave Jonesy a broad smile.

"Bueyo?"

"She must know what's inside". Summer said to Jonesy. "Do you think it is okay to give it to her or is there some ceremony?"

"I don't know of any rituals. I suppose it's all right. After all, it is supposed to be given to an Imoogi," replied Jonesy.

Jonesy took the Orb out of his satchel, unwrapped it and held it before the Imoogi.

"A beautiful pearl for a beautiful pearl." he smiled.

Chapter 20

IN THE EXCITEMENT of the discovery, all three had lost track of everything else around them. As Hugh kept focusing on the scene unfolding in front of his lens, he heard Dr. Bondurant's voice in the background yelling, "Stop!"

It seemed that in the blink of an eye, Lee's plan to contain the situation was smashed. He realized that Hugh's theory about Erik was correct. Erik had seen an Imoogi. He just didn't recognize it for what it was. Lee had expected to summon the creature to him. Having the creature just appear was completely unexpected. Lee tried one more time to call to his friend.

"Stop, Jonesy! Bring it on the beach first. Damnit, Jonesy, STOP!"

Lee finally gave up as he saw Jonesy pull the orb from his satchel and hand it to the Imoogi who was a good fifty feet from Lee's summoning circle. Lee threw his arms in the air in desperation as he realized all his good intentions had just been swept out to sea.

"Looks like your plan didn't work," Sam said looking up at Lee. "I don't know about you but I kinda have a sudden sense of foreboding."

Lee just shook his head in reply. "Let's just hope Jonesy is right about this Imoogi."

For the moment, things looked promising. Lee and Sam watched the Imoogi gleefully take the orb. Then it reached down and hugged Jonesy, Summer, and even Hugh. It was certainly a friendly enough gesture. Then it bowed politely and began swimming back to its cave.

From his rock at the edge of the trail to the road, Erik kept snapping pictures. He was glad he hung back. He wasn't sure how he was going to sell these pictures as an Imoogi sighting. He had been wrong about his original hypothesis. It wasn't some sort of crocodile but instead about a twenty foot long Anaconda type snake. He had to keep pulling the image slightly out of focus to make it look like it had more girth. It could be an interesting discovery on its own.

No large constrictor snakes were known to live in the Korean peninsula but he knew from Hugh's close perspective he would obviously be the one scooping that story. So Erik just kept playing with his focus and shutter speed, and moving around trying to find useful light reflections of the morning ocean. He had to admit the backlight would help him create some image that would be useful for the *WWI*. As he was snapping images he saw Summer and the rest reach out and hug the thing.

"What a bunch of dip shits," he thought. While he didn't believe the movie myths of snakes that big eating people, he realized that constrictors of that size certainly had the ability to kill a person if it felt threatened. Of the three of them, Hugh should have at least known better. The kid had started out as a nature photographer after all.

Chapter 21

GLEEFULLY, THE IMOOGI grabbed its orb, said "annyonghi kaseyo" and headed off towards its cave. She knew the perfect spot in her cave to await the transformation.

"I'm going to be a Dragon! I'm going to be a Dragon!" she thought. *"I really can't believe my luck! So many others like me never became a Dragon. And those that did had to wait thousands of years. And me at the young age of 897! I'm so young to receive such a gift!"*

She reached the entrance of her cave and fully submerged into her underwater home. She kept swimming deeper, imagining the great and wonderful things she would do when fully transformed.

"I'm sure I won't be infinitely powerful, but if I grow wings and can fly then I can at least help my native Korea stave off global warming. I can bring clouds in when Korea is in drought and blow them away when Korea floods. Korea can grow more rich and powerful with my help. Perhaps if I live long enough and grow powerful enough, I can even save the whole world from poverty and starvation. Even from global warming!"

All of a sudden she stopped swimming. She hadn't reached her favorite lair yet so she was trying to swim but a paralysis had come over her and she seemed to have no control over her body.

She almost panicked until she realized this might be what she was hoping for.

"This must be the first phase of the transformation! It's already begun!"

Then her body turned and began to swim back towards the entrance of the cave. Try as she might, she could not resist the bodily movements. It was as if she no longer controlled her own body. Then she felt a cold dark chill come over her. She was not alone.

"Who's there?"

"My name is Azi Dahaka!"

"What do you want from me?"

"Everything!"

Chapter 22

"JONESY! GET BACK here!" cried Lee once the Imoogi had left. With the Imoogi now gone, the three came back to reality. They heard Lee call and excitedly splashed back through the surf towards dry land.

"Oh, my god, Lee! Did you see that!" yelled Jonesy.

"I got it all on film! Can you believe that!" exclaimed Hugh.

"I have been truly blessed to have had that experience," said Summer. "I have never felt such spiritual awareness!"

"Just get back on the beach so we can talk," cried Lee.

Erik didn't see a need to leave his perch. They were all suffering from a mass delusion and he had already vowed not to bust any more bubbles today. He started sifting through the raw images he took on the small screen of his digital SLR. Erik could tell even on the small screen which images were too well lit and which ones were too clearly in focus. He busied himself by deleting those images before bothering to download them.

The others finally clamored onto the beach and gathered around Lee.

"Be careful not to disturb my inscription," Lee said.

"I hardly think we need that anymore," replied Jonesy.

"Well, it has other characteristics that may be useful." Lee said. "Okay, let's change the subject. What the hell was that, Jonesy? Couldn't you hear me calling you to the beach?"

"Sorry, in the excitement I lost myself." Jonesy was grinning from ear to ear.

"Jonesy, you of all people should have known that our best chance of controlling the outcome of this situation was to be sure the Imoogi was standing on that summoning circle before you gave it the orb!"

"Lighten up, Dr." replied Summer. "I was there and I felt absolutely no hostile intent from that beautiful creature. I assure you it was as benevolent as a bottle nose dolphin."

Of the entire group, Hugh perhaps had the most unbiased opinion. Even though he had been caught up in the moment himself, he could understand Bondurant's viewpoint. He also knew that Summer was prone to allow her own advocacy towards animals interfere with her psychic readings.

"Have you ever seen a bottle nose dolphin mate?" he quipped.

"Oh, quit lording your 'badass wildlife photographer' bullshit over my head," she cried. "I'll have you know that…" BOOM!!! She stopped mid-sentence and everyone froze. They heard the sound of falling rocks tumbling from the cliff. A few small rocks tumbled and fell onto the sandy shore and around the corner a few larger rocks tumbled into the ocean.

"Was that some sort of earth quake?" They heard Erik yell from his lonely perch a dozen yards away.

The others looked at each other fearing that while that was a possibility, the coincidence was far too great.

"I think the transformation has begun!" Jonesy exclaimed.

Boom! First they heard it, then they felt it, and then more rocks tumbled from the cliff.

"Hey, guys," Erik yelled to the huddled group. "You might want to stand away from that cliff before you get hit by a rock!"

The rest were in a state of suspended animation. They ignored Erik. It took Lee's firm leadership to snap them back to reality.

"Okay, every one! Gather up behind the summoning circle. On the off chance that something unexpected comes out of that cave, make sure that circle is between you and it."

While Jonesy and Summer were still optimistic about a friendly Dragon popping out the other side, the ominous quakes were enough to convince them to follow Lee's direction. From their position they could not actually see the creature emerging from the sea cave so they all hoped that when it came out it would follow the coastline until they could see it around the corner of the cliff. BOOM! More rocks fell. Hiding behind an etching in the sand they all turned towards Erik as he started yelling at them again.

"Hey, Jonesy! Are we on a fault line? I didn't think Korea was...OH SHIT! There's that monitor lizard I told you about!"

In unison they all snapped their attention back towards the sea. Peeking around the corner of the cliff was a monstrous reptilian face. They couldn't yet see the body, just a long reptilian neck that curved around the corner so it could look at them. The face bore little resemblance to the Imoogi seen just minutes before. The eyes were still large but gone were the innocent baby blues, replaced by squinting yellow viper eyes of a predator. The beautifully colored feather mane was replaced with spiky bones that jutted out from a cobra like hood. The friendly smile was replaced with a mouth full of razor sharp teeth.

Hugh was the first to react. He quickly slung the camera back on his shoulder and hit the record button before he even brought the creature into focus. This was his lucky day. He already had an up close view of an Imoogi and now he was filming the Dragon that it had become. He eagerly anticipated it stepping the rest of the way into view so he could capture its whole body.

"Oh, shit! There's two of them!" They heard Erik cry. "No wait! Three!" as he said this, they all saw two more similarly menacing heads emerge from behind the cliff.

Hugh couldn't wait to see what else was coming around the corner so he cautiously began sidestepping away from the sand circle and towards the surf. *Boom! Boom!...Boom! Boom!*. They all heard the powerful synchronized steps as the monster stepped into full view.

The three serpentine heads snaked their way down to the same powerfully muscled shoulders. On its front quarters were two heavily muscled arms with talon like claws for hands. In its front left claw, it held the orb with the front right claw free to help support its massive weight. The rear quarters were shaped like a lion all the way down to the pawed feet. The overall size of the body was close to the size of an elephant but its skin was unmistakably reptilian. There was no fat on this creature. It bulged with muscles that stretched the skin. Veins could be seen striating across its chest, arms and legs. Firmly planted in its upper shoulders were two large bat like wings that gave a wingspan of over 50 feet.

Being in the midst of two sorcerers, a familiar, a psychic, and a non believer, Hugh was hesitant to speak up, but as the Dragon came into view of his camera, a burning question came to his mind.

"Ahh, pardon my ignorance, but...are Asian dragons supposed to look like that?"

Lee knew exactly what Hugh was thinking. Asian dragons were generally portrayed as long serpentine creatures with elegant graceful features. This creature was large and squat with powerfully built appendages and an amalgam of body parts from almost every frightening creature from the human subconscious. In short, it looked more like a Western dragon. What worried Lee was that, unlike in Asian mythology, there were very few benevolent dragons in Western myths. As Lee searched his brain of the short list of good dragons in Western folklore, he couldn't think of any that had multiple heads. In fact, his memory told him that multi headed dragons tended to be the worst of the worst. Hydra, Tiamat, and God knows who this was! He wasn't going to take any chances. He looked to Sam and invoked the word, "Shiga!"

The coagulated wound on Sam's shoulder reopened and his blood flowed freely again. It was like experiencing the pain all over again. From Sam's view, everyone else stood frozen in time. He knew what he had to do. Sam sprang into action and charged the surf. For the next five minutes only five seconds of time would pass for everyone else. As he ran past the Dragon standing motionless, he fleetingly considered a preemptive strike. He dashed past the beast realizing that a German Short Haired Pointer could gnaw on a beast like that for an eternity without much effect.

Sam broke through the surf quickly enough. Other than the peaks and valleys of the morning tide, the waves, seemingly frozen in time, gave no more resistance than the calm of a still pond. He still couldn't dive deep enough for his quest. He dog paddled out as far as he could, waiting for the next incantation to be uttered from Lee's mouth. He heard in the distance Lee begin to utter the second incantation. He heard the "ka" sound but still swam on waiting for the painfully slow word to finally be uttered from Lee's mouth. "Laaa" Sam kept swimming. "Maaa"

Sam had a thirty second head start into the dead water of the sea before the word "Calamari" was finally spoken. Sam braced himself for he knew this spell would be much more painful. Again the wound opened up, then it felt as if his hair was ripped from his body. His paws, legs and tail painfully split into two as his bones dissolved into mush. His eyes grew and bloated until they felt as if they would burst. His mouth turned into a beak and slowly moved to the center of his bisected limbs that had grown into long tentacles. The brutally painful transformation had turned him into one of the fastest creatures of the deep. He was now a leviathan: a giant squid.

The three headed dragon stared down at the people on the beach to size up who he faced. He thought he had seen a dog but then it vanished. It could have been his eyes playing tricks on him. Azi Dahaka had not used eyes in five thousand years and was finding it difficult to focus. He could tell that four people stood huddled together and further away another person stood alone. As he blinked, his eyes he began to see distinct faces emerge.

While the Dragon had little concern for the small group, he was still weak from his long slumber and he decided not to take too many chances. As his eyes slowly cleared, he saw one of the creatures had only one eye and it seemed to be wearing some sort of armored helmet. Perhaps it was a Cyclops. A Cyclops was still no match for the Dragon but they were generally physically and magically stronger than humans so Azi Dahaka quickly decided to bite its head off.

Hugh was too busy with the technical details of focusing and framing the image to make any reasoned assessment of the Dragon's intent. He was too caught up in the euphoria of the moment to notice that the Dragon had singled him out. Before he knew it, one of the heads reared back and struck. The powerful jaws of the Dragon clamped down around Hugh's camera and wrestled it from his hands. The Dragon then jerked its head to the side flinging the camera more than 100 yards into the ocean. Hugh was too stunned to react. He could only follow the camera, with all his video evidence recorded within, sailing through the air until it splashed into the ocean.

Everyone stood in stunned silence until Summer finally spoke.

"Oh, My God! Hugh! I think he intends to harm you!"

By now, Summer's statement seemed a foregone conclusion. Lee was fairly convinced that his worst fears had been realized. He was about to be witness and victim to the first reported dragon attack in over 1,000 years. The Dragon began to rear back all three heads in preparation for attack. Lee anxiously looked at his watch. It had been almost ten seconds from when he had first sent Sam. He was running out of time and it was obvious he would have to make due with what he had on hand, or in this case, on body. Lee ripped off his shirt and threw it to the ground. He was in incredible shape for a man of his age but much of the muscle definition was hidden behind a blanket of scars that covered his chest, shoulders, and back.

"Everyone!" he screamed. "Get behind me!"

As the others dove for cover, Lee touched a cat face carving over his left breast. One of the Dragon's heads began a steady inhale as another began steadily exhaling fire. As Lee invoked the words, "nine lives," his twenty year old scar opened up and began leaking fresh blood. The force field between himself and the Dragon appeared just as the wall of flame hit it. Lee did his best to stand tall and take as much of the flame as possible so his friends had room to hide behind him.

The "nine lives" incantation did exactly that. It spewed forth a force field that would protect the Magi from exactly nine deaths. He could be shot in the heart nine times or survive nine fatal car crashes before he died. Its biggest draw back was that the sorcerer would still feel the pain of all nine deaths. Another complicating factor was that this Dragon had extra heads to spare. Instead of having to breathe a killing dose of fire, then take a breath and breathe another, one head was breathing for the other. The onslaught of fire was relentless.

Lee felt the mind numbing pain of being incinerated to death followed by an ever-so-brief pause and the homicidal pain began again. He was dying over and over again at an amazingly short interval. If he were to crouch and shield his vulnerable face, neck, and organs he might prolong each life but to do this might not give his friends enough cover.

"*Where the hell was Sam?*" he wondered. He had lost all track of deaths. It was difficult to count to two, let alone nine, under the agony of being burned alive. Fear began to take hold. Was this one it? Did I have any more? Was this my final life? The life I won't come back from? Just as he was about to give into the fear, pain, and uncertainty he felt himself lifted off his feet. He fell into a splash of water.

"*How had the tide risen so quickly?*" he thought. As he began to sink to the bottom, his natural instincts told him to swim to the surface for air. As he tried to do this a large tentacle wrapped itself around his midsection and pulled him under the water. He followed the tentacle to its source. A giant squid was holding him, Summer, Hugh, and Jonesy under the water. It was Sam.

Almost as quickly as the tide had appeared, it began to recede. Lee and the others were dropped back on to the sandy beach and they could once again breathe. Lee looked around and realized the water hadn't gone back into the sea. It had formed itself into a giant wall that stood between the Dragon and Lee's crew. Lee saw that the only thing holding the wall up was the will of one Merman.

Unlike the Disney version of mermen and mermaids, there was nothing about these creatures that would excite the sexual imaginations of a person who had actually seen one. The lower body was of a fish and the upper body was of a primate although it looked less like a human and more like the hairless body of an Austrailo Pithicus. They ranged in length from 3' to 4' and weren't known to have friendly dispositions. The one that Lee saw was big, about 4'2" in length. It balanced itself up on its tail and held its small muscular arms against the sea wall it had created. Lee knew that it was using all of its magical and physical strength to hold up the wall. It glared at Lee with clenched teeth and Lee could hear its voice in his head,

"We don't have much time. Get your fucking people to the sea and dive!"

Lee was too exhausted from his own ordeal to help directly.

"Jonesy! Help him hold the wall!" Lee shouted.

Fortunately for the group, one of Jonesy's strongest magical talents was incantation. While he certainly didn't have enough energy to create a wall of water like this, he could help to hold it in place once formed. There was visible relief on the face of the struggling Merman once Jonesy began to help.

Lee yelled at the others to run to the sea. He then tried to lift himself up but his forearms stung with a maddening pain. Looking down he saw third degree burns on his arms and upper thighs. Lee must have run out of lives. If their rescue had come a moment later he would have been dead.

"I'll help you!" cried Summer as she quickly grabbed him and started pulling him to the water.

Lee looked around and saw Hugh still motionless in disbelief.

"Goddamnit! Hugh! Run for your life!"

Sam's magic had worn off. He was no longer a giant squid but had returned to being a dog. A cold, wet, frightened, and irritated German Short Hair Pointer. None of this discomfort dissuaded him from acting as was the nature of man's best friend. While everyone else was caught up with their near death encounter and current flight to the safety of the sea, Sam was counting his people. One of "his" people was missing.

"Where's Erik?" he said.

At first they all looked back to the rock by the path that Erik had perched himself on. He was gone. Lee thought he understood. For a person who didn't claim to believe in hocus pocus, he must have had his belief system come crashing down on him when he saw the Dragon round the corner. His desire to run away must have been overwhelming once he saw that Dragon attack his traveling companions. Lee couldn't blame Erik's cowardice considering that once the attack occurred, Lee was mostly interested in defending himself and anyone smart enough to hide behind him. Just as Lee was forgiving Erik's abandonment of the party, he caught movement on the path leading to the van. The gaudy Hawaiian shirt and peculiar flight pants were unmistakably Erik's. Most peculiar of all was that he wasn't running away from the fight but towards it..

Chapter 23

THE MERMAN WAS the first to notice the small gun in Erik's hand and deduce his intentions.

"Is that fucker NUTS! This Dragon's going to be eating a dipshit crisp if he thinks he's going to kill it with that pee shooter." (It's important to note here that most Mermen learn English from sailors.)

"NOOO!" Screamed Jonesy. He had made a dire miscalculation today and only from the forethought of Lee and the grace of good luck had no one died yet. Now he watched in horror as Erik charged past the Merman's protective wall and took up a firing position on the Dragon's flank. Blood would soon be on Jonesy's hands.

"Damn you! Run for your life!" Jonesy shouted at Erik.

Jonesy watched in helpless horror as Erik cocked the MP-5 and opened up with a wall of lead aimed squarely at the Dragon. The Merman and Jonesy felt the pressure of the liquid rampart diminish as the Dragon focused its attention away from them and onto Erik. When the Dragon's attack on the Merman's wall had ceased, Jonesy braved a peek around the corner in the hopes of convincing Erik to take cover. He saw Erik firing three round bursts in turn at each of the Dragon's heads. The submachine gun belched out ten different bursts until the unmistakable ping of the action being kicked open signified that the gun had run out of ammo. Jonesy watched in horror as the Dragon reared up all three heads and each blew a deadly blast at Erik from point blank range.

Erik really couldn't believe how crazy this day had gotten. First he had hooked up with these nutcases for an expedition into the twilight zone. Then he'd come clean about what it was he actually saw and they still went through with it, acting as if they had won the lottery after seeing some large sea snake. Then three large Komodo Dragons come prancing around the corner and they got even more excited. Hugh shoved his camera in the face of one of the large reptiles and got it ripped from his hands. After that it was a full blown animal attack. The Komodos were attacking the UFO freaks and none of them seemed capable of defending themselves. Jonesy, who had a pistol on his belt, didn't make a move to fire on the beasts.

Even though he thought this group was a bunch of flakes, he wasn't going to stand by while they got mauled to death. He had dashed back up the trail to the van and grabbed the MP-5 submachine gun he'd seen in Jonesy's locker. When he ran back down the hill, it was with the full intention of killing three representatives of an endangered species. Summer and Hugh, perhaps all of them, would give him hell for killing a Komodo but Erik wasn't a city slickin' environmentalist. Erik was the son of a Montana hunting guide and in his book, human life took precedence over endangered species.

When he reached the beach, everyone was in a panic. They were running or crawling towards the surf. Erik really didn't know if that was a good idea since he had no idea if Komodos were good swimmers. He ran off to the flank of the beasts where he was sure a stray bullet would not miss and accidentally hit one of his group.

Just before he had opened up on the Komodos, he heard Jonesy yell at him to stop. In truth he was surprised he hadn't heard it from Summer but it seemed that muffin eating hippies were all alike no matter what country they came from. They'd rather die than see an endangered species killed.

"*Well not today,*" he thought, "*I'm going to save your ass, like it or not!*" Being a pilot, and the son of a guide, Erik had plenty of training on automatic pistols and bolt action rifles, but very little on sub machine guns. Never the less, most of the mechanisms seemed self explanatory. He found the cocking bolt, pulled it back and chambered the first round. Then he found the fire selector switch. He flipped it to the burst option. With every pull of the trigger, three rounds would be shot out of the barrel. He put the site on the first Komodo and fired.

PaPaPoom! Came the first burst echoing across the beach. Nothing! The gun kicked more than Erik expected and it seemed as if he missed the beast totally. Even if he missed though, the firing had distracted the creature which was good enough for now. He aimed at the next one down the line. PaPaPoom! And then the next. PaPaPoom! It seemed as if he missed every time. The Komodos started coming towards Erik and now it was time to shoot in earnest. PaPaPoom! PaPaPoom!

The Komodos kept advancing as Erik kept missing until one stood squarely in the center of Lee's silly sand art. They all seemed to hesitate after that. Erik wondered if perhaps he had hit one. This would explain their reluctance to continue. Erik kept firing, hoping to kill them or at least force them to retreat. He ran out of bullets before achieving either goal.

Erik was completely stunned and a little humiliated. Every kid from his hometown grew up watching **Die Hard** movies and **Magnum P.I.** reruns. They knew when armed with a submachine gun, the hero could fend off thirty or more "bad guys." The reality proved to be quite different. A submachine gun wasn't exactly a beginner weapon. They didn't have great range and if you didn't know how to handle the kick, they weren't that accurate. Erik was a good shot with a pistol and a hunting rifle but this obviously hadn't translated into accuracy with the MP-5. This miscalculation of his own skill with this weapon had caused him not to bother grabbing extra clips from the van.

He stood in shock with three pissed off Komodos ominously staring at him. The Komodos coughed up some lugis and spat at him in sequence. It was like being spat on by three camels simultaneously. Worst of all it was enough spit to literally drench his favorite Hawaiian shirt in the most awful smelling green slime. That was all Erik needed to push his humiliation over the edge. He was going to go back to the van and retrieve every round of MP-5 ammo and kill every one of these bastards.

When the flames subsided, Jonesy was relieved to see that Erik was still alive and unhurt. Lee must have cast a protection spell on the smuggler, since the only visible damage was a heavy coating of sweat on his shirt.

"Bless your talents, Lee", thought Jonesy.

"Jonesy!" Erik yelled. "You hang in there. I'm going back to the van for more Ammo!"

"No, Erik! Just get to the water!" yelled Jonesy. It was too late. Erik had just expended a thirty round clip without earplugs and was half deaf. He charged back to the van without acknowledging Jonesy's request.

"Lee!" Jonesy shouted. "Erik's going to attack it again when he comes back."

"Oh no!" Lee looked at the Merman. "We can't just abandon him if he's coming back. How long can you hold this wall?"

"Not much longer."

Summer then interrupted, "I think it wants to leave. Why doesn't it leave?"

Sam thought that was the most insightful piece of clairvoyance he'd heard from Summer.

"I can buy that. We are probably giving it more resistance than it expected." said Lee.

"So why doesn't it just leave!" cried Hugh in a panic.

Then they all heard the Merman's voice in there heads, *"Because 'Rambo's' little attack lured it onto a binding circle. It's like a pissed off bear caught in a sling."*

"Oh, No!" said Lee. He knew his circle was not strong enough to control a beast of this much power, but it apparently had enough influence to keep it from moving. If Summer was right and this thing was ready to call it quits, then the only way they could survive was to break the seal.

"I need to break that seal." Lee looked at the Merman. "Is there a point in your wall where someone could jump through the water to the other side?"

"My best guess would be right between me and your friend. But if this Dragon attacks with another endless stream of fire you won't need to worry about it because there won't be a wall left to protect us."

Lee didn't have any more scar enchantments that would do him any good here. He mentally flipped through his crib sheets of useful spells and found a strength inscription that he could scribe under the body of the Merman. This could give the Merman enough power to hold the wall up for another onslaught of fire. The only problem was that he could not be in two places at once. Someone would need to jump through the wall of water and physically kick a hole in the sand carving beneath the Dragon. The third degree burns on his forearms and thighs made it difficult for him to move anywhere without Summer's assistance. The Merman and Jonesy were preoccupied magically holding up a wall of water. Sam was obviously exhausted from his trip into the deep to find the merman. Erik was busy plugging useless rounds into the Dragon. That left Hugh.

Lee had never been in this position before. Somehow he had become the *defacto* leader of this motley crew and on their first outing they were in a life or death struggle with one of mythology's most formidable opponents. Whoever he sent through that wall would be unprotected against the wrath of the Dragon, but it had to be done. If there was even a chance that the Dragon just wanted to get the hell out of there, it had to be attempted even if it meant sacrificing one person's life for the good of the group. Besides, being the person least involved in the fight for survival,

Hugh was by far the most physically fit and athletic of the group and thus the most logical to send into the fire.

"Summer, help me to the merman!" Lee commanded. She did as told. When she helped him to his feet not only could he feel the extra support he needed to move but he felt a mild healing sensation in his burns. "Jonesy! Tell me when you see Erik return."

When he reached the Merman, he began inscribing a new circle around the ugly creature.

"What the hell are you doing, Mage?" the Merman asked. *"You want to bind me too so I can't leave you fucks when this Dragon gets serious?"*

"No. It's a strength inscription. It should help you hold the wall a little longer. Trust me. The last thing I want on my conscious is the death of one of the gods' most favored creatures. If this doesn't work, then I only ask that you hold the wall as long as you can and then escape before the Dragon has a chance to cause you harm."

"I'll give you what I can. This is becoming more complicated than your familiar led me to believe."

"I'm sorry for that. Jonesy!" Lee snapped, changing the focus of his commands. "Tell me when Erik arrives." Lee knew he would be too busy enchanting strength into the Merman to notice.

The Merman didn't fully appreciate the subtlety of Lee's plan. He was straining through the effort of holding up the wall.

"That Dragon is not stupid. He knows what that guy is. He won't attack your friend with magic fire. He'll hit him with real claws." the Merman conveyed to Lee.

"I know, but he's still the distraction we need." Lee looked at Hugh, "Hugh, when I say go you need to leap through the wall. It will be like jumping through the heaviest breaking wave you can imagine, but I know you can do it. When you get through you need to kick a hole in the inscription I carved in the sand."

"Are you crazy! I'll be burned to a crisp on the other side of this wall."

"Not if we wait until Erik arrives."

"Lee, the damn thing has three heads! I'm sure it can spare one for me while the other two are turning Erik into a roast!"

"Trust me, he won't."

"Why is that?"

"Because he's more afraid of him than he is of all of us put together." Hugh didn't really understand what that meant. Neither did any one else but the Merman. Hugh just trusted Lee for what he'd seen Lee do. He had created a force field that protected them against the Dragon long enough to call a Merman to raise a wall of water. Then, he cast a force field around Erik that was powerful enough to withstand all three Dragon heads breathing fire on him at the same time. All Erik had done was pop off a couple of rounds from a weapon that probably didn't even dent the Dragon's skin. How the hell could a Dragon be more afraid of a pudgy washed up pilot than it could of a powerful Magi with all his badass witchdoctor scars blazoned across his body?

Lee finished up the sand inscription under the Merman and began chanting the invocation. Just as he was speaking the last words, he heard Jonesy yell.

"He's coming!"

Hurriedly, Lee finished the incantation. The Merman immediately seemed to relax a bit as if a weight had been lifted from his shoulders. Lee turned his attention towards Erik running down the hill.

Erik was in a flat out sprint grasping the cocked and loaded submachine gun. In his deep front pockets clanked three more thirty round magazines. As soon as he hit the sandy beach, he ran back to his firing position.

"Don't you worry, guys!" he yelled. "I brought enough ammo to take down an elephant!"

Hugh did not exactly understand Erik's boast. In his mind they were dealing with something somewhat more substantial than an elephant. It was obvious that Erik was within seconds of firing at the Dragon and that's when Hugh heard Lee yell to him.

"GO NOW!"

Hugh did not second guess the command. He was dealing with a man who had enough magical skill to have kept them alive this long. Hugh prayed that Lee had some fancy protection spell reserved for him as he dashed towards the wall, leaping at the last second in the hopes of diving through the wall.

The wall was about a ten foot high mass of water that was unnaturally formed into shape by invisible forces created by the Merman. Hugh could feel the violent swirling mass of thousands of tons of water chaotically thrashing about within the wall as the billions of water molecules desperately searched for an escape and a return to the natural flow of fluid dynamics. Having at least tried about every outdoor adventure sport imaginable, Hugh was well qualified to judge the experience. It was much more frightening than swimming through heavy surf. It was more akin to being trapped under a dangerous hydraulic plume whose pressure could trap and pin a river rafter until drowning. Fortunately, the chaotic nature of the fluid flow and the running head start of momentum helped force Hugh out the other side.

Hugh hit the sand on the other side of the wall and gasped for air. Even though he had only been in the water for seconds the crushing force of the water seemed to force most of the air out of his lungs. He rolled to a stop a few meters from the wall's edge. Disoriented, he shook his head to clear his mind and get his bearings. The violent journey had carried him ten feet further up the beach before spitting him out. In an unfortunate coincidence, this had hurled him right under the belly of the Dragon.

Hugh felt like a frightened boy hiding under the table hoping the monsters would not look there. Even in the movies, the table was a stupid place to hide and since this table was made of the four legs and belly of the monster he hid from, it seemed like a foregone conclusion that he would be found. It was not long before one of the three heads peeked under its own belly and locked eyes with Hugh. It began to draw a deep breath as if it was ready to blow the fire that would extinguish Hugh's life. And just when he thought things couldn't get worse, he heard Erik scream at him, "Goddamnit Hugh! You're in my line of fire! Get out of the way!"

"Oh Great!" thought Hugh. *"I'm going to be incinerated, then shot, and then eaten!"* Despite Hugh's expectations of imminent doom, the Dragon did something completely unexpected. The head that stared at Hugh lost interest and snapped its focus around to Erik. In fact, all three heads of the Dragon were solely focused on Erik. What was even more odd was that none of them bothered to breathe fire. All three heads took swipes at Erik snapping with their jaws. This seemed to make no sense because Erik was still out of range of the creature's bite.

The enormous creature only had one claw trapped within Lee's summoning circle. The front left claw that held the pearl seemed permanently stuck in the sand. With Erik's sudden arrival, the other three appendages pulled at the trapped leg in a desperate attempt to flee.

Erik had yet to fire, still waiting for Hugh to clear out, "Hugh! Get the hell out of the way!"

The beast had lost it's futile attempt to escape and its three long necks could still not reach Erik. Then its enormous body began to spin around the circumference of the summoning circle pivoting off its entrapped foot. This jarred Hugh back into action. With the other legs moving, any one of them could purposely or accidentally crush the cameraman into the sand. He jumped, dodged and spun his way clear of the three moving legs until he was clear. Running from the belly of the beast, he could finally see the monster's intentions. The Dragon wasn't breathing fire on Erik, its heads and claws were hopelessly out of range, but in its new contorted position, it could strike at Erik with its long spiked tail.

There was no more time to wait. Hugh lunged at the summoning circle and kicked and scraped away as much of the etching as he could as fast as he could. The claw holding the orb immediately lifted from the sand. He heard Erik open up with a machine gun on full auto. The tail of the beast whipped around and hit Erik in the chest sending him and the machine gun flying across the beach.

For a moment, Hugh thought that the plan to release the Dragon wasn't so great after all. He looked for his quickest escape to the other side of the wall but before he could make a move, a powerful wind seemed to drop from the sky and knock him to his knees. Glancing up he saw that he was directly under the enormous wings of the beast as it slowly lifted itself from the beach and into the air.

Chapter 24

JONESY, LEE AND the Merman collapsed on the beach as soon as the Dragon had lifted up.

"Oh, my God! Oh, my God!" Jonesy kept yelling. "What. . .oh, my God! Lee did you see that? Oh, my God!" Jonesy was pale and shaking and looked as if he might have a heart attack right there.

"Yes, Jonesy, yes, we all saw it." Lee was panting with exhaustion. He looked to the Merman who was now left struggling on the sand. "Grab my arm," Lee said to him. "Are you hurt?"

"Well, I'll probably survive. But do me a favor, Mage. Don't come to me to help you kill this thing. I've got my own problems."

"Okay, I got it." Lee said as he and Sam dragged the Merman into the water. "Thanks. I know that's not much, but thanks." The Merman flopped into deeper water and dove out of sight. "How about you, Sammy? Are you okay?"

"I'm in better shape than you are." Sam said as he licked at Lee's burned arm."

"Ow.! I think I'll get some medicine for this." Lee said. Summer came over to help Lee as she saw him obviously struggling in pain.

"Let me help you, Dr. Bondurant." she said as she helped support him under the arm. "This is a very bad burn. I have some medicinal herbs I brought along. I think I still have some

Balsam of Peru and if so, I can make a poultice that would help ease the pain and allow it to heal more quickly."

"That would be great, Summer. I could use the help," Lee said and he realized that even as Summer touched him, his pain was less severe. She helped him to a rock where he sat as she went back to the van to get her supplies.

Lee looked over at Hugh who was still looking down at his feet where his broken camera had finally washed ashore. Then Lee looked again at Jonesy who was still wringing his hands.

"My God! What have I done?" Jonesy was sitting on the sand near where Lee was sitting. He was weeping with exhaustion and realization of what he had just unleashed on the world.

"Come on, Jonesy. It won't do any of us any good if you fall apart." Lee said. Sam went over and sat down beside Jonesy and put his head on his lap.

"Oh, Sammy. I'm so sorry. I'm so sorry." Jonesy started petting Sam and Sam knew enough to just be quiet. There were a lot of things he could say to Jonesy right now to make him feel worse but Sam knew Jonesy was feeling about as rotten as a human being could feel. Jonesy looked over at Lee.

"Lee, look, look at you! I did this to you. This was my fault." Jonesy cried even more thinking of how his friend had suffered for his mistake.

"Jonesy, we're going to fix this. Just try to calm down," said Lee. About that time, Summer came back with a bowl filled with water and some leaves crushed in it. She had scissors and several roles of gauze bandages that she set on the rock next to Lee. She unwrapped the gauze and put it in the bowl to soak. Then she turned her attention to Jonesy who was near to hyperventilating.

"Jonesy, I sense your panic. Now, Jonesy, take several deep breaths with me." Summer had come to his side now and was seated on the ground in front of him. She took both of his hands in hers and kept her voice calm and gentle. "Breathe in. Breathe out. Yes, that's good now just breathe and relax."

"Lee, I'm so sorry. I'm so sorry." Jonesy kept weeping even though Summer was trying to get him calmed down.

"Okay, Jonesy. Okay. Look, just calm down. We have to use all of our wits to figure out what to do now." said Lee.

"Jonesy. You need to stop now and take a deep breathe in." Summer's voice was actually incredibly soothing and commanding at the same time. Jonesy did as he was told and he let her hold his hands and guide him to a more relaxed place. "That's good. That's much better. Deep breaths. . . .in. . . . .and. . . . out. . . . .in . . . . .and. . . . .out. Good."

Jonesy had actually calmed down a lot as Lee and Sam watched and Lee decided that as flakey as she often was, Summer actually had some helpful skills.

"Are you feeling a bit better?" she asked Jonesy.

"Yes," Jonesy sighed. "Yes, I think so." He released her hands and gently put his hands back on Sammy's chocolate velvet head. "I think so."

"Dr. Bondurant, let's get you bandaged up." Summer said as she stood and began taking the soaked gauze from the bowl.

"Anything that would help take the pain away would be great, Summer. And would you please call me Lee."

"Sure, Lee. I'm going to wrap your chest first," she said smiling. She was elated to be able to be of help to this man she revered. Despite the earlier incident with Sam, after seeing all Dr. Bondurant did during the crisis; she knew she had been mistaken about his abusing Sam. For so many years, she had admired his work and now she was thrilled to work with him, although she had been very intimidated by him. Now, being able to do something to help him and having him tell her to call him 'Lee'! Well, she felt as if she'd arrived. She went about her work, carefully dipping and wrapping, dipping and wrapping until Lee resembled a mummy.

"Well, now that you've got me dressed up for Halloween, you'd better take a look at Erik, Summer. I think he took a hit too."

"Good idea." She said as she picked up her supplies, Erik had come down to where they were all gathered. He looked puzzled and had taken off his soaked shirt.

"Erik, are you okay?" asked Summer looking at red marks on his chest.

"I was attacked by a wild animal! Do I look OKAY?"

"Maybe I can help." Said Summer. "Why don't you let me put some of this on you. It is an herb called Balsam of Peru and it is good for burns of all kinds." She had him sit on the other end of the rock and began her routine again.

"Great! Just what I need. Hippy medicine," griped Erik. "Hope it doesn't smell like patchouli oil."

"Okay, friends, we've got some thinking to do." said Lee. Hugh had dragged himself up off the sand and walked over to where they were sitting.

"I. . .I. . ." Hugh kept stammering.

"You okay, Hugh?" Lee stood and looked Hugh over for any injuries.

"Well. . ." Hugh said. He just held his camera up and the broken lens was hanging by one side. As he stood looking at it, the back popped open and the battery fell out.

Lee put his hand on Hugh's shoulder in sympathy.

"I'll buy you a new camera, Hugh." Lee said. "By the way, you did great back there, kid. You probably saved our lives."

Hugh looked from his camera to Sam and Jonesy and then to Lee.

"Thanks," he said hesitantly.

Just then Lee's cell phone rang.

"Yeah," said Lee.

"Hey, Boss" said Janice. "We got some good news."

"I could use some." said Lee.

"We found out that Erik's real name is Erik Schantz. He is a decorated pilot from the Iraq war."

"Really?" Lee was surprised that this conman had actually been a decorated pilot but it helped him form a plan.

"Yes, the whole crew looks a bit kooky but seem to be on the up and up. I'm emailing the reports to you so you can see it for yourself."

"Okay, well, we need a new plan anyway." said Lee.

"What do you mean? What's happened?" Janice asked.

"We succeeded in finding the Imoogi." began Lee.

"Seriously? That's great! So you didn't need to do a conjuring spell?"

"That's another story. Jonesy gave the pearl to it."

"You mean the orb?" she asked

"Yes."

"And. ." she was waiting for the other shoe to drop.

"And it worked."

"What? You mean . .you didn't. . .you. . . you actually got a dragon?" Janice was stunned.

"Yes, but it wasn't the one we hoped for."

"Oh, my God. What happened?"

"It was a three headed vicious beast that just about took us all out."

"How did you stop it?"

"I conjured a water sprite to help us with a wall of water and then it took off."

"Took off? You mean as in it flew away?" Janice was envisioning scenes from Reign of Fire, a movie made a few years ago with all the worst of dragons.

"Yeah, I mean it took off." Lee sounded despondent which was not very common for him.

"What do we do." Janice was ready for action.

"You guys sit tight for now. Get us ready to go, but we're going to regroup here and try to figure out what to do next. I'll be in touch."

"Well, okay. Let us know how we can help."

"For now, make sure we're stocked with all the gear for a monster hunt, but we've also got Erik's plane which will carry a lot more people and gear. We may not need the jet so you guys just stay where you are and I'll keep you posted."

"Okay, is Sammy okay?"

"Yea, he's fine. Just a little pissed at me."

"Well, you do get him into a lot of trouble sometimes, boss."

"Yeah, I know. Alright. I got to go." Lee said as he clicked off his phone.

Summer had finished wrapping Erik.

"Well, guess we could go trick or treating." Erik said to Lee.

"Yeah, but I don't think we're as cute as a five year old." Lee laughed.

"I guess not." Erik said as he walked back out toward the surf.

"Say, what the hell is this?" He had picked up something on a stick and walked back to the group. He was holding an odd looking snake draped over the stick. It looked very dead.

"I don't know." said Lee.

"Well, maybe you should find out because there's a ton of them over there. Erik walked back to where he'd picked up the snake and the others followed him. As they got close they saw about twenty similar looking snakes, lying in the sand, obviously dead. But they also saw a dozen or more cockroach looking bugs crawling around.

"What the hell?" said Jonesy.

"Okay," said Lee, "I think we need to kill these things. We should take a sample—dead sample of each back to the lab, but I definitely do not think we want to keep any of these alive. I've got a very creepy feeling about this."

Hugh and Erik were quickly disposing of the bugs and Jonesy had gone back to the van to get a couple of sample containers that he always had on hand. He scooped up a couple of the cockroaches, placing each in a plastic container that he could seal. He then put one of the snakes in another container that he sealed tight. Then all three specimens went into a larger metal suitcase that could be tightly closed.

As everyone was heading back to the van, Lee took Jonesy aside and let the others go ahead.

"Okay. Da Soo, I need you to focus now." Jonesy knew Lee was serious when he used his Korean name. He stopped and looked at his friend.

"Yeah, I will." Jonesy still had tears in his eyes and fear in his face but he had forced himself to calm down, thanks to Summer's help, and he knew he could focus on what Lee wanted.

"I need to know what else you found with this orb." Lee was hoping there had been something else. Something they should have known about before and he was cursing himself for not asking more questions earlier.

"Just a few arrow heads and some pot shards from a much later time."

"Was this in a container of any kind or was it just lying loose in the ground?"

"There was nothing left of anything it might have been in. I don't know, Lee, but it has been buried there for over 2000 thousand years."

"And there was nothing else that you saw in the area around it?"

"No, Lee, I would have brought it out." Jonesy looked to be trying to remember the dig and what he was thinking when he found this.

"Do you have photos of it in the ground?" Asked Lee

"Of course, Lee. I always take photo records of my digs. Don't you believe me?"

"I think maybe there was something you missed. I'd like to look at the photos but even more, we need to go back to that site." Lee had stood up now and Jonesy stood as well.

"But, Lee, we've got a Dragon on the loose. I mean we've got to stop this. Make sure he doesn't do any damage anywhere."

Jonesy was letting the guilt set in as to what he had done and he hoped to get it resolved before it got really bad.

"I think we need to know more about what we're dealing with, Jonesy. This was not an ordinary Imoogi turned Dragon. You saw that Imoogi. She was gentle as a kitten. There was something in that orb that changed her in ways we did not expect. We need to know more."

"Yes, yes, of course. Well, the site is about an hour drive from here. It is in the mountains as I told you."

"Alright. Look let's go back into Sokcho, get a hotel and regroup. It's going to be dark soon anyway. I think we should try to find someplace to stay and get out our maps and books and hit the site first thing in the morning."

"Yes, alright. Yes, let's do that." Jonesy was still in shock and willing to let anyone tell him the next move to make.

Chapter 25

EVEN AFTER SUCH an exhausting experience the day before, Lee and Sam managed to wake up early. They had found a motel in Sokcho, a popular tourist town, so each was able to get his own room. They had been too exhausted to even try to eat and Lee and Erik had injuries that were competing with the need for food. So when Sam and Lee woke, they were starving. Lee always brought some provisions along. In particular, he had his own coffee and coffee press with him. Many motels in Korea did not have coffee makers in the rooms. In fact, those that did usually had only instant coffee which already had cream and sugar added. Lee liked real coffee so he had learned long ago to carry it with him whenever he traveled.

He put out some milk and opened a can of food for Sam, who was ravenous after such a workout. Lee had some bagels and oranges he'd brought along so he had that while looking over maps and photos of the area.

"So what are you thinking?" asked Sam after he'd finished his breakfast.

"I still don't have a plan crystallized in my head."

"Well, the sooner we undo what we did, the better."

"Agreed."

They heard a knock on the door and opened it to find Summer.

"Good morning," said Lee.

"Good morning. You guys are up early." She said as she walked in. She was wearing an oversized T-shirt with shorts and slippers on her feet. "I just wondered if you happened to have coffee?" she asked smiling and sniffing the air.

"I do. I always carry it with me. Sit down. I'll get a cup for you." Lee noticed that even somewhat unkempt, Summer was very attractive. She was sort of a hippy version of Paula Zahn or Katie Couric. It was obvious why she had been chosen to co-host the Truth Seekers television show.

"Here you go." said Lee as he put the coffee before her. "I've got some bagels and oranges. Interested?"

"Oh, yes, please. I just ate a granola bar but I'm still starving. I think yesterday we all burned up lots of calories." She said as she began to peel her orange. "So, what's on our agenda for today?"

Just then Jonesy knocked on the door and quickly opened it.

"Okay to come in?" he asked peeking in.

"Sure." said Lee.

"I smell coffee," said Hugh who was just behind Jonesy.

"Come on in. I've got cups." Lee said as he pulled out more Styrofoam cups and put more coffee and hot water in his coffee press.

"Have a seat. Summer, Sam and I were just trying to figure out our next steps."

Jonesy and Hugh sat down and helped themselves to bagels and oranges and Jonesy added a box of Cheez-its and two tins of oysters to the meal.

"Yuu, oysters for breakfast?" Summer squished up her nose. "Way too rich for me this early."

"Okay, so let's get to it." Lee said. "I think we're all agreed we need to send this thing back to where it came from, yes?"

"Absolutely," said Jonesy.

"Yes," Summer and Hugh said simultaneously.

"We don't know exactly how to do that yet, but there are two things we can do in the mean time. First, we need to go back to Jonesy's original dig site and hope to find some more clues about the orb. Second, we need to find a way to keep an eye on the Dragon and follow its moves."

"Well, I'm sure you and Jonesy can handle the dig site with your expertise," began Hugh. "But how can we track a flying dragon?"

"With an aircraft, of course," Lee said. "We can't fight it in the air with an aircraft but we can hopefully keep up with it and maybe be able to anticipate its next move. If we can do that, maybe we can ambush it somehow. I don't know. But Erik should be able to track it."

"Wait. I had hoped this would be the last of Erik's contributions to our quest. Does he really have to stay around?" asked Jonesy who was still miffed over Erik's attempt to con them.

"I'm not so sure we want to get rid of him," countered Lee. "By the way, how is he doing, Summer?"

"Well, he is not healing up as quickly as you seem to be. He woke me in the night and had me rewrap his bandages. I don't think he got to sleep until after 2:00 AM." she said. "I'm sure he's still sleeping now."

"Look, I'm glad he'll live," said Jonesy, "but I don't really want him to stay around. I have had enough of his teasing and his smart ass comments."

"I think you should reconsider." Lee said.

"Why? He's a macho blowhard who pokes fun at every belief any of us has. He makes a living writing made up articles for a phony newspaper and he's a smuggler on top of it!" Jonesy was incensed all over again.

Hugh and Summer seemed to agree with Jonesy, but Lee was quietly pulling out his cell phone and obviously checking his email.

"What? Lee? Spill it—whatever you are thinking," said Jonesy.

"I just think we should reconsider keeping him around. I know he doesn't believe the same things we do, but I'm not sure that makes him an enemy. Look, he risked his life to try to save us yesterday. His methods may have been misguided but he could have just hightailed it out of there and never looked back. He didn't. He came back and got himself injured trying to save our skins."

"That's true," Summer said thoughtfully.

"Also, I had Janice check him out. She's very good at doing background checks, which, by the way, I had her do on you two as well." He said holding up his cell and looking at Hugh and Summer.

"Gee, thanks for the vote of confidence," said Hugh. "Nice to know I'm working with Big Brother."

"Please, don't take offense." Lee held his hands up defensively. "It's just that there are a lot of people who would kill to get their hands on the books and knowledge that Jonesy and I have cultivated over the years. I just don't like to take unnecessary risks. Having new people come onboard a project means I'm going to check them out."

"I hope since you are telling us this, it means we passed muster?" Summer asked.

"With flying colors. Your reputation in psychic circles is impeccable as is Hugh's in journalism. Hugh hasn't been in the work force as long as the rest of us, but all the reports I've had are outstanding." Lee smiled and nodded at Hugh who acknowledged with a nod.

"So what of the record of the gentleman who admits to being a cad and a smuggler?" asked Jonesy.

"He's an ex-naval aviator. Honorably discharged. Journalism has been a hobby since his high school years. Four cruises supporting aircraft carriers, three of those in the Persian Gulf during the Iraq War. He earned a respectable pile of medals including the Distinguished Flying Cross."

"Being a decorated Naval Aviator didn't stop Randall Cunningham from being a scum bag," offered Hugh.

"Pointing out someone is a war monger does not exactly put him on my list of top ten hits." said Summer.

"I'm not saying you have to marry the guy. You don't even have to like him. But with that record plus what he showed yesterday tells me we need to give him the benefit of the doubt. Think about it. For someone with the brains, skills and means to find work as a smuggler, why in the hell is he running Cheez-its across the Pacific ocean when he could face easier skies and much more profit flying drugs to Florida or guns to Africa? Tariff must be the minimum wage of smuggling jobs but it rarely hurts anybody but politicians and big business. I suspect he has a good moral code."

"Well, maybe he is a nice guy hiding in the shell of a sardonic asshole but does that mean we want to deal with him?" argued Jonesy. "Correct me if I'm wrong, but you seem to have recovered much quicker than he has and his injuries didn't seem as severe as yours."

Lee acknowledged this comment with a nod.

"Agreed, but Summer has assisted me with much more than just wrapping my wounds. She also has an innate healing quality about her. Spiritual healing is a common trait amongst psychics and Summer is a true psychic and healer."

Summer was elated with such high praise from Lee but she realized it was a double edged comment.

"My intentions to heal Erik were just as genuine as they were with you."

"Of course they were," assured Lee. "It's just that any spiritual or magical healing you possess won't work on him."

Hugh was still wrapping his head around Lee's statements.

"Are you saying that because Erik doesn't believe in magic, it doesn't work on him?" Hugh asked.

"Exactly."

"But I can think of many patients of mine who didn't believe and yet I know my gifts helped them heal quicker." Summer was thinking about her experience in nursing.

"Yes," Lee nodded in agreement. "But I believe Erik is more than a skeptic. I believe he produces some sort of negative field that inhibits magic."

They all looked at Lee as if a collective light bulb went off..

"Duh! Of course! Why didn't I think of that?" said Sam.

Jonesy raised an eyebrow in subtle understanding. Summer began to piece together her inability to read Erik.

"A what?" Hugh remained puzzled.

"Well, it's just a hypothesis."

"I don't get it," replied Hugh still looking as if he'd missed the joke.

"To understand what I'm talking about, you need to understand a bit about what magic is. It has been theorized by many leading researchers that Magic is the force nature uses to keep balance. In the sixties, chaos theorists just hit the tip of the iceberg when they created mathematical models to predict the degradation of a natural system. The second rule of thermodynamics states that entropy always increases. The complexity theorists of the 80's took a look at the opposite of chaos. They noticed that order could reestablish itself from chaos remarkably quickly.

"Many, like myself, believe that it is 'magic' that helps us reestablish order from chaos and it is also 'magic' that creates chaos from what should mathematically be a stable system." Lee glanced around to see if the others were following his logic.

"To what extent someone can tap into that magic is as variable in an individual as their physical genetics. Some are strong with magic and some are weak. A short fat ugly guy manages to marry a supermodel for her money. A handsome talented star has a drug overdose or drives his car off a cliff before his inevitable Oscar is awarded. The most wonderful future is in store for the most unlikely candidates and the most tragic future befalls the presumed chosen ones."

"Okay," Hugh was beginning to catch on, "so you are saying that magic and other supernatural phenomena are at the root of these scientific theories. You are also saying that some people, yourself and Summer for example, have the ability to use these gifts while others, like me, either don't have the talent or haven't learned how to use it."

"In a nut shell," replied Lee.

"So where does Erik fit in?" asked Jonesy.

Lee thought for a moment pondering the best way to explain his theory.

"Yeah?" prodded Hugh. "How does he create this negative field?"

"Let me first ask you each a question. Summer how old were you when you first noticed your gifts?"

"I was 12 when I first started feeling peoples' thoughts. I noticed I seemed to have healing skills shortly after that. It wasn't until I was in my mid twenties that I really began to feel my true gifts. I was working in a cancer ward as a young nurse and I noticed that the patients I was assigned to seemed to heal quicker. They seemed to have a better chance of going into remission."

"Interesting," replied Lee. "Jonesy?"

Jonesy thought a moment.

"When I was fifteen," he began. "I was studying very hard for my end of term exams. I remember for three weeks I never got more than three hours of sleep. I was so tired one night that I couldn't reach across the table for a glass of orange juice. The next thing I knew the glass slid across the table and into my hand. At the time I thought it was my mind playing tricks on me until years later when you and I began studying the supernatural in college."

Lee then added his story.

"I was at an outward bound camp when I was 16. A friend and I decided to hike around the camp before the sun went down. We were tired from the day's classes and didn't notice the bear until we stood directly between her and her cub. It's the worst place to be in terms of bear attacks. She charged and I just remember thinking, "we mean you no harm. Please don't hurt us." She stopped about six feet from us and slowly walked around us and reunited with her cub." He panned across the faces of his companions until he came to Hugh, "How about yourself Hugh?"

"Well," Hugh stammered a bit, "I have never had any supernatural powers but I did see a ghost once."

"How old were you?" Lee asked. "How did it make you feel?"

"I was 14. It scared the shit out of me. At that age I remember thinking that I never wanted to see that again."

"Did it change your life?"

"Hell, yes! I quit baseball and football. I started hanging out with the skate punks and then the climbers. I wanted any extreme sport I could get my hands on. I realized that if and when I die, I wanted it to be from something tangible. Falling off a cliff, buried in an avalanche, anything but having my soul sucked out of me by the undead."

"And yet a decade later, here you are helping us track down a dragon." Lee smiled.

"True, but I never had the courage to study the spells and witchcraft that you and Jonesy have." Hugh was still unsure of Lee's point. "So we each had experiences. Summer was always open to them, you and Jonesy came back to study years later, and I have done nothing more than study this stuff with a camera. I still don't see how Erik fits?"

"Here is the key similarity in all of our stories. We each had our experiences in our teen years. Indeed, if you ask almost anyone they will admit to having a supernatural experience in their teens. Most people grow up and assume their experience was a result of overactive hormones. They go on to live their lives relying on technology and not magic. Now just assume that your first experience came to you when you were a toddler?"

Lee let them think on that a moment and then he continued.

"Your first experience with the supernatural can often be a frightening and traumatic experience even with ten to fifteen years of cognitive growth. What if it happened when you were still learning to walk and talk?"

"That would be a pretty crappy deal," replied Hugh.

"That could possibly cause permanent developmental damage," Summer mused.

"Indeed it could," Lee agreed. "I think, in fact, it does. I met a man a few years back. Dr. Theo Toernberg."

"I know of his work," Summer interjected. "He is a very famous child psychiatrist."

"Yes. What most don't know is that he is also a psychic healer like you. He has been working for years with children with autism. He has developed a rather shocking theory that naturally he can't publish in the medical journals.

"Dr. Toernberg believes that children who experience supernatural occurrences at such an early age may develop autism. Autism itself is often characterized as the result of a person's receiving too much stimuli from the world around them. They can't filter out stimuli as we can. In an attempt to quiet their mind, they usually try to shut out the world around them. There are varying degrees of autism, of course. Some people are almost catatonic for their entire lives but others are able to channel their energies into certain tasks. They could be a concert pianist or a math genius but can do little else. What is sure, is that very few people with this affliction can have successful social interactions with others and many will even need some degree of constant care."

They all sat listening to Lee's hypothesis. Sam was the first to speak up.

"Hate to bust your theory, boss, but I could think of several mental deficiencies Erik may have, but autism isn't one of them. Hell, he would probably be more tolerable if he drooled on himself while playing Chopin."

"Well, I haven't gotten to Erik yet. Dr. Toernberg has also noted in his practice several young children who appeared to be developing autistic symptoms who seemed to miraculously cure themselves. Obviously this is extremely rare. After these children experienced their miraculous turn arounds, they seemed very responsive to standard psychiatric treatments but almost immune from Toernberg's extra efforts with psychic healing. Indeed, he claims that while he is usually very in tune with a child's emotional state, he finds these children almost impossible to read.

"Toernberg's thought on the matter is that the children who experience miraculous recovery have somehow learned not to turn off the world but instead to turn off the magic."

"What does that mean then?" asked Summer.

"If I'm right…then Erik may have more natural magical ability than any of us. Instead of his gifts being used for empathy, or summoning, or conjuring, his magic repels the magic of others."

"Well, how powerful do you think he is?" asked Jonesy.

"Do you remember the Dragon breathing fire on him?" Lee's companions looked stunned for a moment.

"I thought you did that?" said Jonesy.

"I didn't cast one spell on him. I was too weak from the first attack and too busy helping the Merman. Nope, I had nothing to do with it. Erik took a full blast of fire from all three heads of the Dragon and it did nothing to him but make him sweat."

"Wow," thought Jonesy out loud. "Maybe he could come in handy when we meet that thing again."

"So how does this connect to Erik?" asked Hugh still trying to piece together what Lee was saying.

"I'm just saying that Erik is a bit like a black hole where magic and the spiritual world are involved. It isn't just that he doesn't' believe, it is that magic really does not happen around him. Those of us with magical gifts cannot perform our gifts on Erik. I mean, Sam can't even talk when Erik gets within ten feet of him."

"So how does this help us?" asked Jonesy.

"Well, we have just brought to life a magical creature. But it could not hurt Erik with its breath. It had to use its tail to knock him senseless. It seems to me, it might be advantageous when dealing with a magical creature, to have someone around who is immune to magic. Who knows how or when it might come in handy." Lee looked from one to the other and let them ponder what he'd just said.

"Well, look, the guy is okay. He's a smart ass but he's not a coward and he's nice to dogs, but I hate it that that's all I am when he's around! I just turn back into a big dumb dog!" said Sam.

"Sammy, I don't think you could ever be dumb," said Summer as she reached over and scratched him behind the ears.

"Ohhh, don't stop—"Sammy was loving it. "umm, a little to the left. . .oh, yes, up, ahhh. . .oh, that's great."

"Will you cut it out, Sam!" Lee was laughing. "Look, Jonesy and I are going to head up to the site to check it out. You guys need to figure out how to track this sucker and try to make sure Erik is doing okay. Why don't you stay here at the motel and just try to regroup a little bit while we're out. Sammy, you're with us."

"Right, boss." Sam reluctantly gave up his scratch message. "Thanks, Summer. You're great." Sam licked her hand.

"You're welcome. Maybe Hugh and I could check out Sokcho a bit and scrounge up some real food for all of us. I'll keep an eye on Erik and when you get back we can try to have a decent meal and head back to Seoul?"

"Sounds good. Hugh, sometime today, could you see if you can come up with some ideas about how to track this guy? Give Hank a call because he's good at tracking and he's great with computers. Maybe the two of you can come up with something," Lee asked.

"Yeah, sure. I'm not sure what good computers will do right now.

"Okay, we're out of here. We'll see you when we get back," Lee said as he, Jonesy and Sam headed out to the van.

Chapter 26

LEE, SAM AND Jonesy approached the cave almost reverently, knowing that it was the site of a centuries old event that had clearly been quite remarkable. Lee and Jonesy had their climbers' helmets with head lamps but also carried a lantern to give them better overall lighting. The day outside was cloudy and while the entry area to the cave received good natural light, it got very dark very quickly once inside.

"How did you even find this place?" Sam asked Jonesy, impressed that a human would have come across such a well hidden place.

"I was just exploring the area after I'd found some arrow heads down by the stream. It seemed reasonable that ancient men would have taken shelter in the mountains, so I did a lot of hiking and exploring. I'm sure wild animals once dominated this area," Jonesy didn't have to stoop very low to walk back through the cave.

"Still, to have come back inside and dug here was pretty clever, Jonesy. Was it just perseverance that made you actually dig here or did you see something intriguing?" Lee was stooping lower as he followed his friend deeper into the cave.

"Well, I'd found so many arrow and spear heads near and around the stream bed that it seemed someone must have lived near here. This seemed to be a logical place to take shelter and as I explored deeper into the cave, I found this raised area that didn't seem to have been a natural formation." They had reached the site of Jonesy's dig and he held the lantern so that Lee and Sam could see what he was talking about.

"This part of the ground was raised and I couldn't see how a landslide or something would have caused this naturally. It certainly didn't appear to be a roof fall or cave in so I decided to dig. After a few inches I came to rock and I thought it was a burial site, so I began slowly excavating until I found the orb."

"But, it looks as if you just stopped. Why didn't you excavate the whole site?" Lee was incredulous that his friend who was always so obsessive about proper and thorough techniques on a dig could have just left the rest of the site untouched.

"I know, I know, Lee. I screwed up. I'm not sure what happened but when I found this, I got so excited, I guess, I don't know. . .I just . . .forgot everything else. It, well. . .it's as if I were possessed by something."

"I think you were," said Sam.

"Oh, man! I can't believe this is happening. Lee, you know me. I don't do stuff like this!"

"Yeah, I know that, Jonesy. You are the most methodical digger I know. I think Sam is right. I think maybe you were possessed by that thing. But, all we can do now is try to fix it." Lee was holding the light high so he could see around the area. It was about 6' by 7' flat area with a ceiling clearance of just over 5'. The cave stopped here and didn't go any further into the mountain. "It does seem to be a great natural shelter."

"I didn't find anything else, but then I didn't look any more once I found the orb," said Jonesy sheepishly.

"Well, let's see if we can find something here that may help us understand where our friend really came from." Lee had taken his backpack off and opened his kit of implements. He knelt down near the place where Jonesy had found the orb and began to carefully remove the soil layers. Jonesy worked on the opposite side of the hole. Sam went to the mouth of the cave, sniffed around and then lay down guarding his people and also catching a few zee's.

After about three hours of carefully sifting, digging and brushing, they were feeling hopeless.

"I don't know, Jonesy. I'm not coming up with any other signs."

"Maybe there isn't anything else, Lee." Jonesy sat down and wiped the dirt from his face with a bandana.

Sam came back inside and sniffed around the site.

"There is something touched by humans near here." He kept sniffing around where both Lee and Jonesy had been excavating and finally stopped near where Lee had been working. "I think here. Try going a little deeper here."

Lee followed his friend's advice and after about ten minutes had discovered the edge of something hard and round.

"Sammy, I think you got us there." Lee carefully removed all the dirt from around the item and finally pulled it free. It was a tube of some kind that looked to be ceramic. Inside was a rolled parchment. Jonesy had been photographing Lee's progress as they wanted to document where and how the item was placed. As Lee pulled the parchment out of the tube, he gently uncurled a part of it.

"Wow, this is remarkably intact."

"That's amazing. Can you see any of the inscription, yet?" asked Jonesy.

"Not clearly. I think we need to open this back in the lab, Jonesy. Let's make sure we can keep this as pristine as possible." Lee carefully put the document back in the ceramic tube and placed the tube securely inside a foam backed wrap to help protect it.

Chapter 27

THE SWEAT STREAMING down Grey Fox's face and chest had long ago passed the beading stage and had now developed into a full soaking. This didn't really bother him. It was a mild discomfort brought on from doing one of his favorite activities; dancing. He especially loved dancing to trance music when a decent DJ could be rustled up. The only thing he loved more than the music and the dancing was the subculture of like minded people who attended the conference with him.

Grey Fox was actually Latham Thompson, a computer design engineer who worked for a biotech company that was endeavoring to design the first ever fully articulated artificial hand. It was good work that filled his need to be of benefit to society and his desire to be well paid. Nevertheless, his well paid, do-gooder job didn't fulfill every need and interest in his life. Latham was a "Furry." Furries were a subculture of science fiction fans who had taken to the artwork and mystique of anthropomorphized characters in science fiction stories. Many of them were artists who drew elaborate sketches of animals that had human characteristics. Others dressed up in costumes that gave them animalistic features. Latham was a little of both. He had drawn many sketches and he had created his own costume. His costume was supposed to be that of a bi-pedal fox but, in truth, it looked more like a costume a school mascot would wear.

Wearing a bulky fox outfit complete with the mascot-like head certainly contributed to profuse sweating, but Latham was not about to miss out on any of the fun. He was attending the first ever "Furry" convention to be held in Asia. Osaka, Japan seemed like the perfect place to host the historic convention. The Japanese brought a lot to the "Furry" artwork with their long history of science fiction art and cartooning. This artistic tradition also brought a lot of creativity to the costuming. Many European and American Furries stuck to archetypes of what they thought was cool; foxes, wolves, and lions for men, and cats, or bunnies for women. Asians had a broader view of "cool" animals. There were rats, scorpions, snakes, and even a dragon suit. In all, the mixing of the cultures and sharing of ideas had been well worth the visit.

After a half hour of dancing, Grey Fox was spent. He shuffled off the floor in his large fuzzy slippers. When he reached the bar, he broke character long enough to remove his Fox head to have a beer. As he sipped his cold beer, he felt a tap on his shoulder. He turned to see a large pink beaver with cherub cheeks, buck teeth and freakishly large doe eyes.

"Loopy!" he said as he greeted his friend Larissa from the states. Larissa modeled her character after a favorite Korean cartoon, and in truth, Larissa's personality was very much like the little cartoon, Loopy. Larissa was a sweet and happy young woman and Latham thought she was adorable as Loopy or Larissa.

"Hey, Latham!" she yelled over the loud thumping music in the background.

"Glad to see you made it!" he yelled back.

"Couldn't resist," she replied. "Listen, some of us are taking the party to the roof!"

"Where?"

"The ROOF!" She yelled trying to be heard over the music.

"Why?"

Larissa said nothing but pointed her furry pink paw toward a group who had just walked in. They were led by a man in a large cow outfit. It was "Mad Cow," a notorious "Furvert." Furverts were something of a culture within a culture. There was no delicate way to explain their interests. Not only did they attend Furry conventions for the art and costumes, but also for the possibility of attending animal orgies in full costume, an act they called "yiffing." Larissa and Latham really disdained Furverts in general and in particular Mad Cow. Furverts created really bad press for the Furry culture. Because of some well publicized actions of a few Furverts, the general public got the idea that all Furries were into animal orgies. It was one thing to be labeled weird, but quite another to be labeled weird and perverted.

"Oh, shit!" said Latham. "What's he doing here?"

"I don't know but I want to get out of here before he tries to rub up on me. Petey Penguin and Susie Squirrel got a boom box and some beer. Susie knows a guy who works here, so we've got the okay to go up on the roof and have a more low key party."

Latham didn't really want to leave the dance club, but he knew Petey and Susie were great fun and he certainly didn't want to be around where Mad Cow could cause problems,

"I'm in," Latham said putting his mask back on.

Grey Fox followed Loopy to the elevator and from there they ascended to the top floor and then up the flight of stairs to the roof. The roof was yet another playground in this swank hotel for those who could afford it. Part of the floor was walled in with glass walls for a 360 degree view of Osaka. About half of the floor was open to the air and this was where a large swimming pool awaited the special clientele. Three Jacuzzi hot tubs were on one end of the pool and the other end housed an open bar with a built in pit for grilling. The Furries weren't interested in the grill, but took advantage of the coolers to put their beer in.

"Hey, Latham!" said Susie. "Glad you could join us!."

"Hi, Susie! This is some set up."

"Yeah, now here's the deal. The guy I know is a security guard here at the hotel. He arranged for us to be able to use this tonight in exchange for some of the artwork we sell. We can't touch the hard liquor but we can use the beer taps if we run out of our stuff. I don't want to take advantage of him because I think this might be a great place to come back to and if we screw things up, well. . .you remember what happened in San Francisco?"

"Afraid I do," said Latham as he was reminded of last year's convention where some Furries broke into the restaurant after hours and smashed up some tables, chairs and generally made a mess. The Furries attending all had to pay out of pocket to cover damages so the idiots wouldn't go to jail, but they had been told they would not be welcome to return to that hotel.

"Wow!" Latham said. "This is really beautiful! I thought the only pool here was the one on the 16th floor."

"That's the one for regular guests," said Loopy. "guess this is for the special folks."

Just then, Tigger, a guy named John Clayton, arrived with the boom box and more booze. Several other Furries came in shortly after that and within a half hour, the party was in full swing. It was definitely more reserved than what was going on downstairs, with some folks dancing and others, having stripped to bathing suites, taking dips in the pool. As usual, there were plenty of deep philosophical debates about science fiction issues and in general, everyone was having a good time.

Grey Fox and Loopy were having a blast dancing in their big floppy costumes when suddenly Loopy stopped cold. Latham turned to see what it was. There stood Mad Cow and several of his Furvert compatriots.

"What the hell are you doing here?" demanded Loopy.

"I'm here to do a little yiffing, baby. Preferably with my favorite pink beaver!" Mad Cow and his cohorts laughed as if he'd made a joke worthy of Letterman himself.

"Just leave her alone and get the hell out of here," demanded Grey Fox.

"Don't be such a square dog, Grey Fox." Mad Cow's costume lacked articulated hands but he was still able to do a "square" motion with his hoofed gloves. He then started gyrating his hips back and forth in an obscene way, leaving no doubt as to his intentions. It was a repulsive act in any setting but when done by a guy in a cow costume, it was even more disgusting.

"I gotta get me some pink beaver!" Mad continued to taunt.

"Okay, freak. We caught the sick innuendo the first time. She's not interested," said Latham.

"You don't get it man! I'm like a bull in rut man! And she's like a pink beaver! Get it?" Mad Cow and his pals laughed hysterically.

Larissa's anger boiled over. She wasn't close to anything she could throw, so she took off her heavy beaver head and threw it at him. Mad Cow could not catch the mask with his cow hoof gloves on so instead it just bounced off the pillowy belly of his costume.

"Sweet, dude!" Mad exclaimed. "It's like I just got head from a pink beaver!"

"With nothing left to throw at him, Larissa screamed at him.

"You stupid COW! BURN IN HELL, YOU FUCKING PIG!"

And just like that Mad Cow was engulfed in flames and began screaming in agony. His screams ended just as quickly when an enormous serpentine head swooped down and scooped him up and chomped him in one gulp.

Panic took a second to set in as the terrified Furries observed what happened. Then they screamed and suddenly the scene was ablaze and Furries were being burned and eaten before they could get out of the way. Grey Fox had only seen Mad Cow burst into flame and his reaction was to grab Loopy and plunge into the pool. He had not even seen what had caused the disaster, but thoughts of terrorism ran through his head. He never saw the Dragon, but had felt the heat from the flames and had simply reacted to try to save himself and his friend. His quick, albeit, somewhat bumbling act of heroism meant that he and Larissa were the only survivors on the roof that night.

As Azi Dahaka flew away from the carnage, he couldn't help but feel a little confused and a little sick to his stomach. His favorite meal had always been cows. In his youth, the villagers would sacrifice a couple a week to him. It had been 5,000 years since he had actually eaten anything, so perhaps he just wasn't remembering? Still, the cow he had just eaten had been strange tasting and was very stringy. In fact, all the creatures he had just eaten tasted about the same. They all tasted like stringy chicken. He hated chicken!

Chapter 28

HUGH WOKE UP and rolled off of the uncomfortably firm mattress of his hotel bed. Even in the relatively Westernized city of Seoul, Korean hotels had mattresses that felt more like concrete slabs. It was seven o'clock in the morning and he assumed he would be the first person up. He had left Lee's room at midnight and Lee and Jonesy were still steeped in books and internet searches as they painstakingly translated the cuneiform tablets. If Jonesy and Lee were awake, it was most likely because they had never gone to bed.

Hugh sat down at the desk, flipped open his laptop, and logged on to read the morning news. He clicked through the day's headlines and was unable to resist the urge to browse a few celebrity gossip columns. Even though he pretended not to care about the personal lives of famous people, it was almost impossible to resist glancing at headlines that promised "new revealing photos" of the latest Hollywood starlet. On this date, his shameful curiosity actually led to some useful information. The same websites that flooded viewers with torrid celebrity tales also searched out bizarre stories about regular people. He immediately stood from his desk and ran down the hall and began banging on Lee's door.

After about a minute of pounding, Lee finally opened the door with a groggy angry look on his face.

"Damnit, Hugh! I didn't get to sleep until 3:00 AM. This better be good."

"It is," Hugh said flatly. "Turn on you computer. I need to show you something."

Lee escorted Hugh into his room. The room looked like a paper tornado had hit it. Books and papers from last evening's furious translating session still lay strewn about the room. There were probably a dozen paper cups scattered throughout the room as well. Lee flicked on his computer and logged on. He then handed his seat over to Hugh so the cameraman could bring up the web site.

"Here it is," said Hugh.

"Terrorist attack in Osaka kills 11?"

"Yes, that's the one."

It was a sad statement of world affairs that a terrorist bomb killing only eleven people was not a particularly interesting news story.

"That kind of stuff happens all the time. What does it have to do with us?" asked Lee.

"It didn't catch my eye either until I went here." He made a few more clicks to get to the site he was looking for.

"Former teen star Alysson James to do Playboy spread?"

"Not exactly. When you click on this page the sidebar stories are much more interesting." Hugh scrolled down the list of sidebar stories that appeared after opening the page. He reached the headline he was looking for and clicked into the article. It read, Survivor of Osaka Terrorist Attack Claims to See Three Headed Monster. They both began reading the article.

"The main stream news coverage just reported the official police statement. They probably figured that this poor girl is just nuts."

"Huh? What is a 'Furry' anyway?"

Hugh smirked, "That might have been another reason the cops thought she was nuts."

Chapter 29

"WHAT? UMM...What's a Furry?" Jonesy had been sleeping on the sofa and heard the tail end of the conversation.

"That's what I'd like to know." Lee looked at Hugh to explain.

"It's people who are interested in science fiction art and especially the anthropomorphic art. Some of these folks even dress in animal costumes... sort of a Trekkie only with animals, not spacemen." Hugh explained.

"Why do I get the feeling our Dragon friend decided to have lunch and mistook these Furries for food?" said Lee as he sat down, propping his elbows on his knees and dropping his head to his hands.

"Well, if he did, I suspect he got a very nasty surprise. Doubt that human flesh covered in polyester fake fur is very tasty. Certainly not like a nice juicy steak," said Sam.

"Lee, we need to get to Osaka to interview this lady. The cops think she is a lunatic but I think we know better," Hugh said.

"You think Erik would fly you over?" asked Lee.

"I'll check," Hugh said as he headed out the door on his way to Erik's room.

"But this is awful," Jonesy started pacing the floor. "He'll find out there are cities and people and who knows what he'll do next."

"Which is why we need to get a handle on this text now," Lee said. "Erik and Hugh can go interview this lady and see if she saw what we think she saw. If so, we need to be ready to track him down."

"Yes, yes, okay." Jonesy was still shaken up and exhausted to boot. Lee knew his friend had not fared well through this whole thing. While he seemed to have lost the driving obsession when the orb was given to the Imoogi, his sense of the personal guilt over the outcome was beginning to overwhelm him. It was up to Lee to keep him focused so his knowledge could be used to try to get the upper hand.

"Okay, Jonesy. Go take a shower and wake up. I'll get some coffee and breakfast going. We need to be fresh to start working the problem, okay?" Lee asked as he picked up the phone to call room service. Just as he was hanging up, Hugh knocked on the door and came in followed by Erik.

"Hi, Erik. Hugh told you?" Lee asked.

"Yeah, a Furry convention? Sounds like it's right up my alley."

"So you're good to go?"

"We can leave as soon as we get to the airport. It'll take me about 40 minutes to get the Pegasus prepped and get our take off cleared but then we're out of here." Erik was halfway out the door as he was speaking. "Hugh, how long will it take you to get ready to go?"

"About five minutes. What about Summer, Lee? Do you want her to go with us or stay here?"

"You know, it probably will be a good idea to take her. Maybe she can get a read on this woman and let us know if she thinks she's for real or not. Sammy, can you go see if Summer's up?" Lee turned to his buddy who jumped up and wagged his tail as he headed for the door.

"If who's up?" came a voice just outside the door.

"Mornin'." Erik said to Summer as he turned to see her.

"Good morning. What's going on?"

"We'll tell you on the way," said Hugh. "Grab your stuff and meet us at my room in five minutes. We're heading to Japan."

"What? Why?" Summer was confused.

"Summer, just go now, please. Hugh will tell you on the way." Lee said.

Chapter 30

BREAKFAST CAME AS Jonesy got out of the shower. They ate quickly and then went back to work on the translation. The text was Ancient Persian but there were some symbols neither of them knew. Lee had emailed a friend in London, Ardrahan Cheddar, another of the original "Indiana Jones" crew from college. Ardrahan had gone on to teach at their alma mater but had specialized in Ancient Languages and had done some fairly extensive work in Ancient Persian. Lee was hoping he could translate some of the parts he and Jonesy couldn't figure out.

Lee put a call through to his friend, hoping he'd read the email by now.

"Hello" came the familiar voice.

"Ardi! How have you been?" Lee was genuinely fond of Ardi and hoped he could help them.

"Well, well, Dr. Bondurant. Why is it much too long between phone calls or visits?" Even though Ardi had lived in London for twenty plus years, he'd never lost his northern accent. Lee could just picture him sitting with his legs propped on his desk, puffing on his pipe, looking every bit the English gentleman professor with his thick graying mustache, slightly longish mussed gray hair and his wire "granny glasses" perched on the end of his nose. Lee would bet he was wearing a tweed jacket with suede elbow patches.

"I have no excuse, Ardi, just busy as usual. But the phone lines work both ways, you know," Lee chided.

"Touché, my friend, touché. So you said you have found something that is quite remarkable? I'm intrigued. What is it?"

"We have found what I believe to be a journal and I'm still trying to decipher it."

"Is it in good condition? I mean can you actually see the words?"

"It is in remarkable condition and the characters are pretty clear considering the age."

"So, I'm assuming it is older than I am," Ardi joked.

"Ardi, this thing is older than dirt," Lee said. "Jonesy and I have dated it to about 300 B.C. It was written on parchment that we've dated to 5th century B.C. And it appears to be Persian but there are many symbols neither of us have ever seen before."

"You actually found a parchment that old? That's amazing! Where on earth did you find it?"

"Actually it is part of a find that Jonesy made in Korea."

"You mean that old slacker finally found something worthwhile?" Ardi chuckled. "How is the old boy?"

"He's well, Ardi. He's here with me now."

"Tell him I'm extremely jealous, as always. He has a way of turning up intriguing mysteries now and then. Has a knack for it, you know."

"Well, he definitely turned one up this time. Look, Ardi, we need to know this information. . .like yesterday. I can't really explain more than that but can I email you some photos of this and see if you could decipher it that way?"

"Well, if the photo is clear enough, it should work. Why don't you try sending me a page or two now and I'll let you know if I can make it out. If it looks as if we can't see it clearly enough, you'll just have to get it to me in person. But, even if I can interpret the photos, I'd still like to see this document up close and personal. Is that alright?"

"Of course. We'll make sure you get to do that."

"Brilliant! Well, let's have a go, shall we? You have my email so send it as soon as you are ready. I'll be waiting by the computer and ring you up as soon as it comes through, yes?"

"That's great. Here's the number where you can reach me." They exchanged numbers and when Lee hung up, he and Jonesy carefully unrolled the parchment enough to take digital photos of the problem areas. He then uploaded them into his computer and sent the email.

It seemed to take forever for Ardi to ring them back. Meanwhile, Lee and Jonesy were trying to photograph every inch of the document. It took two of them because they didn't want to unroll too much at a time for fear of causing the parchment to crack. They had finished the first piece of parchment and were beginning the second when the phone rang.

"Hello," said Lee.

"Ardi here, Lee. I've got the photos pulled up and they look pretty clear. Why don't you go ahead and send me the rest and I'll start working on it now. There are a few things here I'm not sure of so I'll have to pull up a few books but I think I'll be able to decipher it."

"That's great, Ardi. Okay, we'll begin sending you the rest of what we have. I'll call you back when we've sent everything."

"Righto. Talk to you soon, then. Cheero, Lee, and tell Jonesy he owes me a dinner for this one. I'll take it in Firenze whenever he's ready. I'll get the Chianti."

"I'm sure he'll oblige. Thanks, Ardi." Lee smiled as he told Jonesy what Ardi's payment would be.

"Well, let's hope we get the chance to have that dinner," Jonesy said, still looking worried.

Chapter 31

LEE PORED OVER the notes Cheddar had sent him on the translations he'd finished. Like most translations, much of the substance of the writing required analysis to be properly placed in context since many languages had vocabulary without direct counterparts. He printed Cheddar's work and checked his watch. Quickly calculating the time difference, he realized that it was 11:00 p.m. in London. He decided he would have to risk a late night call. There were too many open questions that Cheddar could answer and save Lee hours of extra research.

"Hello?"

"Hi, Ardi. Hope I didn't wake you," Lee said.

"Not at all. I was hoping to hear from you as soon as you had a chance to look it over."

"We've got you on speaker, Ardi. Jonesy is here with me."

"Hello, Ardi. We hope you've had some additional insights?"

"Hello, Jonesy, old boy. Well, I thought you might be interested. I am rather glad you called, actually. This is a fabulous find, my friends, especially since it was discovered in Korea." Ardi was clearly intrigued.

"So, it is a form of Persian cuneiform?"

"Yes, it is an Avestarian script, actually."

"What does that tell us?" asked Jonesy.

"Well, that was the writing used by the most famous of the Persian empires. The same writing used by Darius, the Great, and many of the other Persian kings. It basically ceased to exist after 300 B.C.," Ardi explained.

"What do you mean?" asked Lee.

"Well, most spoken and written languages evolve into something new over time. This one just stopped being used altogether."

"Do we know why?" Jonesy asked.

"Alexander, my friends. My God! Have you fellows been so consumed with your Shamanistic religious studies that you have forgotten your high school history?" Cheddar teased.

"Well, I admit that is a flaw." Lee chuckled. "Other than the Oracles, the Greeks tended to view magic abilities with suspicion and hostility. Not too much fun to investigate those parts of history. I leave that to you guys."

"Well, the good news is that you are going to want to start because you have got yourself a find that will turn the world of Greek history on its head."

"How is that? I thought you said this was ancient Persian?"

"It is and that's the point. You see, this form of writing did not have the chance to naturally evolve into something new because as Alexander advanced, so too did the art, literature, and philosophy of the Greeks. This Avestarian cuneiform was simply replaced with Greek. I'm sure you've heard about this. It has been called the 'Helenization' of the world. Most historians consider it a good thing, and more or less, I suppose it was. Many of the peoples Alexander conquered had no written language or philosophical tradition at all so it had some benefits. Unfortunately, for a society that already had its own alphabet, philosophy and art, as Persia did, any benefits of Helenization came at a great cost to its own traditions."

"I admit a little naiveté about Greek history," Lee said, "but I don't recall much discussion about the negative aspects of the fall of the Persian Empire. I always assumed they were the 'Bad Guys.'"

"Of course you would! History is written by the winners. Even in our world today, it can be difficult to expunge all bias and propaganda from the news media and this is coming from a profession that actively tries to offer an 'unbiased' view to the world. In three hundred B.C.E., journalists didn't exist. And that is what makes this document so special."

"Go on," Jonesy urged.

"This is a history, or perhaps a better description would be 'travel log', told entirely from the perspective of a Persian man fleeing Alexander's conquering army."

"Humm." Lee's thoughts were racing. "Who was he?"

"Well, that was a bit hard to suss out, actually. I thought at first maybe a priest or a scribe but after reading the text in its entirety, I have come to believe he was a warrior of some sort and this was the journal of his quest. That, in itself, is quite remarkable since it would have been rare for a warrior to have been able to read and write."

"A warrior fleeing Alexander?" asked Jonesy. "Was he a deserter then?"

"I don't think so. At times, he seems to lament his fate, wishing to fight the Greeks. He also recounts several encounters with brigands. If these were true, he must have defended himself quite bravely to have survived such encounters. Indeed, he claims to have been sent on his mission by King Darius himself."

"What was the mission?" Lee asked.

"It appears he was to prevent some artifact from falling into the hands of Alexander. I'm not sure exactly what it was. There is no direct translation. I believe it may have been some sort of precious stone but that is conjecture only."

Lee and Jonesy looked at each other realizing that it was the orb the warrior was probably protecting.

"Did he say why it was so important to keep Alexander from having this artifact?" Jonesy asked.

"Ahh! That is where we get some interesting reading. He seems to think of Alexander as a power mad youth with no respect for antiquity or the lessons learned from history. He was probably not far off in his assumption. Alexander supposedly untied the Gordian knot by hacking it to pieces. Most modern thinkers like to say 'good on you, lad. That is original thinking!' But, if you put it in historical perspective, he solved an ancient puzzle by destroying what amounted to an artifact. Quite distasteful, if you ask me."

"The Persians weren't worried Alexander would destroy it. They were worried he would use it." It was becoming clear to Lee.

"What's that?" Ardi asked.

"The scroll. . .we found it near some sort of orb. . .a large pearl about the size of a softball."

"Really? Oh, my God, Lee! You may have found the one treasure the Persians were able to keep from the Greeks! May I see it?"

"Well, not exactly. We don't actually have it anymore." Lee said looking at Jonesy uncomfortably.

"Oh, my God, man! Was it stolen?" Cheddar was very excited now.

"Not exactly. . .well, Ardi, it's complicated."

"Well, you need to get it back! We have to study it! By itself, the scroll is a fascinating insight on Alexander's invasion from a new perspective, but with that orb, this may be the most significant archeological find since the discovery of Machu Pichu!"

Lee sighed in frustration. If he had only known all this before, maybe he could have talked Jonesy out of his temporary insanity.

"Ardi, were you able to translate the rubbing we sent you?" Lee had sent a rubbing of the cuneiforms from the metal holder of the orb. Jonesy had at least remembered to do that before giving the orb away.

"Yes, that style of cuneiform is much older; probably one of the first examples of writing ever. It is ancient Zorasterian from about 4000 B.C.E. . .was that found with the orb?"

"Yes, why?"

"That's odd. I thought it was from a tomb marker or a monument of some sort."

"Why?" asked Lee. "What does it say?"

"Here lies Azi Dahaka."

"Who the hell was that?"

"That, my friends, was the most powerful Dragon in Persian mythology. Vicious brute according to the legends," Cheddar said matter-of-factly.

Lee sunk his head in his hands. Why did it have to be "the most powerful" and a "vicious brute?" Just summoning any dragon would have brought trouble.

"Okay, Ardi. I'll call you back once I've processed some facts." Lee sounded exhausted. "You think you could do a quick report for us on any myths surrounding this particular Dragon?"

"Not a problem. I'm so excited about this, I'll be up through the night anyway. I'll put on some Earl Grey and with luck, I may be able to email you a report by mid morning."

"Thanks, pal. I'll be waiting."

"Well done. Cheers then."

"Talk to you later." Lee sounded quite dejected now as he disconnected the call. He looked at Jonesy who seemed to have shrunk before Lee's eyes.

Sam was the first to comment.

"So, basically, we just possessed Barney, the purple dinosaur, with the spirit of Godzilla."

"Oh, my Got! Oh, my Got! What have I done?" Jonesy began his litany again.

"So what now?" Sam asked ignoring the once again semi hysterical Jonesy and looking to his master.

"Research. This time we get our facts straight before we make another monumental blunder. My guess is that 'Dragon Slaying' is somewhat of a lost art."

"Probably true. I'd guess because no one has needed a dragon slain in the last millennium because no one has been stupid enough to summon one in the last millennium." Sam said as he went over to get a drink from his water bowl. Then he went to the sofa, jumped up and closed his eyes.

"This is a job for Super Dog and I'm just Sam," he said as he curled up to sleep.

Chapter 32

LEE AND JONESY flipped through Cheddar's report on Azi Dahaka with growing concern. The part that concerned them the most was an old Zoroastrian prophecy that claimed that Dahaka would return and slaughter 1/3 of all life on earth before it was finally slain. A population cynic might have thought that a necessary evil to stave off global environmental and economic catastrophes that seemed the inevitable by product of an over populated world. Lee and Jonesy weren't cynics. They were, in their own small way, crusaders for a hopeful future. Furthermore, neither of them, Jonesy in particular, wanted a part in the slaughter of two billion people. There had to be a way to prevent this fate. Lee picked up his phone and dialed Cheddar.

"Hello?"

"Ardi, this is Lee."

"I take it you have read my report?"

"Yes and we have some questions. May I put you on speaker?"

"By all means."

Lee clicked the speaker button and hung up the handle.

"Jonesy, I assume you are there?"

"Yes. Good to hear your voice."

"And yours. So you two are saying the rubbing I translated was from a metal holder which contained a large pearl?"

"That's correct," said Lee.

"but the pearl is missing?"

"Correct again," Lee responded. Lee and Jonesy looked at each other with remorse. Had Cheddar been in the room with them he would have certainly seen from their faces that it was more than just missing but both had decided to keep Cheddar in the dark on the specifics. Cheddar had never believed in magic. He was not much of a field archeologist and as such had not had many of the experiences that had led Jonesy and Lee to study arcane arts. Ardrehan Cheddar was instead known for his uncanny ability at deciphering inscriptions and ancient languages. He spoke seven modern languages fluently and could read the writing and hieroglyphs of four ancient languages as easily as reading the newspaper. Archeologists the world over came to him for help deciphering the parchments, scrolls, and tablets they found at their dig sites.

"Well, at least one account of Azi Dahaka describes him as a dragon," Cheddar began. "But the idea of a pearl or orb of some sort does not quite fit with Persian dragon mythology. That is much more an Eastern idea. Perhaps this box instead held the head of a mace?. Maybe a famous weapon that he used in battle?"

"Huh?" inquired Lee in a confused tone.

"Did you not read my whole report?" Cheddar sounded a bit offended. "The Zoroastrian myths describe him as a dragon but non-Zoroastrian Persian myths describe him as a man with two snakes growing from his shoulders. My personal guess is that if he did live 5,000 or 6000 years ago, he may have been a cleric or warrior who had two pet snakes draped around his shoulder to spook the knickers off his foes. There is also reference to his 'wounds pouring forth foul reptiles and vermin' or that's as close a translation as I can get to. Again, probably be something the guy could throw out to make it look as if it were coming from his body somehow."

Lee and Jonesy looked at each other Jonesy wrote a note to Lee "the snakes and bugs we found." Lee nodded.

"Wow! Well, Ardi, we were more interested in the Zoroastrian version of events."

There was a long pause on the other end. It was obvious from the silence that Ardi was either stunned or offended. Finally his voice broke over the speaker.

"Damn your stubborn eyes, Lee. You graduated with the same intellectual credentials I did and you're looking at this find with blinders on. You may have discovered physical evidence that a mythological figure from the past actually existed! It would be as stunning a discovery as finding Noah's Ark. We could argue that Azi Dahaka was a real person and not just the creation of ancient story tellers. And here you are telling me that you are only interested in the one, the less likely, telling of the story. Have you lost your scientific objectivity?"

Jonesy and Lee looked at each other with ironic smiles after the chastising from their colleague. Indeed they were positive that Azi Dahaka did exist. They knew for a fact that the Zoroastrian myths got the story right. Dahaka wasn't a man with a few snakes draped around his shoulder. He was a real, honest to god, three headed winged Dragon that spit acid and flame. And he was on the loose.

"Okay, Ardi," began Jonesy. "We agree that you have an interesting point. Let's just say that certain characteristics of the dig site lead us to believe the artifacts we have found more closely fit with the Zoroastrian legends."

"Just what characteristics?"

"Let's just say that certain specifics will need to remain an academic secret until the site has been fully excavated," continued Jonesy in a diplomatic tone.

Cheddar considered this for a moment. He understood that field archeologists were very protective of their digs until they were sure no legal or academic difficulties would arise. More importantly, they needed to be wary of the word getting out to treasure hunters. Cheddar acquiesced, knowing that once the full dig was uncovered, he would be free to publish his own interpretations of the findings.

"Fair enough, Jonesy. It's your dig after all. We'll explore your Zoroastrian angle a bit. The problem is the Zoroastrian legends say he was chained by the hero, Frēdōn, in a cave atop Mt.Dermawendgi. So what does this holder have to do with that?" Cheddar challenged.

Lee stepped in to steer the conversation in a more useful direction.

"Let's say for the sake of argument that the orb we found was a 'dragon orb?'"

"Your problem there, as I stated before, is that dragon orbs or dragon pearls, whatever you choose to call them, come from Chinese and other Asian traditions. Not from Persia."

"Agreed," admitted Lee. "But when were those myths put to writing?"

"Well. . .," Cheddar paused for a moment. "I have never researched the first reference but I would guess near 1000 BCE."

"And how about the Zoroastrian myths?"

"The Avestan, the stories that contain the Zorastrian version, were also about 1000 BCE."

"Ahh, but you said that the current form we are familiar with is the result of a redaction written about 300 BCE." Lee had read the Zoroastrian portion of Cheddar's report very carefully.

"True," Cheddar pondered that for a moment. "I suppose details may have been added, subtracted,…possibly even changed. Where exactly do you want my mind to wander to, Lee?"

"Well; consider. Azi Dahaka legends originate in 3 or 4 thousand BCE. They are passed orally for thousands of years before the Zoroastrians write their version of events. Then seven hundred years later, the legend is included in a redacted piece of literature, which, I add, is all we have to work with."

"Ahh," Cheddar then caught on. "And since trade, technology, and ideas continued to flow east to west in this period of oral story telling, it is possible that dragon orbs, be they an idea or an artifact, were traded as well. And, in the thousands of years since they have been forgotten in one culture but remembered in another."

"Exactly, and by the time of the Zorastrian telling of the tale, metal working has advanced to such a degree that it seems more logical that our hero used chains to bind the creature instead of a big pearl that captures his soul," finished Jonesy.

"It is an interesting hypothesis that conveniently allows a Western dragon to share characteristics with its Eastern brethren. Unfortunately, because oral traditions are, by their nature, un-excavate-able there is no archeological or linguistic way to prove this," Cheddar continued in a triumphant tone. Ever since university, Cheddar had reveled in winning academic debates.

"Correct," replied Jonesy. "But at least it gives our long dead warrior an excuse for abandoning family and country in time of war and trekking across the world's longest continent." Jonesy and Lee were satisfied. They were not interested in publishing an article for academic review. They only needed to confirm who it was they were dealing with. With that part of the puzzle solved they now had to stop a world catastrophe.

"Okay, Cheddar," interjected Lee. "Let's skip to the end of world prophecy."

"Frightening as are most prophecies," Cheddar began. "Still the destruction of 1/3 of all life on Earth is a shade cheerier than the Bible's book of Revelations."

'Thank God we didn't call forth that Dragon!' thought Sam. He didn't say it out loud knowing that it would be tricky for Lee to explain that his dog was just making another wise crack.

"Who exactly is this hero, ahh," Lee said flipping through his notes, "Kirsasp?"

"It's a shame not more is said about him, actually. Both from the Zoroastrian name of Kirsasp, or his Persian spelling of Garshasp, he is credited with killing two dragons. In our traditions, tomes are written about St. George, Beowulf, and others who have only managed to kill one dragon. If we pretend for a moment that the prophecy comes true,"

"And it is!" Sam thought.

"then Kirsasp would become the undisputed reigning king of all dragon slayers, with three to his credit."

"Well, what exactly does he do?" asked Lee.

"Unclear, really. Supposedly, his corpse has been magically preserved so that when the time comes he will rise from the dead and kill Azi Dahaka."

"When is that?" asked Jonesy.

"After 1/3 of the world is dead."

"Does some priest resurrect him?" Lee asked searching for a clue on where to search.

"Not according to the legend. He just senses his time has come, he hops up from his long sleep and kills the beast."

"And what then?" queried Jonesy.

"He probably rules the world. He'd be a different sort of hero than we are used to. Even benevolent despots of that heroic age thought nothing of human rights, democracy, free will and all that rot. Theirs was a time of wars, slaves, concubines, whores, and heroes! You took what you wanted and gave the peasants the scraps and demanded they love you for it. A simpler time really," Cheddar said ending on a sarcastically cheery note.

"Okay, thanks, Ardi," Lee said drawing the conversation to a close.

"Not a problem. Glad to help."

"I may have to call again about all this. Will that be alright?"

"Certainly, Lee. And if you gents don't explore my hypothesis on this matter I promise you that I will happily publish my own opinion on your discovery."

"You are welcome to do that as you always are, Ardi," Jonesy replied.

Lee hung up the phone and looked at his friend and his familiar. "Opinions?"

"My opinion is that I did a damn fine job keeping quiet!" barked Sam.

"Good point," agreed Lee. "I don't think you have kept your mouth shut that long since Erik was near by."

Jonsey chuckled, Sam growled.

"Well, it seems our worst fears have been confirmed," Jonesy said in a more serious tone.

"Agreed. But I don't stomach the idea that we have to sit idly by and watch the world fall apart."

"What do you have in mind?" Jonesy asked.

"Maybe this Kirsasp is our best bet. I just don't want to wait that long for him to show up and save the day."

Jonesy knew his summoning friend well enough to know where he was going with this.

"You think that is even possible?"

"Maybe if we can get close enough to his burial site?" Lee wandered aloud.

"If this plan includes me turning into a squid you can count me out," Sam said snidely.

"Have you ever even attempted a spell like this?" Jonesy said almost shocked.

"Never," Lee said flatly. The thought of it made him squeamish. He may have summoned many supernatural creatures in his time but the difference was they were all living when he called.

"So how do you plan to do this?"

"First we need to get to New Orleans. I know a guy there who can help us."

"A friend?"

"Not exactly."

Chapter 33

THE SECOND ERIK laid eyes on Larissa, he tossed out any notion that he would exploit her for the WWI. He had taken some good shots of the Komodos and framed them in such a way as to appear to be something different. That, plus some photo-shop work would make a good foundation for an article or two. When Hugh had mentioned one survivor from the Osaka terrorist attack had claimed to see a dragon, Erik figured, why not? But when Hugh, Summer and he had met Larissa and her friend, Erik had quickly changed his mind. She was just too sad a figure to make a fool of publicly, no matter how ridiculous her story.

Both she and Latham, her fellow survivor, seemed to have suffered little physical trauma but both seemed to be deeply out of touch with their emotions. Erik had seen looks like that before. He'd landed a load on the Carl Vincennes only to find out that on his return flight he would be carrying the body and personal effects of a Marine Hornet driver that had biffed his landing the day before. He had to stay an extra day on the Vincennes as the ship prepared for its full honors send off. Six thousand people on board and they all spoke in solemn tones and held their head low. In the ceremony prior to Erik flying the corpse home, every person involved in the accident stood in full dress regalia with anguished looks in their eyes. The maintenance crews, landing signaling officers, and the catapult crews all had hollow looks in their eyes. Looks that said, 'God, I'm sorry you're dead, dude, but I sure hope it was pilot error and not something I did.' Erik saw that same look in Latham and Larissa. They would spend the rest of their lives struggling with 'survivor's guilt' and wondering if they could have done something to have saved the others. And behind it all, wondering 'why them and not me?"

On the other hand, Hugh and Summer seemed to have abandoned the high road. They were unrelenting in their questioning of Larissa's account of the 'Dragon' attack. Feeling uncomfortable with the whole scenario, Erik quietly excused himself and headed to the counter for another cup of coffee. Secretly, Summer was relieved since his absence allowed her to begin searching Larissa's emotions. What she found was disturbing. As Larissa recounted the attack and described what she saw, Summer couldn't help wonder what really inhabited the orb. Had it somehow possessed the Imoogi and worse yet, was it bent upon more destruction? God only knew when or where it might strike next.

When Erik finally got his over priced cup of coffee and found another table, he realized Latham had followed him. Erik looked at him curiously and motioned for him to take a seat. Latham was tall and lanky with an athletic appearance. He certainly didn't seem to fit the description of a sci-fi die hard but Erik figured anybody had the right to make of themselves what they wished... even if it was a little weird.

"Not too interested in what your friend has to say?" inquired Erik.

"It's not that," Latham said sheepishly. "It's just that I couldn't really see too well that night...I was wearing a big mask, couldn't see much of anything, really."

Erik felt bad for the guy and tried some comforting words.

"You saw enough to get into that pool. Probably saved her life."

"Sometimes that's not enough." Latham sighed deeply. "I didn't really know what was going on...so I can't corroborate her story."

"So, you don't believe her then?"

"I didn't say that." Latham seemed startled by the observation. "I've never known her to make stuff up. But I guess," he continued hesitantly, "maybe it's easier to believe a dragon would do something like that."

Erik sipped his coffee.

"Maybe it's too hard for her to accept that man could do that to another man." Erik mused sympathetically.

"Something like that," Latham quietly agreed. "You go through your whole life never imagining something like that will happen to you. You know, getting mugged or having a car accident, those are things we all sort of accept. But this kind of random violence makes no sense to me."

"Yeah, me either." Intellectually, Erik knew that creating feelings of paranoia and tearing away feelings of safety was exactly what terrorists hoped to achieve but it still didn't sit well with his view of the world.

Erik felt his phone buzzing and answered.

"This's Erik."

"Hi! This is Lee. Where's Hugh? I tried calling but his phone is off."

"He's doing an interview right now. What's up?"

"I see. Well, when he's done tell him to call me okay?"

"Sure. Anything else?"

"Yes. Jonesy and I need to fly to New Orleans for a few days. We should be back in four or five days."

"Okay?"

"Look, when you guys finish up there do you have anything pressing?"

"Not really. Why?"

"I'd like to extend our little arrangement if I could. At least a week or two."

"What's the rough figure?"

"I'll pay you $500 a day when grounded and a $1000 plus fuel expenses when flying. I don't have time to stick around for your return so it will have to be a verbal agreement for now."

Erik thought about that for a moment. Getting paid $500 for sitting on his ass in Korea was better then getting paid $0 sitting on his ass in Anchorage waiting for Nariff to arrange another shipment. Lee had already paid Erik $2000 in cash just to fly Hugh and Summer to Osaka and back so he knew the rich archaeologist was good for it.

"That sits good for me...You thinking of making this a regular gig?"

Lee paused on the line thinking about that. He certainly wasn't going to give up the luxury and speed of his Lear jet, nor the long time and trusted association with his two pilots but there might be certain advantages to bringing Erik on to his small staff. He had certain talents that were handy in a pinch and the small cargo plane he flew could handle a lot of cargo at a reasonable rate.

"Well, let's call this deal shook on and consider the other as the time comes."

Erik was happy with that.

"Sounds good to me," he said. "I'll pass the message on to Hugh and see you in a week. By the way," he said as an afterthought.

"Yes?"

"You think this terrorist bombing has anything to do with those Komodos we saw on the beach?" Erik asked, wondering why in the hell Lee was even interested in all this.

Lee didn't know what to say. Erik certainly wouldn't believe the truth if he told him. He finally decided to be vague and let Erik try to rationalize in his own mind what was going on.

"I do actually. That's why I'm off to New Orleans. I need to research some leads."

Erik didn't prod any further. He figured of all the personalities involved in this misadventure, he was the one Lee would put on the need to know basis. For many people, that would be a tough pill to swallow but after six years in Naval aviation and one year smuggling, Erik was okay with that so long as there was a paycheck at the end of the tunnel. Whatever the case, he figured Lee was a competent man. Whether the guy was a philanthropic do gooder or he worked for some secret government agency, all Erik needed to hear was that he thought there was a connection. He was happy to sign on to any venture that might get back at the bastards who turned that poor pretty girl into a basket case.

"Hey, Erik...I have a question for you."

"Shoot."

"Why aren't you in there with Hugh interviewing that girl for your magazine?"

Hell," Erik laughed. "I can come up with a crazier story than that when I'm sober!"

Chapter 34

J.P. WOKE UP with a splitting headache.

"Oh, uh. . ." he groaned. As he opened his eyes, he knew he wasn't at home. He had to clear his head to think.

"Uh. ." he groaned again as he tried to sit up.

"Wha. . .?"

J.P. turned to see the black hair trailing over a naked woman lying next to him.

"Who the. . .he. . .," he grumbled as he tried to remember who she was and why she was here. Well, okay so he figured he knew why she was here, but "who is she" was still a mystery. She just groaned and fell asleep again. J.P. sat on the edge of the bed, aching head cradled in his hands, and tried to shake away the booze and drugs of the night before.

"Oh, yeah," he was starting to remember last night. "The party after the party," he muttered to himself. He remembered he'd gone to the dinner after the lectures. It was a pretty typically boring dress dinner for all the judges and their spouses. He had attended so many of these things over the years, he could hardly remember where he was.

But as he heard the surf and felt the ocean breeze come through the open door of the lanai, he remembered he was in Hawaii at the International Judicial Conference. He'd been a good boy for three whole days, attending lectures, meeting and greeting his colleagues from around the country as well as around the world, and trying to sound and act "judicial." But it was finally too much and, after all, it was the last night of the conference. How many times did he get to be away from his wife and in an exotic place where booze and drugs and women were plentiful? So he had hooked up with this lady, couldn't remember her name but she was pretty hot, not young, he didn't really like them too young—no experience usually meant boring. She was probably in her early forties but a very sexy lady and obviously ready to party. She hit on him about midway through the drinks and dance stage and asked if he'd wanted to go somewhere "less public." He jumped at the chance.

She took him to her car where things got pretty hot and heavy and then she pulled out a bag of coke and they snorted a few lines. Next thing he knew, they were in this bungalow on the beach. Wow! It had been some night! But he had to get back to his hotel and make it to the last half day session. He didn't want anyone wondering where he was or what he was doing. He certainly didn't need any whispers getting back to his wife.

He went into the bathroom and got into a cold shower, hoping it would wake him up and clear his head. It did. When he got back to the bedroom, his partner had arisen and didn't look too bad after the night they'd had. She was standing in the open patio door, naked, letting the ocean breeze caress her body. She had a cigarette in one hand.

"Well, good morning," she smiled at him seductively.

"Good morning," he said and came over to her. "You look amazing."

"You look pretty good yourself," she said as she put her cigarette down and wrapped her arms around him. She brought one hand down and slipped it into his pants but he moved away.

"Oh, no!" he laughed. "Look, it was a great night, but I have to get back. There will be those that notice my absence."

"But isn't that half the fun?" she asked teasingly.

"Mmm. . .don't think so," he answered. "Look, I'm embarrassed, but I don't remember your name."

"We never used them and don't need to. It was a fun night. Just remember that," she said as she waltzed into the bathroom and closed the door.

J.P. Morton managed to arrive at the breakfast session only thirty minutes late and had even called his wife before he left the room. She asked why he hadn't called yesterday.

"We had some long session and then there was this dinner for the last night. I was really beat when I got back."

She'd been satisfied with that but then she was always satisfied with his excuses and didn't seem aware of his frequent trysts so he felt no need to confess and disturb her peaceful life.

Following the breakfast and the boring tirades of judges who proclaimed their righteous indignation of the way of the world while doing all they could to circumvent the law in their own lives, J.P. and the others went into their final session which was being presented by the Honorable Sharon Brandon, Justice of the Tenth Circuit Court of Appeals from Oklahoma.

JP. settled himself at his table and looked up on the dias as Her Honor was being introduced. There stood the woman he'd just left this morning.

The bio of the judge said she was married with three children, two in college and one clerking for the US Supreme Court. Her husband was a prominent land developer and they obviously were well heeled. J.P. blushed as he realized what had happened.

"Well, guess we both have reason to keep quiet," he thought.

The judge was making her impassioned plea about the courts' role in preserving the family unit and the integrity and sanctity of marriage. She had been a Republican appointee and "family values" had been her stock in trade. She opposed abortion, gay rights, and she even publicly condemned divorce although admitted it was a fact of life in our broken society. Her public image was one of the devoted wife and mother and humble public servant. Obviously, her private image was quite different.

There was a brief coffee time on the patio following the judge's speech and the justices had the opportunity to chat once again before the adjournment session. J.P. couldn't resist the opportunity to approach the judge and tell her what an inspiring speech she gave. She offered him her hand in thanks and was as cool as ice. No one would have thought they'd ever met before, let alone that they had been snorting cocaine and engaging in sexual behavior that was far from anything approved by "Emily Post's Family Values" book.

They stood a moment, chatting with a few other justices about the lack of morals and the general decay of the society and suddenly they heard a scream from a few yards away. They looked up to see flames engulfing one side of the patio and they felt something swooping by overhead. The flames spread so quickly, few had the chance to escape. Sheer terror and panic had struck the group and a few people were trampled in the melee. J.P. had grabbed the judge and threw her on the ground under him, but the flames very quickly consumed them and those they were near

Chapter 35

LEE HAD COME to the Crossroads bar alone. It was a dingy basement club on the outskirts of the lower 9th ward in New Orleans. The Crossroads was a new blues club purposely built in the remains of one of the few surviving buildings from Katrina. It was a three story concrete building with very little in the way of classic New Orleans architecture. In fact, it was something of an ugly building but it had obviously been built strong enough to survive in an area where little else had. Even though the bar opened post Katrina it still billed itself as the "bar that survived the flood." It was clever marketing, if somewhat misleading, but the Crossroads backed up its hype with booking some of the best blues artists in the world.

Lee had dressed the part of a blues aficionado. He wore a black sport coat and pants and a dark brown turtle neck sweater. Most people in the club were dressed in similarly dark colors. Some even dressed in "Goth" attire complete with dark eyeliner and black lipstick. It was an oddly eclectic crowd. If you could imagine every subculture that liked to dress in dark colors, they were represented in the Crossroads. Lee was sitting at a small table by himself when the opening act came on.

It was the Crossroads Band, the blues quartet that comprised the four co-owners of the bar. Every Thursday, Friday, and Saturday the Crossroads Band would come out and play a three song set to open who ever was headlining for the evening. Even though it was only a three song set, anyone who knew blues traditions knew that one song could go on for twenty minutes if the band and the crowd were ripe for an improvised jam.

The band started with a dark and somber piece. While lyrically the Blues tended to have sad or depressing topics, there was nothing in the structure of the music that required the instruments be played in the same way. The most common Blues structure was a repeating twelve bar structure. Within that structure, the musician could play somber notes, upbeat notes, and everything in between. If the band held the structure, they could let the melody drift almost seamlessly from one to the next. The Crossroads Band was particularly adept at this. They played tonight for a solid thirty five minutes without stop. They started with a somber slow song and transitioned into an upbeat, almost jazzy song, and then again back to a fast paced but eerie sounding conclusion. Lee was no aficionado but he was always impressed by a band that could do that. Many bands tried to shift tempo and melody, the Beatles and Jethrow Tull in particular, but they often sounded like the musical equivalent of a person who did a poor job downshifting their car. When Crossroads played, you didn't realize they were playing a new song until two minutes after they were playing it.

Lee always admired talent like that. Knowing what he did about the occult connections to the Blues he was also suspect of talent like that. Lee was the kind of believer who thought that Led Zepplin or Black Sabbath may indeed have sold their souls to the devil. He was also pretty sure that if Marolyn Manson or Rob Zombie had struck a deal they had been royally screwed.

As the band concluded, the front man and bassist, Freddy Dixon, thanked the crowd for their applause and announced the evening's headline band. Freddy was a stout man in his mid fifties. He wore an all black suit with a black shirt and silver tie. He carefully packed his bass in it's case as the next band quickly set up. Lee saw him exchange some friendly words with the new performers and then he left the stage for the back offices. Freddy was the man Lee had come to see.

Freddy Dixon was one of the world's foremost practitioners of Hoodoo. Hoodoo was the magical skill set that was commonly associated with the Voodoo religion. What Hoodoo offered that most other magic didn't was a direct link to the dead. Lee summoned sprites, elementals, and other magical creatures, Jonesy called forth the raw essence of magic itself, but few except the practitioners of Hoodoo ventured into the world of the dead. In Renaissance parlance, Freddy Dixon was a Necromancer.

Dixon emerged from stashing his bass in his office and took a seat at Lee's table. Before saying a word to Lee he nodded towards the cocktail hostess and flashed her two fingers. She quickly arrived with a tray full of three bottles of wine and two glasses. Without so much as a hello, Dixon motioned to Lee.

"These are from my private collection. Which one would you like?"

Lee examined his choices. He was certainly glad the Creole culture has an affinity towards good wine which rivaled that of his neighbors in Tuscany.

"This will be a treat. I've been in Tuscany so long I almost forgot what a French Bordeaux tasted like. How about the Chateau Mouton Rothschild?"

"Good choice. This bottle is only 5 years old but I have a 1973 in my office."

"That was the year Rothschild was promoted to a first growth by the Medoc AOC correct?"

"That's right."

"Well, now you are just bragging. Don't suppose you would go get that one."

"I don't like you that much, Lee."

"Fair enough. The five year old will do nicely."

The hostess popped the cork and poured Lee half a glass, allowing Lee to go through the whole tasting ritual. She finished pouring the two glasses, left the bottle on the table and hustled back to her duties.

"Your band is doing quite nicely. I'm very impressed with your talent. How is the rest of the business going?" asked Lee in a cordial manner.

Dixon wasn't much for small talk.

"Cut the crap, Lee. You didn't come here to talk about my bar or my music."

Lee was taken aback. His upbringing and academic training had taught him to adhere to a certain sense of cordial decorum even amongst rivals.

"You still like to cut to the chase I see."

"Hey, I'm from E. St. Louis, man. Don't have time for anything else. My business and my band require a lot."

"I hope your success has not come at too high a price, Fred."

Dixon's eyes narrowed at Lee's suggestion.

"Everything comes at a price, Lee, but when you have talent and a good head for business you don't need to strike any bargains, if that's what you're implying."

Lee felt a surge of frustration and anger at his old rival's arrogance.

"Never said you did…but you have helped many make that deal."

"Everybody has a right to choose. All I did was tell them who to call."

"I guess that brings me to my point." Lee hesitated before continuing. Lee was not planning to use Dixon's powers for personal gain. He didn't need to get more wealth, he didn't need the love of another, he wasn't here to sell his soul. Nevertheless, asking Dixon for help felt like a Faustian bargain on it's own. He slid a folded piece of paper across the table to Dixon.

"I need to contact this man."

Dixon was stunned. He just stared at the paper for a moment. The only thing that had separated Necromancers from Summoners was that Summoners drew a distinction between raising the spirits of the Earth and raising the spirits of the dead. If Lee had come to Dixon with a name, he was obviously into something important enough to cross that line.

"I'll be damned!" Dixon finally blurted out.

Lee said nothing. He just stared off into space awaiting Dixon's answer. Dixon's first impulse was to tell him to take a hike. He couldn't do that. He was just too curious as to who it was that would make Lee compromise his principles. He picked up the paper and read the name. Puzzled, he folded the paper and put it back in his pocket.

"Who the hell is that?"

"A Persian. Dead maybe three or four thousand years."

"Jesus, Lee! How the hell you expect me to call a Persian who's been dead that long? Why don't you find an Arab to do this for you?"

"Modern Iran isn't quite as open as America is. The last known Necromancer from that part of the world was detained shortly after the '79 student revolt. He's either dead or still rotting in prison."

"You'll need more than me for this." Dixon took a sip of wine and looked thoughtful. "I think I know someone who can help. She's a medium...a priestess."

"Can you trust her?"

"With my life."

"Fair enough."

"I don't work cheap and neither does she."

"I'm not worried about the money."

Dixon took another sip of his wine and looked skeptically at Lee.

"Your views on Hoodoo are fairly well known," he said at last.

"True. But I never said you didn't have the right to practice it. I have just questioned the ethics of some who have."

"Yeah, well my brother was basically run out of the country by others like you."

"Your brother was selling his services as a Zombie maker to the highest bidder. He never considered who he was turning or why. Not particularly ethical in the use of his powers."

Dixon flushed with anger.

"I still don't see why I should help you."

Lee's mind shuddered at the damage the Dragon was causing as they spoke. He leaned forward and stared into Dixon's eyes.

"Because, Freddy, if we don't find that guy, a disaster will come that will make Katrina look like a backed up toilet by comparison."

Dixon took another swallow of wine and met Lee's stare.

"Who is this guy you want to raise?"

"He's a Dragon Slayer."

Chapter 36

"**A**WAH HA know, mon?" Naiyah was surprised to hear from her old friend, Freddy. Years back when she'd first come to New Orleans, she started singing in jazz clubs and met Freddy Dixon. She sang while he played and together they'd made a good name for themselves and made a little money, too. They'd tried being lovers for awhile but that didn't seem to work, so they settled into a nice friendship that was still there even though they didn't see each other much anymore since Naiyah had left the business.

"Ah, Naiyah, my boonoonoonous lady." Freddy said. "I wanna meet wit you soon, okay? I have a man who need to go beyond the grave to aks a question. You help us?" Freddy hadn't been excited about seeing Lee Bondurant again, but he was glad it gave him the chance to hook up with Naiyah Morgan again. He remembered her incredibly sensual voice when she sang along with his bass. He also remembered how beautiful she was and the last time he saw her, about a year ago, she hadn't aged much over the twenty years. If anything, she was even more beautiful as a mature woman. But Freddy had long since decided he and Naiyah were not good that way. They were better as friends.

"I do dat fine. Wah know dis mon?" Naiyah was from Jamaica and spoke Patois almost exclusively and especially when she spoke with old friends.

"He is Dr. Leroy Bondurant. He Summoning mon."

"Wah fo he need me? Fi he summoning mon, he summon. Don need talky talk wid da dead."

"It's complicated, Naiyah. You meet wit us?"

"Ok. When fo yo want come?"

"Now."

"Okay. I be here."

As Freddy clicked off his cell phone, he looked at Lee.

"She'll see us now."

"I have a friend I want to bring." Lee called Jonesy who was waiting in a coffee bar a block away. "Hey, Jonesy. We're going now. Meet me out front."

"Who is this Jonesy?" asked Freddy.

"He's an archeologist and long time friend of mine. He and I are working this together so I want him to join us, too."

Lee stood and left money on the table for the waitress. Then he followed Freddy out to the front where they saw Jonesy approaching with Sam. Lee made quick introductions and they followed Freddy down an alley. It was dark and creepy and in New Orleans, after all, and Jonesy was very uncomfortable.

"You sure about this, Lee?" whispered Jonesy as they trailed a few feet behind Freddy.

"Well, not necessarily but I don't know that we have a lot of choice here. I think Sam will pick up on anything that is out of whack, right Sammy?"

"I'll try." Sam said. "Just keep me away from the bayous."

"Why?" Jonesy said alarmed. "What's in the bayous?" He had heard all kinds of horror stories about swamps and vampires and zombies and didn't want to have anything to do with that.

"Alligators." Sam said.

"Oh, oh, okay." said Jonesy. This whole adventure had been way more Indiana Jones than Jonesy had ever wanted and he was still quaking in his boots. But it had all started because of him.

After a block of walking through the dark alley, Freddy came out to a street filled with people obviously enjoying the music, the food and the drink at the different places along the street.

They were behind Bourbon street but still in a very active part of town. Freddy crossed an intersection and headed down another side street until he came to a little shop with a crystal ball hanging on the metal sign holder over the door. The window showed a dim orange light in the interior and was covered with signs of occult objects. The sign painted on the window said "Madam Naiyah."

As Freddy opened the door, there was a soft "tinkle" notifying the back that someone had come into the store. Jonesy and Lee looked around to see candles, robes, T-shirts, earrings, crystals, incense, tarot cards and all manner of occult souvenirs. Obviously, these items supplemented the income Madam did from readings or séances or whatever it was this woman did.

Lee wasn't sure what he was expecting, but when the curtains at the back parted, he found himself surprised. The woman that exited was probably in her thirties or maybe forties but certainly no older than he was. She was almost as tall as he and she had on a long gauze yellow caftan with charm bracelets on both wrists and a huge gold medallion hanging from her neck. He couldn't make out the emblem from the dim light but he could make out that this woman was an extraordinary beauty. Her hair was almost an auburn brown and she wore it long and pulled back and up into a pony tail of tight braids. She wore very large golden earrings dangling almost to her shoulders.

"Naiyah!" Freddy walked over and hugged his friend. "Good to see you."

"You do no eber come roun, no mo, Freddy." But she was smiling a smile that gave Lee another surprise. She had looked so austere and regal coming in the door and then she smiled a smile that was warm and kind and almost gentle. He was intrigued by the contradictions in this woman.

"Naiyah, this is Lee Bondurant and Sam Da Soo." Freddy led her to the two men.

"Jonesy." Said Jonesy as he bowed and smiled at her.

Naiyah smiled at Jonesy but walked right up to Lee.

"You da summoning mon, yes?" She extended her hand to shake hands with him.

Lee took her hand but was momentarily struck dumb as he looked into this woman's dark, almost black eyes. He felt as if he'd been struck by lightening or something.

"Wah chew no talk, summon mon?" Naiyah then saw Sam and bent down to take his head in her hands and give him a nuzzle. "Ah, yo da talkin' one, yes?"

Sam said nothing since he wasn't sure how much he should reveal but he was as flattered as he'd ever been and believed he had just fallen in love.

"Ah, yo boonoonoonous." she scratched behind his ears and he found his tongue dropping out.

"Uh, this is my dog, Sam." Lee finally said. "We're both glad you met with us on short notice."

"Wah chew tink, I don no yo come dis day?" She gave him a sarcastic smile and said "Wah chew tink I do, summon mon? Bake cookies? I see tings, mon. Das wah I do. I see tings and I see you come dis day to me. Now you here wah chew need talk wid dead mon? You don need talk no dead mon—you bedder talk wid me!" She said as she walked to the front door and locked it, turning the sign from "open" to "closed". Then she led them to the back room.

"Siddee down, genlemen. Sam, yo boonoonoonous soul, siddee wid me." She petted Sam as he moved next to her chair. The men sat around the table which was a round mahogany table with nothing on it but a small dish with a well used candle sitting in the center.

"Now, you gon tell me wah chew don need talk wid dead mon?" she brushed back her draping sleeves so that her bare elbows rested on the table and she looked at Lee.

"Yes, well, I. . .we. . ." he said, motioning toward Jonesy, "we need to see if you can contact an ancient spirit."

"Spirit don know age, spirit jis spirit."

"Okay, well, this man died nearly 3000 years ago."

"3000 years? Wah chew wan go disturb dis mon now?"

"I can't really go into that. I just need to know if you can learn where he was buried. We know it was somewhere in Ancient Persia."

"You gon summon dis mon?"

"Look, can you contact him and find this out or not?"

"Don never know wah com true. But don gon do spell wid no money."

"Oh, yes, yes, of course. I'm sorry. How much do you charge for a séance?" Lee was reaching for his wallet.

"Five hunnard dollars for dis."

Lee took out $1000 and laid it on the table.

"Wah yo gib me dis?" She asked.

"Incentive." Lee responded. "It's very important that we contact this man. I'm willing to see that you are well paid for your help."

"Spirit come or don come, cain no wich an spirit don care bout money." But Naiyah took the money and rose to put it in a box on the credenza behind her. She picked up a match box from there and then resumed her place at the table. After lighting the candle, she held her hands out for each of them to hold hands around the table.

She took two deep breaths and closed her eyes. They all just sat quietly for what seemed like several minutes and then she let out an audible sigh. Lee and Jonesy looked at each other and then at Freddy who just sat with his eyes closed. After what seemed like another several minutes, Lee saw the candle flicker and then he saw Naiyah open her eyes.

She began speaking in a very low voice and in a language that sounded vaguely like Farci but not quite. Lee was glad he'd decided to record the session, even though he didn't ask Naiyah about it. He felt if they did get anything, it would be too important to rely on his memory or Jonesy's. He looked at Jonesy with a look of bewilderment and Jonesy silently returned his concern.

She spoke for awhile and then was silent and finally Lee asked.

" Kirsasp, I must have your help. Will you tell me where your resting place is? Where is your burial site?" He had no way of knowing if he was talking to Kirsasp or not and since he didn't understand what Naiyah had been saying, he wasn't even sure if this was even the time to ask, but he'd come here to find out one thing and he needed to at least try to ask. He looked across to Freddy and saw him sitting with his eyes open now looking at Naiyah with what appeared to be astonishment.

Naiyah spoke again in the deep voice and it sounded like gibberish to Lee. They listened to the voice for another few minutes until they saw Naiyah sigh deeply again and drop her head to her chest. She sat quite still for several moments, still holding Lee's and Freddy's hands. Finally, she breathed deeply and raised her head. She opened her eyes and looked around as if she didn't know where she was.

"Sorry, bredren," she said in her own voice. "Da spirit he don want come to dis place." she released their hands and stood to turn to the credenza. She picked up her money box and opened it, removing the money that Lee had given her.

"What do you mean, Naiyah? Someone spoke through you," said Freddy. "Didn't you feel him? Or hear him?"

"Wah chew mean, someone spoke true me?" She stopped and looked at them all in bewilderment.

"Yes, Naiyah, we heard a voice, a very deep voice and it was speaking in a language I'm not familiar with but we think it was an old Arabic tongue," Lee said. "Don't you remember?"

"Someone come true me? I don hear nutin." She looked puzzled.

"Yes, Naiyah, you were speaking in a language I never heard before, woman. How'd you do that?" Freddy had seen her before when he knew she was faking and he had seen her when she was not. Even in a real trance, Naiyah was always aware of what happened afterwards. She could usually remember hearing what the spirit had said.

"I don know no udder langige cept Patwa and Englie." Naiyah sat down again and looked from man to man. "Dey udder one do talk?" She seemed confused and disoriented.

"Yes, another one spoke through you. I don't know what he said but I have a friend in England who is very good with languages. I'm going to call him and repeat as much as I can of what you said to him and see if he understands. Naiyah, are you alright?" Lee was convinced her séance had been real, even though he and Jonesy had concerns before hand about her authenticity.

"I be fine, I be fine." She was still holding the $1000 in her hand and Lee reached over and closed her hand around the bills.

"Keep this, Naiyah. You earned it. And I'd like to know if we might be able to come back if we haven't gotten all the information we need. Would you agree to see us again and try to bring this spirit back?" He was still holding her hand.

"I don know. You call me." Her thick Patois had slipped into a more relaxed New Orleans drawl. "I always remember." She seemed to be talking to herself. "Dis time no memory."

"I don't think you need to be afraid, Naiyah. He has no reason to come back to you unless we call him. We are going to him. We are the ones he'll be interested in, not you, so you should not be afraid, okay?" Lee was trying to reassure her since she still seemed shaken by the séance.

"Okay, okay, but chew don mess wid dis mon. I don tink dat's good to talky talk wid da dead. You don't bring him up. Bad tings happen." Now she seemed to be pleading with Lee.

"We'll be okay. We know what we're doing and it's important. Believe me, I wouldn't be doing this if it weren't really important." Niayah finally pulled her hand away from Lee and stood up. The men stood and Sam walked to the curtain to go back into the shop.

"Jes be careful, summon mon." Naiyah said as she watched them all go. She closed the door after they'd gone and locked it behind them.

Chapter 37

"WE'RE ALL CLEAR from navigational radios, Lee. You are free to use the phone and internet if needed," said Hank as he entered the passenger cabin of Lee's Learjet.

"Thanks, Hank. Go get yourself a catnap."

"Just where I was headed," replied Lee's pilot.

Some believed Lee's renovation of his Learjet was for his comfort, but in truth he had fashioned it for his pilots. A Learjet did not have the range of a jumbo jet and because of this, the plane usually had to make several stops to fly internationally. Two pilots were only needed for takeoffs and landings, so the individual "suites" allowed one to nap while the other flew.

Lee opened his flip phone and checked his voice mail. "Hugh left a message," His face grew grim as he listened. Sam and Jonesy stared intently at him while they waited. "Two more reported attacks, one in Hawaii and another at a PETA conference in California. At least those were really cows killed there but ten people were killed at a Judicial Conference in Hawaii."

Jonesy moaned and put his head in his hands.

"Cheddar left a message," he said.

"What's it say?" Jonesy was grasping at anything that might offer hope. After Naiyah's séance they had emailed the recording to Cheddar hoping he could decipher the language.

Lee didn't respond as he busily logged on. The two sat silently, watching Lee's expression as he read the e-mail.

"Not what I'd hoped," he said.

"Anything useful?" Sam asked.

"I guess the spoken dialects are much harder to decipher than the written ones. Apparently the way we speak evolves much quicker than how we write."

"Damn!" sighed Jonesy.

"There is one thing that he feels good about."

"What's that?"

"It seems that two words were uttered several times. 'Hamun' and 'Sistan'. Cheddar says that Sistan was the city that Kirsasp supposedly founded and there is a lake, Hamun, that is not far from it."

That renewed Jonesy's hope.

"Well, we were asking him where he was buried. Perhaps he could understand us but we could not understand him?"

"My thoughts exactly," replied Lee without returning Jonesy's optimism.

"What's the bad news, boss?" Sam knew Lee well enough to know his master was worried.

"Hang on a sec. I'm doing a Wiki search on the two locations," Lee hurried through his search, found the latitude and longitude and cross referenced with a mapping program. "Shite!"

"What!" cried Sam and Jonesy in unison.

"They are both located in Iran...just west of the Afghanistan border." He sighed deeply. "100 miles east and this would have been so much easier."

"What did Freddy say about the spell you bought?" said Sam.

"He said get within 100 miles of the body. But since we are not exactly sure where he is buried that still means getting ourselves into Iran."

None of the three spoke for a moment. They all stared off into space, thinking their own thoughts, hearing nothing but the low hum of the jet engines. Finally, Jonesy spoke up with reluctance in his voice.

"Well, we do know one person with some experience getting things into places they aren't supposed to be." Jonesy said hesitantly.

"How much do you suppose that would cost us?" asked Sam.

"We're about to find out," Lee said, already dialing the number on his phone.

"Erik?"

"Yeah." responded Erik on the other end. "You need me to find Hugh again?"

"No. I called to talk to you."

"'Bout what?"

"How much do you owe on your plane?"

"Nothin', why?"

"How much do you owe on the work you have put in to your plane?"

"Ahhh, that's a different story," Erik said chuckling. "Probably 30 grand or so."

"How would you like to pay that all off and fly her free and clear?"

Erik hesitated as if he was about to make a deal with the devil.

"And what would that cost me?"

Lee paused knowing this would be a hard sell.

"You sitting down?"

Chapter 38

THE NEIGHBORHOOD OF Itaewon in Seoul, South Korea was a place where anything could be bought by anybody. It catered to the Western Expats living in Korea. In most large Western cities, there are neighborhoods that are created around immigrant communities. There are China-towns, little Koreas, little Vietnams, even Russian towns in areas with enough Russian immigrants to support it. What may come as a shock to Americans with little experience traveling abroad, is that the same sorts of Westernized neighborhoods exist in major metropolitan cities in the East. Itaewon was a Little America of South Korea. On one block, there was a McDonald's, two Starbucks, and a host of specialty clothing stores representing major U.S. brands. There were Western pubs, Western restaurants, Western bookstores, and, of course Nariff's, Western grocery store.

Erik was one of the many "businessmen" who helped support the Western fares sold at Itaewon. Some of these businessmen conducted their affairs in a completely legal fashion, such as the North Face dealer and the Starbucks' distributor. Others, like Nariff, were just a little grey, and still others were completely illegal. It was one of the latter that Erik had come to meet. He was here to meet Tom Jordan. Although unconfirmed, the word on the street was that Jordan was a fixer for the CIA. That word "fixer" meant that he didn't exactly do illegal acts but more or less arranged for illegal activity to occur. Specifically, he was the contact guy for just about any CIA supported smuggling activity on the Pacific rim.

Erik was meeting Jordan at one of the Starbucks. Although the decorum, menu, and prices were practically identical to a Starbucks in America, the architecture of the building it was in matched most architecture of industrialized Asian nations. It was housed in a rectangular mini skyscraper. This particular building was split down the middle with the Starbucks inhabiting one half of the three story structure. The first floor housed the baristas and a handful of tables, couches, and chairs. Most of the lounge and table space was split between the second and third floors. On first glance, it looked rather cramped for a Starbuck's, but once you discovered the other two levels, there was actually more lounging space than a typical American Starbucks. On a slow Saturday afternoon weeks away from peak tourist season, the third floor was practically empty.

As Erik reached the third floor with his scalding hot Americano in hand, there were only two other people in the room. Civilian clothing could not disguise they were American servicemen from the nearby base. They had short haircuts and a cocky "I've been in the shit look" which, from Erik's experience, meant they probably hadn't.

The two servicemen had perched themselves next to the window looking down on the streets of Itaewon. Erik took up residence on the opposite end of the room in a comfortable lounge chair. It wasn't long before he heard more footsteps springing up the stairway. The man who emerged from the stairway was tall and lanky and looked to be in his mid twenties. He had long hair that was neatly pulled into a pony tail and a thin beard that was neatly trimmed. He wore stylishly faded blue jeans and a T-shirt. Across one shoulder was a brown leather messenger's satchel. In a way, this man was more in uniform than the two soldiers. He wore the trappings and had the mannerisms of one of the thousands of young, college educated English teachers who were hired by Korean school districts and tutoring companies.

Erik couldn't help but think that Korea's perception of Western culture must be thoroughly skewed. The only Westerners who had an interest in living in the country seemed to be on completely opposite ends of the political and economic spectrum.

As the man approached, Erik could see the beginnings of age lines around his eyes suggesting he was older than he first appeared. When he sat across from him, Erik could see the thin beard was hiding some sort of scar across his jaw line. Playing the part of a hippy English teacher was a clever disguise. In a post 9-11 world, many people did not give the CIA the credit they were due. If this man was an example of the norm, then it could be argued that CIA tradecraft was still second to none.

Jordan extended his hand across the table.

"You must be Erik?" He said with an affable smile.

"You must be Tom?" The two shook hands and then Jordan reached into his satchel and pulled out what appeared to be a cell phone.

"What's that?" asked Erik.

"Spook gadget. It emits a few different sound frequencies on the high and low end. It makes listening in a hell of a chore."

Hearing news like that gave Erik mixed reactions. On one hand it seemed like a good idea, on the other hand there was no way for Erik to know that it wasn't a recording device. He couldn't help but think that he was getting in over his head but then he couldn't think of anything more ridiculous than trying to sneak into Iran.

"Let's be up front, shall we," began Jordan. "I have word you want to work for me. Is this true?"

"I'm looking for one run, not a full time commitment."

"The problem is that I already have a pilot. Couple actually. Why would I want to jeopardize long standing working relationships for a guy who wants to make one quick run and then get out?"

Erik could see his point but he was hoping that the scuttlebutt he was hearing from Nariff was close to accurate.

"I hear you're planning to take your route one leg further to the west."

Jordan cocked his head in surprise.

"Where did you hear that?"

"I won't kiss and tell if you don't."

"You'd be willing to go that far?"

"Yes, but I'd be flying some of my own cargo in with it."

It was a tough call for Jordan. In his line of work the ends do justify the means and sometimes that meant allowing a little bad to exist in order for the greater good to prevail. It was because of the nature of these dirty deals that the CIA had been caught so many times in bed with right wing insurgents, drug dealers, and gun runners. The CIA had to be fairly forgiving of an agent who made a poor decision but it would certainly redirect your career from the field to a cubicle.

"I'd need to inspect the cargo," demanded Jordan. "Need to make sure you aren't sending the Iranians parts for their F-14s."

Erik had expected that.

"I've got no problem with the cargo but I'm flying me plus 5. You don't need to meet my passengers."

"I beg to differ. How do I know you aren't ferrying terrorists?"

"Because, Iran already has plenty of home grown militants. They don't need to smuggle any in. Besides it will be obvious when you see the cargo. It's mostly camera equipment. I'm working for a film crew making a documentary."

"Hope this doesn't shock you too much, but in my line of work that isn't much better than a militant."

"They aren't interested in your crappy little airstrips. When we land at a site, your ground crew can greet us with guns just to be sure the cameras are happily stored in their cases."

"That still doesn't give me any control over what they film while air born."

"Who cares what they film? Once we get east of China it's going to be barren steppe land all the way west. Footage like that could be anywhere in the world for all we know."

"Fair point, I guess," Jordan leaned back in his chair and took a few sips from his coffee, considering the proposal. "What equipment are you on?"

"C-1 Trader."

Jordan seemed visibly impressed as he raised one eyebrow.

"A little old but a sturdy airframe."

"Built to handle rough landings and short takeoffs."

"So refresh me on your capabilities."

"She has a 1300 mile range, max takeoff at about 29,000 lbs which leaves me about 10,000 pounds of cargo. I need 1,000 of that for passengers and 1,000 for cargo that gives you about 8,000 pounds to work with."

Jordan pulled a notebook and a mini-calculator from his pocket and began running some numbers.

"That will suit my needs." He closed the book and the calculator and looked off into space. "This is a risky flight. You sure you are up for this?"

Chapter 39

ERIK WAS COMING close to the completion of the fourth leg of the long flight. In the last 25 hours, he had flown for almost 20. Five hours at a stretch. It was grueling but then so too were most long distance flights. In the opening days of the Afghanistan invasion, B-2 pilots had recorded 40 hour flights without a landing. He couldn't imagine what that would have been like yet the B-2 pilots flew in pairs. Because of the load limits of the C-1, Erik could not afford to invite Hank or Janice, Bondurant's pilots, to share in the work load. In the co-pilot seat he was accompanied by one of Jordan's operatives, a thirty something man named Hunter Taheri.

Hunter Taheri, if you believed that was his real name, was somewhat of a surprise when all interested parties arrived at the Wonju airport. Erik felt that he had been up front when he indicated that part of his cargo was passengers and was a little miffed that Jordan had just added a passenger to the manifest without mentioning it during the negotiations. Jordan had said that he needed his own man on board to ensure that Erik's passengers didn't snoop around in his cargo.

"Ever hear of a padlock?" Erik had snidely commented.

Even though most of his military experience had been in logistics, he knew enough about operations to realize that Hunter was probably not just baby sitting the cargo but part of it as well.

Erik wasn't just re-supplying agents in Iran, he was delivering one as well.

Hunter was something of a Chatty Cathy. Erik figured it was a byproduct of the guy's job. He usually hated people who talked too much, but on such a long stretch flight, he didn't mind as much. Taheri was a handsome man and very well spoken. If you believed his story, he was the son of an Iranian oil engineer who had whisked his family to Houston, Texas, shortly after the student revolt in '79. He grew up in a bilingual house and spent a couple years with Marine force recon. It was always suspect to trust a spook, but Erik felt that at least part of the tale was true. He was, after all, being sent in to Iran for some reason and the CIA probably wouldn't recruit that sort of operative from the patriotic Mormon polygamist community.

Hunter wasn't the only surprise Jordan had sprung on Erik. He had also vastly altered the flight route. If he had traveled overland, they would have been there by now. Hunter had arrived with aeronautical charts with a planned route that avoided China and Afghanistan all together. Instead they flew all the way around Asia; Korea to the Philippines, Philippines to Thailand, Thailand to India, India to the center of the Arabian sea. Jordan had planned this route hoping to take advantage of the peculiar characteristics of the plane Erik was flying. He was hoping the old carrier airplane could make one last landing on the Indian Aircraft carrier INS Viraat.

According to charts, they were within 100 nautical miles of the Viraat so Erik broke squelch and attempted to contact.

"Viraat, Pegasus 123 on flight follow."

There was nothing so he tried again.

"Viraat, Pegasus 123 on flight follow. You copy? Over."

"Pegasus 123, this is the Viraat. Your transmission we are receiving," came a voice with a thick Indian accent.

"We are 100 nautical from rendezvous. Can you course correct?"

"What?" came the reply.

"We are 100 nautical miles from planned rendezvous point. Can you give us a heading? Over."

"Oh a heading! I did not know what you speak of." There was a nervous giggle and then some dead air. "Our radar has not seen you, yet."

"Copy. I'm Cherub. I'll climb for fix."

There was another long pause. Erik was wondering if they were hearing him or not. Then came the squelch on the other end.

"Excuse me, sir? What does being a cherub have to do with this?"

In the world of radio communication, various code words and expressions had emerged to help minimize the amount of radio time required to convey a message. Police and truckers liked ten codes while firefighters and military created their own jargon and lingo to convey messages quickly. In no other service was this clipped lingo more prevalent and necessary than in carrier aviation. Lots of guys used the postage stamp analogy but Erik preferred the bottle cap analogy. A carrier isn't a fixed position. It's moving through the ocean at thirty knots and the deck is pitching and rolling with each wave. To understand how complicated this task is, go to a party and get drunk. As soon as the room begins to spin, go to the nearest beer cooler and pull out a bottle. Pull off the cap and toss it across the room. Once you have located the bottle cap on the floor, if you locate the bottle cap on the floor, attempt to take one huge step and jump onto the bottle cap landing on your right big toe. If you can perform this task without spilling your beer, you are carrier pilot material. If you can't do this, you will need a lot of help to land. It's usually less than a minute between final approach and landing on the deck. In that minute, you need to give a lot of information to the people trying to help you and in turn they need to give you a lot of information. Therefore, code words and jargon are essential to a successful carrier landing. It was becoming clear to Erik that the

Indian Navy was speaking the same language, but not the same jargon as the American Navy.

Erik explained his last transmission.

"Cherub…I'm flying at 100 ft. I'm going to climb high so your radar can see me and give me a vector…I mean compass heading."

"Ahhh! Good Idea…Why do you call it cherub?"

"I'll explain later. Just tell me when you see me."

"I understand. Good luck to you, sir. Out."

"Copy, thanks. 123 clear."

As Erik pulled up for altitude he looked at his guest sitting in the co-pilots seat.

"Just what kind of carrier are you putting us on?"

"An Indian one," replied Hunter.

"They built it?"

"No, the Brits did in the late fifties. Then they converted it to a vertical take-off carrier in the early seventies and then they sold it to the Indians in the mid eighties."

"Vertical take-off! You mean Harriers and helicopters!"

"Yeah, well the Indians are building a new carrier with catapults and arresting gear and in preparation they rebuilt some of the original gear that existed on the Viraat."

"When did they 'rebuild' this gear?"

"I think she came out of dry-dock a month ago."

"And how many times has this rebuilt equipment been tested?" Erik said nervously.

"Well, that's kind of the thing…" Hunter replied sheepishly. "Their pilots are afraid to use the arresting gear and the catapult. So in order to use their ship, we agreed to be the test subjects."

Erik's jaw dropped.

"I don't recall agreeing to that!" Erik was furious.

Hunter just gave him an embarrassed grin as if to say, "sorry buddy I just work here." Erik wanted to give him an ear full but it was too late now. They were too far out in the open ocean to divert to any other location. Erik peered into the passenger compartment over his shoulder. He made eye contact with Hugh and gestured.

"Hey, toss me that thing above your head!" he yelled.

"What thing?" asked Hugh.

"That helmet!"

Hugh looked up and saw a flight helmet hanging above his head. He grabbed it and passed it to Erik. Erik rarely wore a helmet while flying in civilian life, but he thought it might be a good idea for this landing. He donned the helmet, strapped it down and plugged it into the communications panel.

"Thanks!" He yelled back to Hugh.

"Do we need to wear one, too?" Hugh looked very worried . "Nahh!" replied Erik.

"Are there any more?" asked Hugh.

"Nahh!" replied Erik.

"Are we going to crash?" asked Hugh.

"Probably not," replied Erik.

"Then why are you wearing a helmet?"

Erik paused.

"So I can look like Tom Cruise!"

Hunter was beginning to realize the impending danger. He leaned over to Erik.

"Do you have one of those for me?" he asked.

"Fuck you, spook!"

As he climbed to 1000 ft and pulled level, he heard the Viraat break squelch.

"Pegasus 123, this is Viraat on flight follow."

"Viraat, Pegasus 123 go."

"We have you on radar. Pull left 272 and maintain your altitude."

"Copy 272."

Erik did as he was told, first banking and then feathering the rudders to take a heading of 272 degrees.

"Pegasus 123, do you have our frequencies for air control and landing control?" asked the Viraat. The controller was referring to the different radio frequencies that Erik would have to cycle between in order to communicate with pertinent personnel during his landing. In all aviation, there were at least two different air traffic controllers to deal with on a long distance flight between major airports. First, the landing controller at the specific airport, sometimes called pattern control and in this case called air control. Second, the Flight follower; these people guided the aircraft from one airport to the other. They set safe altitudes and headings so as to avoid mid air collisions. They also called an aircraft every fifteen minutes to verify location. If an aircraft didn't respond, a search and rescue could be quickly mounted at the last known coordinates. In carrier aviation, they added one last controller, in this case called landing control but in U.S. Navy parlance he or she was simply called 'Paddles.' This was an experienced aviator who could talk a pilot in during the final moments before he landed on a carrier deck and 'hooked' an arresting wire that would prevent a plane from sliding off the end of the deck.

Erik checked his records of the frequencies he had quick dialed into his communication gear.

"I believe I have the proper frequencies, let me confirm. Pattern control is 122.7896. Paddles is 125.8765. Confirm?"

"Correct…I think. Air control is 122.7896 and landing control is 125.8765."

"Affirm."

"What?"

"Affirmative…yes….those are my frequencies."

"Copy… good luck to you, sir."

"Pegasus 123, clear," Erik said clearing the channel. He looked over at Hunter and said, "It would help with my confidence if he didn't keep saying 'Good Luck.'"

Erik promptly switched to the air control frequency and called for contact. The air control copied down pertinent information about the plane he was flying and his current fuel load. This was important to gauge the counter weights used on the arresting wires. The wires had to play out a plane like a fisherman would a big fish. If the weight was too high the cable might snap and if it was too low it wouldn't stop the plane in time. In either event, the plane was likely to slide off the end of the runway, fall into the ocean, and possibly be run over by the carrier steaming at full speed. Erik called it "doing a Wiley." Wile E. Coyote had a knack for falling off a cliff and then having the anvil dropped on his head.

Soon after this conversation, two Harrier jump jets arrived to escort Pegasus to the Viraat. The weight of the situation was frazzling Erik's nerves. Sitting in the co-pilot's seat, Hunter could sense impending doom. "Everything is alright...right?" He asked, half hoping that Erik would deliver some reassuring words.

Erik looked his useless co-pilot in the eye.

"I haven't made a carrier arrest in over a year, my plane hasn't done it in two decades, the Viraat hasn't used arresting gear in almost three decades, and the crew and LSO of the Viraat have never marshaled a carrier landing using wires. I look at your dumb face and see two hundred pounds of fuel I could really use right now. Shut up and let me concentrate!"

Terrified, humiliated, and feeling guilty, Hunter turned his gaze from Erik and stared blankly out the window. As he looked out to barren ocean as far as the eye could see, he caught his first glimpse of the Viraat. Thirty thousand tons of steal and decking looked like a dot on the horizon compared to the expanse of hazy horizon blending into dark grey sea.

"Goddamn that thing is small," he thought to himself. Looking outside gave him no hope so he dropped his gaze to the blizzard of dials, gauges and switches that splattered across the cockpit in an arrangement that made sense to no one save the pilots. Deciding that confusion was better than horror, he concentrated on all the extraneous minutia the Pegasus had to offer.

The Viraat called, letting Pegasus know it was ready for final approach. Erik flipped to the frequency of the Landing Signaling officer for the final approach.

"Paddles, Trader 123." In U.S. Navy protocol, the LSO doesn't care what squadron you fly with and as such your call sign switches to simply the name of your airframe, in this case a C-1 Trader. This is the final check to ensure the arresting gear is set to the proper weight for the aircraft arriving.

"Is this the Pegasus flight?" asked the LSO.

"Yes," replied Erik. The Indians were speaking English just fine, it was the lack of 'jargon' that meant they were speaking different languages. In the next minute, they would have to bridge this gap in a hurry. With flaps down and carefully adding power to compensate for the turn, Erik banked 180 to line up with the deck. His eyes never left their target.

"Pegasus 123, when you see the ball, feel free to let me know of this," called the LSO. At least he knew to call the Fresnel lens the ball. The "meatball" was a landing aid that helped carrier pilots ensure that they were on the proper glide slope for a safe landing. It was a single light shown into a prismatic bank of lenses. The light would appear in different lenses across this bank depending on the plane's orientation to the correct approach path. By looking at which lens was showing, Erik could easily tell if he was too far right or left and if he was too far high or low. In the clipped parlance of a U.S. Navy LSO, he would have simply said, "Call the Ball!"

Erik was still speaking this foreign dialect and responded as his training dictated.

"Paddles, Trader 123, Ball, point eight." Which meant "LSO this is Pegasus flight. I see the meatball. I have 800 pounds of fuel on board."

This confirmation was there so the LSO could make one last double check of the counter weights on the arresting gear to ensure no mishaps would ensue.

"What?" came the Viraat's LSO reply.

Erik had no time to educate the man on proper radio procedure. He called back.

"Forget it. Just guide me in."

"Understood! Right Rudder!"

From Erik's angle that didn't look quite correct, but he had been so trained to quickly follow that LSO's advice that he applied a bit of right rudder.

"Oh No!" cried the startled LSO. "My right your left!"

"Shit!" Erik screamed as he applied the left rudder. The overcompensation of the rudder had the effect of applying air breaks to the Pegasus. Erik quickly applied throttle to compensate for the loss in speed. All that happened in the blink of an eye but then the gravity of the situation slowed his mind to a crawl as he realized the deck was right there. A little luck and crafty rudder work had brought the Pegasus back to the centerline of the deck, but it was now too slow and too low.

It was bolter time. A bolter is when a plane needs to give up its attempt to land, add power, and fly around for another attempt. Erik assumed the LSO was screaming that in his ear right now but he was too focused on the business at hand to pay attention to anything the man said. His hands were full adding power to the throttles and steering the plane. If he had a real co-pilot, the co-pilot would be reducing flap angles and retracting the tail hook in preparation for the wave off while Erik fought for speed and altitude. As it was, the flaps were fully extended making it harder to gain speed and altitude at a critical moment. The Pegasus fell so low the ball went out of sight as Erik stared at the ass end of the Viraat with the deck above him. For a moment he figured "This is it! I'm going to pile drive myself in to the stern of this crappy old carrier!" Then his efforts began to pay off as the Pegasus began to gain speed and altitude. Almost as if on cue, the Viraat caught a big wave causing its bow to rise and its stern to drop. The meatball came back into view along with the open sky that seemed invitingly safe. The bolter was going to be successful. They would live to see another attempt.

Erik saw the deck pass underneath the Pegasus and was reaching to pull up the flaps when it happened. BAM! The passengers of the Pegasus felt the plane slam into the deck followed by an immediate deceleration to zero. The tail hook had caught a wire with the wheels still in the air. First, the plane was slammed down into the deck and then the plane was pulled to a violent stop. Carrier landings were violent enough without first being slapped onto the deck. Erik hunched forward in his harness straps feeling a bit abused. He looked to his right, seeing that Hunter had soiled his pants. Erik nudged his CIA benefactor and pointed to the bridge of the Viraat.

"If you had waited five more minutes, I'm sure they have a restroom inside."

Chapter 40

THE EXCITEMENT OF the Viraat landing now seemed an eternity ago as the engines of the old C-1 Trader spooled down after landing in Iran. There was almost no sound left to hear in the vast expanse of the arid Iranian plains. No one was talking yet and the only noises were the faint sound of the breeze drifting across the land and the crunchy sound of gravel as the exhausted passengers of the Pegasus paced around the aircraft. Everyone seemed to have the same idea. After a day and a half of flying and refueling, flying and refueling, it was nice to just walk off the cramps. No one wanted to break the silence that had been denied them by the airplane's twin turbo prop engines.

Hugh examined the small dirt strip that constituted the air field. There wasn't much to it, just a patch of level dirt that had been cleared of brush. There were no structures or buildings anywhere close and the only road was a two track that led off towards what appeared to be a small river. The only trees visible were down by the river bank. There was no welcoming party from Hunter's contacts, but neither was there a Republican Guard.

After several minutes of stretching, Hunter crawled back into the Pegasus's hold to inspect his share of the cargo. The others, Lee, Sam, Jonesy, Summer, and Hugh milled around silently until they had unconsciously gathered together.

"Do you think we are close enough to the burial sight for your spell?" Hugh finally asked Lee.

Still a little tired, Lee kicked at the dirt.

"According to Dixon, we can cast this spell within a hundred miles of the corpse and it will still work. That should save on the archeology needed. If it doesn't work here, we travel up river and keep trying. We know he was buried on this river somewhere."

"Let's hope he is close," said Jonesy. "Remember that we have snuck into a country that is not on friendly terms with our respective governments. Furthermore, they are certainly not receptive to the talents that you and I possess. The more time we spend here, the more we chance being detained."

"I shudder to think of that possibility." A chill ran up Hugh's spine at the thought.

Lee turned to Summer.

"Do you have any sense of his presence?" he asked.

"Respectable psychics commune with the living...not the dead," she replied flatly.

Lee looked up examining the surroundings.

"Well, we need to rest up. It has been a long, stressful trip and we will need our wits about us when we do this. I also don't want to carve a summoning circle out in the open where the wind can blow it away. I say we gather our gear and make a camp by the river bed. There is shade and water there and it looks like a good place to rest and start our work."

Hugh followed Lee's gaze.

"Fair enough. Looks like it's about a kilometer. If we distribute the gear we could make it in two trips. What about Erik?"

Lee looked into the cockpit window where he could see Erik still working on his post flight checklist.

"He will probably want to stay with the plane and I am not sure I want him near us when Jonesy and I get to work."

"Yeah, I guess so." Hugh then walked back to the passenger door and up the gang plank, "Knock knock! Coming in Mr. Cloak and Dagger Dude. Don't shoot."

"Yeah, nothing to see here. Come on in."

As Hugh's eyes adjusted to the dark inside the plane, he could see Hunter unfastening the ratchet straps that had been fixed to his shipment of boxes.

"Look, we are going to grab some of our gear and head down to that river…maybe look for a camp sight."

Hunter poked his head out the window to see the tree line Hugh was talking about. He knew that his contacts had assured him that area around the airstrip was free from watchful eyes. This was one of those "hope for the best" moments that field operatives sometimes experienced. If he picked the right local talent, then things were probably fine. If he was dealing with double agents, then there was nothing he could really do lacking any formal military assistance.

"That seems fine, but I'm afraid you'll need to leave the camera boxes here. My hosts should be here within an hour and I'm sure they wouldn't appreciate being photographed."

Hugh thought about that for a moment. Leaving the camera behind was a tough pill for a journalist to swallow, but the people who fought Hunter's kind of war weren't the type to accept embedded journalists with open arms.

"Well, we'll need to take two trips, anyway. We'll save the camera gear for the second haul."

Erik then emerged crawling between the pilot and co-pilot seats into the passenger hold. He looked tired and worn from the long hours of flight but there was still an urgent look in his eye.

"Nobody's moving anything, yet. The job's not done."

"What do you mean, Erik?" asked Hugh.

"We have to get this plane moved into the brush over there and then get some netting over the top." He opened a locker near the cockpit. Inside were three large bundles of desert camouflage netting. Behind the netting was a firefighter's ax and a shovel. He handed one to each. "Get to work clearing a space for the plane. Save all the brush you chop so we can stick it in the netting."

After the long flight, hard manual labor didn't seem appealing to Hunter or Hugh and their expressions made that evident. Erik knew the exact words to persuade them.

"Your precious cargoes won't be anything but evidence in our not so phony trials if some plane happens to fly over this supposedly abandoned airstrip."

That motivated everyone to begin the laborious task of disguising the plane from above. They chopped brush, pushed the plane into position, draped camouflage over the Pegasus, and finally interlaced brush into the netting to make the plane invisible from all but the most careful inspections. After understanding the need for this operation, everyone pitched in on the back breaking job, all except Sam. Lacking opposable thumbs gave Sam an excellent excuse to find the nearest shade, lie down, and pant.

As soon as they were finished, Lee insisted they gather gear and begin the trek to the trees. He wanted to get the manual work out of the way as soon as possible so the group could get some quality rest in the shady trees down by the river. Sammy had cheerfully avoided the labor involved in moving the plane but would not avoid being pitched into service moving the camp and camera gear. Lee pulled out a doggy harness that had saddle bags and various straps to secure gear.

"You have to be kidding me? Not that old thing again."

"Sorry Sam," said Lee. "If we are going to make it in two trips, we all need to carry our own weight."

"I have hated that thing since you bought it for me as a pup. You were so excited at the time. Told me 'oh looky here boy! Now we can go backpacking together.'"

"Well, we did go back packing together!" said Lee defensively.

"We did? I don't recall any...oh wait! You must be referring to the 'post divorce, discover myself, hike' across Africa! As I recall, you were almost beheaded by some militant warlord and I was almost eaten by a lion...oh and you could have mentioned that hippo's are extremely territorial before I pissed on his side of the river! Backpacking is great fun!" he said sarcastically.

Lee looked at his best friend sympathetically.

"It wasn't all bad was it? I mean, if it hadn't been for Africa, you wouldn't be exactly who you are today."

Sam thought about how he had been "just a dog" before Africa. Now he was "just a dog" again only when he was near Erik. He hated being near Erik! Erik was actually a fairly funny and interesting guy and he was kind to dogs, but Sam had to admit he liked being able to talk and that couldn't happen when Erik was around.

"I guess Africa wasn't all bad," he grudgingly admitted.

"Look, it will be much better, and safer, to get the camp set up as soon as possible. It's already hotter than Hades inside that hull and soon enough, anything out in the open will be close to 100 degrees. The sooner we do what needs to be done, the sooner we can get back to Manarola and relax."

Sam drooped his ears and looked up at Lee with his beautiful sad brown eyes.

"Well, OK. Put it on. It's just that…wearing that thing is so humiliating! I look like a pack mule."

Hugh had been overhearing the conversation as he loaded his bag of gear. Painfully hoisting a rucksack that weighed close to 100 lbs on his back he looked at Sam.

"Not a bad idea, Sam. Lee, next time you make a talking animal make it a pack mule."

Sam could take shit from Lee but he wouldn't put up with it from the youngest person in the group.

"Screw you, punk! I'm 135 in dog years. See how much weight you can carry when you're that age! You know, I would be more apt to take criticism from a dumb jock like you if you could manage to hit the play button on your camera the next time you see a three headed dragon! And another thing, you Bark Bark Bark Bark!" Sam looked around confused and felt someone pat him on the head. It was Erik!

"Go get him, tiger!" said Erik. "I'm glad to see he barks at someone besides me."

"Bark, Bark! Bark, Bark, Bark!" was Sam's response.

"STOP IT! Sam!" Lee said harshly, attempting to ease his dog.

"Easy, boy. I'm on your side," Erik said as he dropped a piece of beef jerky as an offering.

Sam quieted himself and looked at the jerky. In Manarola, Lee's lavish lifestyle had afforded Sam a diet of fillet mignon and chicken Florentine but on the road he had been on a dog food diet for three weeks. He quickly devoured the jerky as Erik moved on to finish his work.

Erik finally finished tying down the last lanyard that secured the camouflage netting. He pulled his floppy hat from his head, wiped his brow, and entered the Pegasus. After a few moments of rustling around in the cargo hold, he emerged from the plane with a lawn chair and a cooler. He set the lawn chair up under the shade of a wing and sat down. Pulling his hat over his eyes he reached into his cooler and pulled out a beer. The long hours of flight had exhausted him and it was time to drink a beer and take a nap.

Summer looked at Erik in disgust.

"I sense he doesn't intend to help us move the camp." She whispered to Hugh.

Dumbfounded Hugh stared blankly into the eyes of the "Truth Seekers" resident psychic.

"Ya think?"

By the time Lee and the others had arrived at the river bed with the second load of gear, the team had endured a day and a half of flying in a slow noisy relic of the Vietnam war, manhandled that relic off the runway and camouflauged it, and finally made two heavily laden trips to the riverbed camp. All were tired, but Lee had been correct about the nicer arrangements. The trees afforded nice shade and the breeze was mild and cool. The small river looked clear but Hugh took precautions to filter everyone's drinking water all the same.

Jonesy had taken the liberty to start the camp stoves and was in the process of fixing dinner. In the many years of field work, Jonesy had become a master of backcountry Korean cuisine. He fixed a spicy stew with kimchi, potatoes, pork and as a main course, fixed a Korean style stir fry with rice, vegetables and oysters. While Lee had never been a fan of Korean fish dishes, the rest of Korean cuisine was world class. Lee was always impressed with Jonesy's ability to whip up a good meal on small backpacking stoves.

By the time the meal was finished, everyone was ready to catch some shuteye. It was 3:00 o'clock in the afternoon. Lee set his travel alarm to wake him up at 11:00. A good solid eight hours of sleep should refresh everyone for the evening's work. Lee rolled out his and Sam's bedding under a tree and fell asleep with Sam by his side.

Chapter 41

THE RUMBLE AROUSED Erik from his slumber. He awoke still in the lawn chair, a half drunk beer precariously gripped in his right hand. Blinking his eyes a bit, he checked his watch. It was 5 PM. He took a swig from his beer. Warm flat beer flooded his taste buds. He quickly spat it out and tossed the can to his feet.

"Yuk!" he exclaimed as he stood.

He looked out through the netting draped over his wing at the vehicles approaching along the two track, two jeeps and a large military crew carrier. That was the compliment of vehicles that Hunter said to expect but they were two hours late. Erik was hoping the occupants of the vehicles hadn't been replaced by Iranian Secret Service. He walked over and nudged Hunter who was dozing in a hammock slung under the wing.

"Hey, spook! Wake up. Your psycho killers are here."

Hunter's eyes shot open and he jumped out of his hammock.

"Christ they're late!" He fumbled through the travel vest he wore and pulled out a pair of mini binoculars. "Yea that's Rahnny. Wonder what took him so long?"

"Think it might be a trap?" Erik worriedly enquired.

"Always a possibility." Hunter shrugged.

The roles of an expert calmly doing his job and the tag along scared close to uncontrolled defecation, had been switched 180 degrees from the carrier landing on the Viraat. This time Erik was scared out of his wits. "Look, I got a pistol in my locker. You think maybe I should go get that."

"Oh, I doubt that would do much good." Hunter replied coolly.

Erik, who had passed many rigorous flight physicals, swore he felt his heart flutter.

"Well, then, what should we do? What do you guys do when a meeting goes down wrong?"

Still gazing through the binoculars Hunter answered.

"You mean when we are deep in enemy territory without any Navy SEALs or F-18s to back us up?"

"Yeah, like that."

He pulled his gaze away from the approaching trucks and looked at Erik with a cocked eyebrow and a crooked grin.

"We get a star on the wall at Langley."

Erik knew enough about spooks to get the reference.

"Think they might give me one, too?"

Hunter sighed and shook his head.

"Sorry, bud. You're not on the official payroll."

"Ahh fuck!" replied Erik. He reached down to his cooler and pulled out a fresh cold beer. He took a few long swigs and deciding he may not have enough time to get one last buzz going, he took a few pulls from his hip flask as well.

"You're not going to like this, Erik, but you'll have to trust me. I need you to face your lawn chair the other way and take a seat."

"So you can shoot me in the back of the head?"

"Actually, so I can convince these guys you haven't seen any faces," Hunters expression was dead serious. "Just give me time to warn them you are here and give them a chance to cover up if they choose."

"I never really felt comfortable with my back to a truck load of loaded guns."

"Well, it sucks I know, but I can guarantee you that if they think you can recognize them on the streets of Tehran they will kill you."

"Cheez-its!"

"Huh?"

"My next job…nothing but Cheez-its!" Erik spun the chair around, sat down, and took another long pull off the flask. It was a full minute of hearing rumbling vehicles before Erik heard breaks squealing to a halt and clutches dropping engines into idle. Doors were opened and then he heard a few pairs of feet plop down onto the crunchy sounding dirt.

Two men began speaking in a language that sounded like jibberish to Erik. He could make out one of the voices as Hunter's,

"Rahnny badachicka badachicka muybadachica!"

"Tahari! Badackika badachica unpocobadachica!"

The two carried on for a few more badachikas and then Erik heard the unmistakable sound of back slapping and assumed they were giving one another the manly hug with lots of back slaps. Erik always wondered why men who hugged had to do so in this rough and tumble way. As if to say, "Lothar! You are my very good friend! I would like to hunt many more furry animals with you so we may share in the eating of the still pumping heart! I shall now hug you in a totally masculine and non gay way!"

Then he heard his name.

"Badachica badackica chingga te' cavarone Erik Hartman."

Hearing one of his pseudonyms come up seemed pointless at this juncture. The whole point of his many taglines was to make tracing his true identity a bit more difficult. But in this case, with a few trucks full of Iranian militants at his back, did it really matter if they put a bullet in Erik Hartman or Erik Schantz? All it meant was that if an unnamed star was put on the wall at Langley it would be for a guy that never existed. The Schantz family would just assume he'd passed out on an ice float and drifted out to sea.

Rahnny's reaction didn't sound promising,

"Ha! Lugie spit! hack hack cough!" The hacking and spitting sounds went on for almost a minute with a few syllables thrown in for good measure. It was the excited way of speaking that Americans were familiar with from news reports. Erik assumed that when someone started speaking like this it meant some F-18 pilot mistook their three year old on a big wheel for a semi tractor trailer loaded with WMDs. He tipped up the last ounces of his hip flask and chased it with a large guzzle of beer expecting the brain exploding gunshot to come at any moment.

Then Taheri started chuckling.

"Hey, Erik. It's all clear. Come on over. Rahnny wants to meet you.."

All clear? Had he heard that? There was no way he had heard that. Being the ultimate control freak rationalist that he was, he had never been forced to put so much blind trust in a guy he hardly knew. Yet, as he stood and turned around, the truth of it was evident. Though Rahnny and all his nefarious accomplices were masked, it was obvious by body language that they meant him no harm. In fact, Rahnny eagerly walked over to take Erik's hand.

Rahnny started babbling in Farsi again and Hunter began to translate. "He says he admires your courage for coming this far. No other smuggler has ever had the courage to fly into Iran." Hunter waited while Rahnny continued to speak. "He says they must rely on mule trains through the passes on the Pakistani border. Many mules die in the mountains and we lose many supplies." Hunter listened for another moment and then proceeded again. "He is very impressed that such a large airplane could land on a ship."

Then Rahnny started speaking excitedly and held his hands out low over his crotch as if he was cradling two soccer balls.

"He says you must have very big balls!" translated Hunter chuckling.

"Thanks, spook, but I don't think that one needed translation." Erik laughed. He then checked the time on his watch. It was time to get busy. "I hate to interrupt the introductions, Hunter, but part of the deal was that these guys bring some fuel."

"Oh, of course," replied Hunter. "It's in the troop carrier."

The three walked to the back of the large troop carrier. Erik had expected an automated pump, but what he found instead was several large 55 gallon drums of fuel. Each of them would have to be manually lifted into place and pored into his fuel tank. It was going to be a heavy job indeed.

Chapter 42

B Y 9:00 PM, Lee was wide awake. It was two hours before his alarm was set to go off. His belly tingled with nervous energy. In the next few hours he would have to perform a summoning ritual with Hoodoo techniques he was barely familiar with in the hopes of raising a mythical dragon slayer from his 3000 year old slumber. The stakes were high. If he allowed the Dragon to continue his wrath unabated, the myths read that it would destroy 1/3 of all life on earth before the hero, Kirsasp, returns to destroy him. When the Zorastrian mages prophesized this, the catastrophe would have meant hundreds of thousands of lives. In 2009, it would mean more than 2 billion dead. Lee and Jonesy had decided early on that they had to do something to avoid this but, calling Kirsasp prematurely could be a double edged sword. That is to say if they were successful at all.

From his own study of West African shamanism, he had performed a ritual and scarified himself, Sam, and Jonesy with a protection glyph that was supposed to ward off the attack of the undead. It was his hope that if Kirsasp proved uncontrollable, the three of them could distract attention long enough for the others to escape, but the Glyph was designed to ward off vampires and zombies, not the most powerful hero from the oldest known monotheistic religion.

Too many things could go wrong. The summoning could fail and the Dragon would continue his wrath. The hero could fail and be slain by the Dragon. Or, the hero could succeed and vanquish Azi Dahaka, but then, what do we do with the hero?

Lee rose from his sleep deciding that the best thing for him to do to calm his nerves was begin work on the summoning circle. He tried to be as silent as possible so as not to disturb the others, but as he rose to a seated position he saw the dark shadow of Jonesy sitting near the cooking stove. He stood up and walked towards Jonesy. As he drew close he could hear the burners on the stove and see his friend warming something in a copper tea pot.

"Good evening, Dr. Bondurant," greeted Jonesy.

"Good evening, Dr. Sam." Lee followed his friend's formality.

"Please sit," Jonesy said.

"You are up early." Lee took a seat cross legged on the ground next to Jonesy.

"It's a very important thing we must do. I could not sleep. I see by your early revival that you feel the same."

"There is so much that could go wrong tonight."

"Indeed." Jonesy looked thoughtfully into the dim light of the camp stove.

Hoping to get his mind off his nervous belly, Lee tried to redirect the conversation.

"What are you cooking?"

"Nothing. I'm simply warming a traditional Korean medicinal wine. It's called Takju."

"What's it for?"

"Courage and concentration. We will need it tonight."

Lee then felt a warm presence lie down next to him. He didn't need to look at the dark starlit figure to know who it was. Sammy laid down next to his master and nuzzled his long snout onto Lee's lap. Sam made a few deep sighs as Lee scratched behind his ear. No matter how careful a person was to not disturb a sleeping pet, it always seemed as if your pet would come to you on a sleepless night. This was even more true when your pet had his own magical powers.

Jonesy turned the stove off and lifted the kettle from the burner. He poured a cup for himself and Lee and a small bowl for Sam.

"Here you go my friends. Drink up."

Sam sniffed his small bowl and winced a bit. Lee took his first sip. It was awful! It tasted like warm milk mixed with sugar and vodka. He almost spit it out but seeing Jonesy's expectant expression he choked down his first swallow.

"It's good for you. Drink," implored Jonesy.

Lee smirked and finished the cup with a forced grin.

"Oh, my God!" cried Sam after he took his first taste.

"Finish it...It's good for you," commanded Lee hoping to avoid a scene.

Sam forced himself to get through the rest of his bowl of Takju. It was obvious to Lee that drinking the Takju was an important pre-fight ceremony for Jonesy. Koreans were passionate about their food and drink. Their tastes tended towards the extreme which meant that to Westerners, Korean food and drink was either world class or worse than garbage. Regardless of other opinions on their culinary tastes, Koreans seemed to unanimously think they were the best cooks in the world and it was important for them that you pretend to agree less they lose face. There was no middle ground when it came to food, especially when they said "it's good for you."

Jonesy was casting spells on various items they would need throughout the ceremony while Lee got to work with the intricate carvings of the summoning circle. It was a multi cultural effort in magic. Jonesy was a Korean who practiced a Western style of enchantment and Lee was an American who practiced a form of ceremonial summoning found in West African shamanism. Together they pooled their collective talents to cast a spell used in Haitian necromancy to raise a middle eastern Dragon Slayer from a 3,000 year old sleep.

While Lee concentrated on the circle carving, Jonesy began blessing the various items with magical powers. First a ceremonial knife, then a living cock, then an old gas lantern, and finally an antique serving bell. The advantage of Jonesy's style of magic was that almost anything you could imagine could be created or enchanted on the spot with no elaborate props or preparation. The disadvantage was that the mage had to use his own magical energy to do this. By the time Jonesy had completed the final enchantment, he was physically and emotionally drained.

"Shit! I thought you guys were going to wait until eleven!" cried Hugh. He had obviously just woken up and had discovered the trio diligently at work.

Jonesy, who had completed his work, sat exhaustedly by the camp stove warming up some more Takju.

"Neither of us could sleep, so we decided to start work early."

"Let me wake Summer and go get my camera."

"Okay," Jonesy replied as Hugh marched back into the darkness to prepare his gear.

By the time he returned with Summer, Lee and Sam had nearly completed their work as well.

"You know the deal, Hugh. No close ups of my circle and if you happen to catch my face on film it needs to be blotted out later," said Lee. It was another reminder that, even though the two had worked closely over the last few weeks, when it came down to it, Lee was very protective of his secrets.

"I understand. Trust me, if the Dragon shows up, the last thing anyone will care about is how we got him here. Jonesy, do you mind if I have Summer interview you?"

"I'm a little tired but I guess its okay."

The three quickly set up for the interview as Lee finished his work. Summer hadn't worried about doing any makeup as the entire event was to be filmed on night vision. For some reason all respectable spook documentaries had used night photography ever since the release of the fictional movie, "The Blair Witch Project."

"Dr. Sam. Can you please tell us the significance of the items you have before you?"

"Certainly, Summer. You see, in the ceremony you are about to witness, we will use these items to help us summon 'Kirsasp' the Dragon Slayer."

"I see. I will certainly like to ask about Kirsasp in a moment so we can understand his significance in all this, but first, please go into detail about each of the four items."

"Cut! Cut!" called Hugh. "Summer, let's start with Kirsasp and then go into discussing the trinkets. It will be easier to edit for the show."

"Certainly," replied Summer, deferring to Hugh's judgment. She reset herself for the interview and then continued.

Chapter 43

1 ST LIEUTENANT BERNARD "Burns" Gomez bounced along the rough Iraqi roads in the passenger's seat of an armored Humvee. He was the assistant commander of E company, 1st Battalion, 555th Engineering Brigade. He was on the second month of his second combat deployment to Iraq. With a total of seventeen months in combat zones, he would have been considered an experienced combat vet by the standards of most previous wars but many of the soldiers who had been with the brigade since 2003 were on their third tour.

The job of the company was primarily IED removal. Improvised explosive devices were the biggest killers of military and civilian personnel in the Iraqi campaign. Every IED the company destroyed meant lives saved in this messy war. Gomez was proud of the job he and the company did. The men of the company were seasoned, well trained, and professional. The young lieutenant had the utmost confidence in his men.

Gomez had always been a confident young man. In high school athletics, at the Academy, and even in his first tour, he had always been confident in his abilities. But his self confidence had changed radically with his recent promotion. Platoon commanders tend to drill by playbook. They are taught the most common combat situations a platoon might find itself in and then taught the most effective ways to prevail in those situations. Add to that, the fact that the Lieutenant is usually followed closely by a Sergeant that probably knows these maneuvers better than you do.

For a young Army officer, things change a lot the second you move up to company. A company commander has a lot more leeway and flexibility in terms of battlefield decisions. With that added flexibility, comes a lot more responsibility as well. Some say that running a company is the most difficult job an army officer will do throughout his career. Tonight, Gomez certainly felt that to be true. Captain Bingham had received a minor shrapnel wound and had been sent to Kuwait for a four day medical R&R. That left 25 year old 1st. Lt. Gomez, with not even three years military experience, in charge of the lives of 200 men.

"Easy 1-1, Easy 6-2," Gomez said into his radio.

"Easy 1-1 go ahead."

"What's your status?"

"We have arrived at the scene. The eight-two platoon seems to have a perimeter set already. I have detailed my squads to reinforce them. Over."

It was always a nervous situation when E company got called out. In this case, a patrol from the 82nd Airborne had called for engineering assistance to investigate a suspicious tractor trailer left abandoned on a highway. The good news was that an abandoned trailer was such a large object that it was hard to miss. The bad news was that a tractor trailer was so big there was no telling how much explosives could have been packed inside it. What's worse was the thought that it may be a Trojan horse. E company had done such a damn fine job finding and safely disposing of IEDs in the last month, there was a rumor running around that the local militia had put a price on their heads. For all Gomez knew, the abandoned truck had been put there to lure members of his company into an ambush. These were some of the extra burdens of command, the extra decisions that had to be made, that made Gomez feel uncomfortable.

Checking his watch and position of the convoy, Lt. Gomez responded to his 1st platoon.

"Okay, Easy 1-1. Be advised we are 5 minutes eta. Keep your eyes peeled. Break. Easy. 3-1 you copy?" The "break signaled that he was finished talking to his 1st platoon and now wanted to speak with his 3rd platoon.

"Yes sir," came an almost high pitched reply.

The 3rd platoon Lt. was the newest officer in the company. He had graduated his military specialty course less than one month before the 555th had been deployed. Gomez had a special assignment for the 3rd, but the platoon got the job based on the experience and skill of the acting platoon Sergeant, Staff Sergeant Hickman. Hickman was a go getter headed for a commission or Special Forces whichever came first.

"Once we get there, I'm going to detail you boys to expand the perimeter and patrol for any ambush they may try to set up while we are busy."

"Yes, sir," replied the young Lt. "Sir, specifically where would you like us to patrol?"

Gomez had other things on his mind right now and didn't have time to be more specific.

"Hold a sec. Break. 3-2 you up?"

"Yes sir." Replied Sgt. Hickman.

"Do you understand the intent of my order?"

"Yes, Sir."

"Good. Help 3-1 put that together for me."

"Yes, Sir."

"Thanks. Hicks, 6-2 clear," there was mild concern about embarrassing the young Lieutenant but the only people with radios were sergeants and lieutenants and they all understood that the sergeants ran the platoons.

The convoy finally arrived at the scene. It was a large four lane avenue in a blacked out section of Bagdad. The Humvees from the 82nd and the 555th platoons had parked in rows so that they could be used for cover if snipers from the buildings opened up. The buildings on each side of the boulevard were mostly two story office and business buildings. Gomez hesitated before leaving the relative safety of his Humvee. Something didn't feel right. He was positive he had just led a company of engineers into a trap. But then again, it could just be that this was his first time leading the company on his own. He forced himself out of his bulletproof shell and quickly jogged to where he saw two lieutenants and a hand full of sergeants squatting behind the cover of the Humvees.

"Fost, what's up?" Gomez asked as he arrived.

"Sir, this is Lt. Roylance from the 82nd."

Lt. Roylance gave a casual yet courteous salute.

"Sir, we came upon this about an hour ago. We got word in the morning briefing that someone had stolen a whole truck load of cattle that was bound for the green zone. We all thought it was a good laugh at the time but we saw that sucker abandoned out there and got to thinking maybe they wanted the truck more than the cattle. The militia could sure pack a lot of explosives in that som-bitch if they wanted to. So I told my guys to keep a wide birth and called you guys."

Gomez looked down the road to the abandoned truck.

"Goddamn, it's dark tonight! Fost, gimmie your binoculars."

Lt. Fost did as told and handed Gomez his night vision binoculars. Peering through the eerie green illumination, he examined the scene. The tractor was about 100 meters away and looked as if it had slid into the borrow ditch beside the road. In the altered reality of the night vision binoculars, it was difficult to determine what, if any, damage had been done to the tractor trailer.

"Okay, Roth," Gomez said addressing the company's Master Sergeant. "Get the 'Rover' out and let's go have a closer look."

"Yes, Sir."

The Rover was the company's IED detonating robot. It was about the size of a kids' go-cart but built like a mini tank. It was slightly armored, but not designed to take a full point blank blast from an IED. Instead it was equipped with a robotic arm and high quality camera gear. It could drive into a suspected IED sight, investigate at close range, and plant a charge to detonate any IED.

"Okay, Fost, Roylance, here's our situation. It may take us 30 minutes to set up and investigate this thing. What's the perimeter like? I don't want any surprises while we are sitting ducks."

Roylance was the first to speak since his platoon had arrived first.

"Well, I had my guys clear and search the buildings to the east and west. They were clean. Right now, I have sharpshooters on each rooftop with counter-sniper objectives. They haven't reported anything yet."

"How 'bout you, Mitch?" Gomez asked Fost.

"I had 1st and 2nd squad shore up the Humvees and 3rd squad cleared the building left of Roylance's east position. We don't have a shooter to put up there."

Gomez looked at the building that Fost was referring to. It was one story taller than everything nearby. It would be nice to have a gun up there.

"Hold on a sec," Gomez then keyed his radio. "2-1, 6-2."

"Go ahead."

"Don't you have a kid who just graduated sniper school?"

"Affirmative."

"Okay, give him a buddy and send 'em up here to tie in with Lt. Fost."

"Copy that."

"Status on Rover?" Gomez asked.

"Be rollin' in five."

"Copy 6-2 clear."

"2-1" the 2nd platoon leader replied. Merely saying your call sign without any other communication indicated you were done talking.

"Okay," Gomez looked at the two lieutenants and a half dozen sergeants that crouched before him in the darkness. "Anything else? Any other threats?"

"Nothin'," replied Lt. Roylance in a worried tone. "We have cleared everything nearby and haven't seen shit. It's almost spooky."

"Agreed," said Fost. "The whole place seems deserted."

Gomez considered these statements. It might not be as bad as the junior lieutenants were making out. Perhaps, there wasn't an ambush in store for him? Perhaps it was just a big goddamn IED that the militias hoped someone would be stupid enough not to notice. Just then Rover came trucking buy with its remote control operator and the Lieutenant from 2nd platoon following closely behind.

"Fost, your sniper is over there," said the newly arrived lieutenant.

"'Scuse me," said Fost and he rose to go brief his new arrivals.

"Cop a squat, Travis," Burns said to the new Lieutenant. He handed him the pair of binoculars. "Okay, that semi over there is your objective. Could be rigged with a shit load of shit. Can you run that thing that far out?"

"Yeah, no problem, Burns," the lieutenant replied without pulling his eyes from the binoculars. Travis keyed his radio, "2-4 this is 2-1. Come on up and set the charge in Rover."

Gomez then looked around at the conflagration of officers and senior sergeants that had huddled around. One rocket propelled grenade would take out most of the leadership for the whole company.

"Okay, everyone, we have our plan. Now, get back to your platoons and get it done."

After the bomb tech set the explosive charge in the robotic hand of the Rover, everyone dispersed to their assigned units. Only Gomez, his Master Sergeant, and the Rover operator remained huddled around the little TV monitor that displayed the Rover's progress.

Gomez looked up as the little armored robot rolled its way across the dark empty street towards the abandoned tractor trailer. The monitor was on green screen night vision until the robot drew close. Then it switched on its lights to get a better view of the abandoned truck.

From up close, things looked more peculiar. The truck had several dents in the cab and trailer. Scorch marks seemed to be present at random locations throughout the bed and cab. It looked less like a truck that had been turned into an IED and more like a truck that had been hit by an IED. That was the most puzzling part of the scene. If the truck had been a victim of an attack, someone must have heard it and reported it by now. IEDs didn't just go off without someone noticing. When the Rover got close enough, the Specialist controlling it panned the camera under the cab of the truck to begin his search. Immediately, the lights illuminated the eyes of a man dressed as an Iraqi workman. The man seemed frightened to death as he looked into the lens of the camera and before anyone could react, he bolted from hiding under the truck and ran past the camera of the Rover.

"6-2 this is 2Overwatch!" shouted the sniper from second platoon into his radio. "I got visual on some dude running out of that Semi!"

Gomez keyed his mike and spoke as calmly as he could.

"2- Overwatch! Hold fire!" Then he looked at his Master Sergeant, "Get Nobelzada up here now!" he shouted referring to his interpreter.

The Master Sergeant keyed his mike and made the call.

"6-8! 6-3!"

"Go ahead, SSgt!" came the speedy reply.

"Get your ass up here, pronto!"

"Affirm!"

Gomez was caught in the classic Iraq war dilemma. He had a job to do, a company to protect, and a civilian population to protect all at the same time. An Iraqi who had been hiding under the cab of a derelict tractor trailer had just been found and was now running towards his Humvees. There was no way to know if the man was the survivor of an attack and running for safety, or if he was a suicide bomber making a mad dash to his target.

Specialist Nobelzada, a defense language institute graduate, was at his company commander's side within seconds.

"What do you need, sir?"

Gomez didn't mince words.

"Tell that son-of-a-bitch if he doesn't stop now we'll shoot to kill!"

"Sir!" the specialist replied. He then yelled out at the charging Iraqi.

The Iraqi slowed to a walk and raised his hands in the air. He yelled back at the interpreter.

"Sir, he's saying 'help me.'"

"Tell him to stop or we will shoot him."

After the translation, the Iraqi continued to advance at a fast walk.

"Sir, he says we're all going to die here!"

"Tell him that he will if he doesn't stop!"

More words were exchanged as the Iraqi continued in his fast pace.

"He says we need to run for our lives sir!"

"Okay, that's it!" Gomez wasn't going to fuck around with this guy. He was giving every indication that he was a suicide bomber on a mission of intimidation. "2-overwatch this is 6-2."

"Go ahead, Sir!" came an excited voice on the other end of the radio.

"Weapons free! Take the shot!"

Pop! Was the first response from the sniper. Several seconds later the radio crackled with a shaken voice.

"6-2, 2-overwatch. Target down."

Unlike the movies, real snipers were not cold blooded assassins. They were soldiers trying to do their duty. In a questionable situation like this, there was obvious uncertainty on the other end of the radio. It was Gomez's job to reassure his young soldier that he had done the right thing. He looked through his binoculars to see the man was down and then called his sniper team.

"2-overwatch. That was my call. Good shot, guys!"

"Copy 6-2. Thanks."

After the excitement, he looked to his Rover operator.

"Okay. Specialist. Let's continue the search."

The young man did as ordered. As the Rover continued its mission, Gomez began to dread what he would find...or not find on the corpse that lay motionless in the empty street. He was positive he had made the right call but that wasn't going to make him feel any better if no explosives were found. Shaking his head to clear his thoughts, he focused on the screen in front of the Rover operator.

The little robot traveled along the side of the abandoned truck, peering beneath the under carriage looking for bombs. When the rover reached the halfway mark, the operator saw something interesting in the monitor.

"Huh? What the hell is that?"

"What do you see, Specialist?" Gomez asked.

"Well, you see that thing over there?"

"Under the carriage?"

"No no. On the other side of the truck. It's kinda behind the far tire right there."

"Oh yeah...Huh. What do you think it is?"

"Beats me? Looks like a big animal foot."

The Master Sergeant chuckled at that.

"Yeah, right. It's probably just a funny looking rock."

"Probably so," replied Gomez. "Hey look! We are about at the location of the side door. Can you telescope that camera up a bit so we can peek inside the trailer?"

"Yes, sir," said the specialist raising the camera. The side door of the trailer seemed to have been bashed in instead of out. That indicated that the truck was likely the victim of the attack instead of the origin. As the robot's little camera peered in, there was a scene of utter carnage. The truck had been carrying cattle. This much was evident by the volume of dismembered cow parts that lay strewn across the innards of the trailer. They didn't see any obvious human remains, but with the mass carnage within it was impossible to rule out that possibility without a closer, hands on inspection.

"Goddamn! What a blood bath," stated Sergeant Roth.

"Let's pray its all cow," Gomez responded to his Master Sergeant. "Specialist, continue the search under the carriage. When you get to the corner, turn it around and try to bring it back on the other side of the truck."

"We'll try, sir."

The Rover drove down to the end of the truck and turned the corner. There were several more cow carcasses littered on the road behind the battered truck. They were torn in pieces similar to the carnage within the trailer.

"Oh! What's this?" said the Rover operator. Lt. Gomez and Master Sergeant Roth drew closer to the tiny screen to see what he was referring to. "Looks like something is feeding on the remains."

Gomez eyed the dark object with suspicion.

"Light up the flood lights so we can get a better look."

"Copy, sir," the specialist said as he turned on an extra set of bright lights to illuminate further into the darkness.

The four soldiers expected to see a pack of wild dogs feeding on the remains of blown up cows. Instead they saw a huge serpentine head attached to a scaly neck that disappeared out of the frame of the video monitor. It snapped its attention to the flood lights and as it did, the large black pupils shrunk to tiny vertical slits surrounded by yellow eyes. They could see the creature sniffing at the Rover. The Rover seemed to hold little interest for the giant snake head. Then a forked tongue began lashing out into the air as if searching for something. The head suddenly snapped its attention towards Lt. Gomez's column of Humvees. Almost as suddenly as it appeared, the reptilian head was gone and the Rover was staring at the remains of cows.

"What the fuck was that?" cried Roth. Gomez said nothing. He grabbed his night vision binoculars and scanned down range towards the truck. Every one began to hear a banging on the metal sides of the tractor trailer. Gomez still could not make out much in the green light of the binoculars but he could tell that the trailer was rocking with every loud bang.

"6-2 this is 2- overwatch! We are hearing some commotion coming from that semi-."

"All units, this is 6-2! Keep your radio discipline! Something's going on at the trailer. All sniper teams, weapons free! Repeat, all sniper teams, weapons free! Break! 2-1 and 1-1 you copy?"

"2-1!"

"1-1!"

"Get your Dragon teams armed and ready!" Gomez ordered. The dragon referred to the squad portable tank killing rocket launchers carried by each platoon. If he had known just how ironic a command that was, he most likely would have ordered a retreat instead.

Peering through the binoculars, he heard one more large bang and then the whole tractor trailer tipped over on its side. Revealed behind the tipped over truck was something big, yet Gomez had yet to figure out what it was. Night vision equipment took all color out of your vision except for shades of green. This tended to give an object a two-dimensional appearance, even in binoculars. Because of this, soldiers trained to recognize what a threat might look like in night vision. Gomez knew what an AK-47, a Rocket Propelled Grenade, and even an enemy tank, might look like in this altered reality, but what he was looking at now didn't register friend or foe. It seemed as if it had three long necks, perhaps three giraffes standing close? There was a large body, perhaps just one elephant? But then something spread from the body of the elephant. Was it enormous bat wings? Then it was gone!

"What the hell?" Gomez pondered out loud.

"Sir, what is it?" asked Roth.

"Specialist! Drop your charge and get the rover home fast!" was the Lieutenant's terse reply.

"Yes, Sir." A hundred yards away the mechanical robot dropped the plastic explosive close to the tipped over truck and then maneuvered itself to begin its lonely march back to the Humvees. Its battery of cameras was now focused back towards the column of parked vehicles. It became the only reliable witness to the events that unfolded.

Three streaks of fire scorched across the desert air to incinerate the sniper teams perched on the roof tops. The radio erupted with panicked calls as did the mind of Burns Gomez. He was right! It was a trap. The militia had RPGs hidden in the truck!

"Specialist! Fire the charge! Take out that fuckin' truck!" he screamed.

The Specialist hit the remote control button that activated the explosives the Rover had just laid. He heard the BOOM! and felt the dull thump! in his chest. The video monitor went fuzzy for a moment and then came back clear. The little armored robot had survived a very close detonation. It kept on trucking towards the 555th's position.

"6-2, 2-overwatch! You copy?"

No response.

"82nd sniper teams...east or west...you copy?"

No response.

"Roylance! Gomez!" He screamed in his mike.

"Roylance!" came an equally worried voice.

"SitRep?"

"No contact with snipers east or west! My one and two squads are crawling through the rubble to look for survivors!"

"Shit!" thought Gomez. Just then he heard more chatter on the radio.

"Sir, they must have a helicopter! There is something over head. We're firing!" Though the man didn't acknowledge himself,

Gomez recognized him as one of the sergeants from second platoon.

Fifty yards away, the dedicated robot recorded the event for posterity. The flash of a Dragon rocket launcher streaked into the air in hopes of downing the 'helicopter.' The rocket missed and flew off into the dark sky. Seconds later three balls of flame descended from the pitch black sky.

Gomez saw the Humvees from behind him light up. Seconds later, he could hear the cries for help on the radio and out loud. He was being hit from in front and behind, and if his panicked sergeant was correct, possibly from above. It was his worst nightmare. Ambushed from three directions and he had no clue where they were coming from. He had to accept the truth. His command was cut off and out maneuvered. He needed to get help and pass on his command code if he were to be taken.

Dispensing with code name protocol and chain of command, he called the only trusted person within radio earshot who wasn't totally fucked.

"Hickman, this is Gomez!"

"Go ahead, boss," replied the loyal sergeant.

"I'm a broken arrow," an awful admission by any commander. It meant that your command had been compromised. "Call Battalion. Get us air support! Get us armored support! Code word is Darius. You copy?"

"Yes, Sir! Code word Darius. What about us, sir? We can be there in one minute!"

"Negative! Do not advance! You will wait for air and armored support and then advance from the south side. Understood, Hicks?"

There was a long pause before the Staff Sergeant acknowledged, "Yes, sir."

Gomez had possibly signed the death warrant for everyone in the firing line. It would be fifteen minutes before the air support would arrive and longer for the armor. He couldn't be sure, but from the decimation around him, he had already lost the better part of one of his platoons and the platoon from the 82nd Airborne wasn't in much better shape. He had quickly decided that it was better to lose 2/3rds of the best IED killers in Iraq than to sacrifice his last operational platoon in a futile effort to save the rest. Like a Captain going down with his ship, there was a part of him that hoped he wouldn't survive to witness the consequences of his decisions.

By now all hopes of command and control seemed lost. Three of his Humvees in the rear of the column were in flames. Survivors of the attack were pouring out of the flaming vehicles. Some who were on fire hit the ground and rolled around in a panic hoping to snuff the flames before the flames snuffed them. In the background he could hear radio traffic from his third platoon calling Battalion for support. Erratic and undisciplined gunfire began erupting in all directions. From the report of the rifles he could tell that it was his men spraying the surrounding area hoping enough lead might kill or suppress the unseen attackers.

"ROTH!" Gomez yelled. "Did we lose both Dragons?"

Trying to control his own shock and horror, the Master Sergeant quickly surveyed the smoky flaming scene, "No, sir! Over there!"

Gomez followed the Sergeant's outstretched hand, "I see 'em. I'll tie in with them. You get everyone in the trucks. We are going to hop the boulevard and head back home. Concentrate your suppressive fire in that direction!"

"Done, Sir! Be careful!"

Gomez didn't respond. He just grabbed his M-4 service rifle and sprinted towards the Dragon team. He wasn't five strides away when he heard an explosion behind him and felt the blast from a wave of heat knock him to his face. As he shook the clouds out of his head he looked back to see the position he'd just left alight. Sgt. Roth and the young specialist were certainly dead or dying along with two more burning Humvees and God knows who else. He would have thought that more RPGs had been fired from the front but the flame and heat caused seemed more like a napalm strike. Napalm usually fell from above.

He stood up, put the thought of his dead soldiers behind him, and kept running towards his Dragon team. When he reached the team, they seemed completely stunned. They had a loaded rocket but had no clue what to do with it. Their Humvee was located close to a Humvee from the 82nd. There was a soldier standing in the turret of the Humvee screaming at the Dragon team.

Just about every soldier in an airborne unit had a personal set of night vision goggles. This man was no exception. The man was yelling and pointing above. Gomez guessed that he must have located the 'helicopter' that was attacking them.

"You there!" Gomez said to the turret gunner. Do you see him?"

"Yes, sir....But..."

"NO BUTS! Fire your weapon and my guys will aim off your tracer rounds!"

"But, Sir?"

"GODDAMNIT! Fire your weapon soldier!" With that the gunner from the 82nd began firing at his target. Every 5th bullet out of the fifty caliber machine-gun was a tracer round. At night a tracer looked like a laser beam streaking across the sky. Gomez shook his crew back to reality and gave them an order to follow, "Follow the tracers boys! Knock 'em out of the sky!"

Just then Gomez got a good look at the weapon that was killing off his men. It wasn't a rocket launcher, it wasn't napalm. It looked like a giant flame thrower. Unlike any other flame thrower he had ever seen, it appeared deadly accurate and had a range of over 100 feet. Flames shot from the sky and engulfed the gunner and the Humvee he fired from. The Gunner made no awful screams. The flame was so hot the man must have died instantly. Gomez hit the deck to hide from the heat.

When he looked up this time, he saw his Dragon team aiming at the source of the flame. Just as he felt hope that they might prevail, the real horror of the situation revealed itself. Two large serpentine heads emerged from the darkness and into the orange glow of the fiery surroundings. One grabbed the Dragon gunner, the other his assistant. With nothing left for defense but their own blood curdling screams of protest, each man was snapped in half by the powerful jaws of the beast. The real 'Dragon' had arrived.

The beast finally landed on terra firma and the rest of its atrocious form came into the light. The heads on the right and left seemed to be scanning its surroundings looking for more threats and victims. The head perched in the center focused all its attention on Lt. Burns Gomez. It drew to within inches of his face. The Dragon's eyes grew to slits and a gleeful grimace full of blood lust formed on its enormous mouth.

Gomez had lost his command. He had lost most of his men. Now it seemed that he had also lost his mind. He reached into his collar, threw his dog tags to the side, and grabbed his crucifix. He was determined not to lose his faith.

"The power of Christ protects me!" he prayed in a shaky voice. "The power of Christ protects me."

A voice came into his head. A dark voice. A voice he couldn't quench out by plugging his ears, "And who is this Christ, little man?" The Dragon reached out and snatched the tiny crucifix with its' giant birdlike claw. It held the little artifact into the glowing light of the fires and curiously glared at it. It then flung the crucifix into the nearest fire and looked at his victim again. "You will hold no other gods but me!"

"The power of Christ protects me," Gomez continued in a catatonic trance.

"Let me say this again...if you want to live. I won't begrudge you the gods you have worshipped in my absence but let's get one thing straight. I'm back now. This is my shitty little world and you are my shitty little people. You will hold no other gods before me!"

Gomez would have given his own life for his men and giving it to his God was only nobler. He continued his suicidal chant in the face of pure evil. "The power of Christ protects me!"

"Have it your way FOOL!" Azi Dahaka reared up all three of his head in preparation for incinerating 1st Lt. Bernard Gomez.

Gomez prepared his last prayer, "Dear Lord, accept my sacrifice! Forgive me my sins and protect my family." Showing what defiance and courage he had left, he stared into the devilish eyes preparing to kill him.

All three heads inhaled air that would soon become fire. Just as they seemed ready to strike, their attention snapped. One by one each vicious head of the beast looked off into the distance. It was hard to see emotion in the devilish faces of Azi Dahaka but the middle one seemed to take on a look of astonishment. Gomez clearly heard the devilish voice in his head one last time, "Kirsasp?" And just like that the Dragon forgot about his prey. Unfurling its unholy wings from its grotesque body, the Dragon lifted from the ground and flew off into the night sky. Gomez collapsed to the ground and began to cry.

Chapter 44

BECAUSE THE IRANIANS hadn't brought a mechanical pump to help with the fuel transfer, the job was reduced to a backbreaking effort. They had to manhandle the 55 gallon drums to the roof of the crew carrier, then run a hose between the can and the plane, and let gravity do the rest. It was fortunate for Erik that the Iranians had to get the fuel off their truck in order to make room for their shipment, otherwise he feared they may have just loaded up their stuff, dumped the fuel and been off. Erik didn't have to do much manual labor, he mostly supervised, but he was still regretting slugging a beer and a flask of whiskey. While it calmed his nerves when he was certain of sure death, the buzz wore off in about an hour and now he was more tired than before he'd taken his nap.

While exhaustion tugged on his eyelids, he dared not fall asleep with fifteen armed men crawling about his airplane. He kept himself awake with small talk. It turned out that Rahnny knew English very well and was able to converse without the aid of spitting and hacking.

"I've seen the F-14s the Republican Guard keeps in their hangers. Very impressive aircraft. Was this the plane you flew?" asked Rahnny.

"Oh, no. I flew a C-2. It's like the updated version of this guy," he replied patting the Pegasus on the hull.

"You mean a guy with your courage didn't fly a fighter?"

"Yeah, well that's kind of a long story. I was second in my class...had I been first I could have picked my own plane."

"Second? That's still pretty good. They still didn't give you a jet?"

"Navy politics. I was a ninety day wonder. A shake and bake officer. They like to save the fighter planes for the Academy and ROTC guys."

"Wow! Too bad."

"Ahh. I did Ok. I got a lot of medals." Erik shrugged defensively.

"Really?" Rahnny said, surprised to hear a cargo pilot could win medals in the American Navy. "What medals?"

"Well, they give you one for graduating from basic," Erik cocked an eyebrow and looked in the air thinking about the medals he had. "Then I got one for learning how to shoot a pistol...one for shooting a rifle...'course that one was cheating. My dad taught me how to do that when I was 12." He thought some more. "Then I got one for delivering supplies to Iraq...oh yeah and then the Tsunami."

"Really?" Rahnny seemed shocked. "Weren't those things just part of your job?"

"Navy has a medal for everything". Erik chuckled. "It's all image. If you ever become an Admiral, you are supposed to have like twenty of the damn things splattered all over your chest. The press never bothers to ask if it was for rescuing an overboard sailor or getting an A+ on your typing exam."

Rahnny threw his hands up in disbelief.

"I can't believe it! You mean you have all those medals and you have none for bravery?"

Erik gave him a wry smile.

"Actually, I do have one."

"I knew it. A man with your balls has to have a medal! What is it?" Rahnny exclaimed satisfied.

"I have the Distinguished Flying Cross." Thinking back on the incident made Erik laugh inside.

"Of course! What was it for?"

"The letter read something like 'delivering urgently needed medical supplies to the carrier, George Washington, while at night with seas heavy enough to suspend all flight operations,' or something like that."

"Oh, my God! To land on a ship must be frightening enough. To do it in such conditions? I can only imagine."

"Actually, it was in broad daylight and the seas were calm." Erik finally laughed out loud as he thought back to the incident.

"I don't understand?" Rahnny asked and looked at him confused.

Still laughing, Erik continued.

"The 'urgently needed medical supplies' were actually a case of fifteen year old Ladaigh scotch. The Admiral had a penchant for Islay and I happened to know where to get it on the cheap."

There was a long dumbfounded pause as Rahnny considered this. He then broke out in laughter.

"Hunter is right! You are a sneaky slimy son of a bitch! You were born to smuggling my friend. I hope we can do more business."

Erik was hoping to never have to make such a risky arduous journey again but he was happy to play along so as not to get shot. As the conversation went on, a darkness enshrouded the starlit scene from above. Almost everyone at the plane was on edge immediately. The darkness lasted only momentarily but everyone's eyes went skyward.

"What the hell was that?" called Hunter.

"Spy plane maybe?" offered Rahnny.

"No way...too big. And even the B-2 makes noise when it's that close," responded Hunter.

"What the hell was what?" Erik was as confused as the others.

Chapter 45

"KIRSASPMON OH COME de mon. Kirsaspmon
oh come de mon." Lee had been chanting this over
and over for the last fifteen minutes as Jonesy and
Sam stood by expectantly, waiting for their parts to begin. Hugh
and Summer stood in the background filming and delivering
hushed commentary. Lee had finished the summoning circle
and had started a small campfire in its center. As the summoner,
his was the voice of the proceedings, chanting the summons to
the long dead hero. He was also the conductor. When he felt
the magical energy was right he would direct Sam and Jonesy to
begin their respective tasks.

After a moment and without breaking his concentration or his
monotonous chant, he signaled to Sam. Sam carefully stepped
into the circle being careful not to disturb the carvings Lee had
etched into the dirt. In his mouth, he carried the pottery shard
Cheddar had sent them. Cheddar had believed that it may have
once been a possession of the long dead hero. Sam dropped the
shard into the fire and then retreated.

Then Lee motioned to Jonesy to begin his task. Careful not
to disturb any carvings, Jonesy stepped towards the fire with the
struggling cock in one hand and the knife in another. Sacrifice
was something that neither he nor Lee had ever performed but
he rationalized his actions with the fact that chicken was a large
part of his diet. His experience as a fisherman had taught him to

slaughter an animal as efficiently as possible. With a deft wielding of his knife he lopped off the head of the cock letting it fall into the fire. He turned the body upside down letting the blood drain onto the ground beside the fire. Then slicing the feet from the lifeless body he dipped the feet into the puddle of blood. Tossing the carcass into the fire with a quick prayer he then exited the circle.

With Lee still in his trancelike chant, Jonesy dabbed his forehead with the chicken's bloody talon. Then it was Sam's turn for the same treatment. Finally, Jonesy dabbed his own forehead. The three were now ready for the final moment.

"Kirsasp, hear our chant," Lee said.

In unison all three chimed in.

"Kirsasp, hear our chant!"

"Kirsasp, hear this bell!" then Sam grabbed the dinner bell in his snout and began a rhythmic ringing.

"Kirsasp, follow the light!" Jonesy lit the old propane lantern.

"Kirsasp, come to us!"

Hugh was busy capturing the whole thing on film. If he believed that it would work at all he certainly was not prepared for how it would work. There was no waiting around. The second after Lee made the last call, a figure emerged from the flames. The man was average sized by modern standards but standing 6'0" 3000 years ago must have made him a giant. He strode forward wearing nothing but a loin cloth, a leather helmet and thick fur boots. In his right hand he carried two spears and in his left he carried a circular wooden shield. Strapped in a belt that was draped over his shoulder was a short bronze Roman looking sword. If Hugh hadn't been witness to the Chupacabra, the Imoogi, Azi Dahaka, and a myriad of UFO sightings, he would have thought a gay stripper had stepped from the flames.

The arrival of Kirsasp so suddenly pulled Lee and the others from their trance and back to reality. Kirsasp pranced forward with an arrogant pride that only a hero from 3000 years ago could pull off. He walked forward and stepped easily out of the summoning circle. Lee, Sam, and Jonesy knew exactly what that meant. Their spell was powerful enough to call Kirsasp but not control him. Lee immediately began thinking of a plan B.

"Bla Bla Bla! Pendejo! Bla Bla Bla!" cried the long dead hero.

"He wants to know why you have called him," said Summer.

"You can understand him?" asked Sam, surprised that Summer may actually prove to be useful.

"Yes. I can hear his thoughts, sense his emotion, feel his pain," Summer replied emotionally.

With Kirsasp so easily striding beyond the influential grasp of the summoning circle, Lee wanted to quickly inform him that they meant no harm. "Well, tell him we are friends!"

"I'm a psychic not a telepath! I can hear his thoughts but I can't send my own."

Angrily Sam barked, "Is there anything on this earth psychics are good for?"

"Azi Dahaka!" Lee said quickly. He hoped that the long dead hero would understand.

"His pain makes him violent!" cried Summer as Kirsasp began to ready a spear to throw at Lee.

"Azi Dahag?" continued Lee hoping to get it right this time. The problem with written languages that date back that far was that no one had a clue how they actually were spoken.

Kirsasp was ready to throw the spear just as everyone heard the flapping of the wings overhead. How the Dragon had arrived so fast was a mystery. It must have sensed his eternal foe's rise from the dead.

Kirsasp broke eye contact to look skyward. As he saw his foe circle above, a devilish grin came across his face. There was no more glorious enterprise for a hero of ancient Persia than to fight a worthy opponent. There was no more worthy opponent than a dragon. Kirsasp, a veteran of two previous dragon fights had already known victory and glory as a Dragon Slayer. And now an opportunity had come yet again to slay a dragon. Not just any dragon, this. No, this was Azi Dahaka!

Through the green illumination of the night vision camera lens, Hugh was the first to catch a glimpse of the Dragon. The shock of the beast coming into view was instant and immobilizing. Hugh's first encounter with this creature had been so unexpected that he had relied on survival instinct alone without regard to consequences. Now those consequences seemed all too real. Hugh was a young man used to feeling confident in himself; athletic enough to be a world class climber, talented enough to be a highly regarded videographer, and tenacious enough to be a quality journalist. But now at the moment of truth, he was the least qualified person in the group; the only one without magical talents and psychic skills. He pulled his eyes from the horror emerging in the camera and stared across the orange glow of the campfire. He could see Sam tucking his tail between his legs and cowering behind Lee. Even that scared dog had a better chance of surviving than he did, thought Hugh.

Just then Hugh felt a hand grab the back of his shirt. It was Summer. She had grabbed him and with a force of strength only possible in such moments of terror, she flung him away from the fire towards the stream bank. When he rolled to a stop, Hugh could feel the heat from the blaze the Dragon had lit. Desperately he flailed around until he felt Summer. Returning the favor he grabbed her and pulled her closer into the safety of the bank.

"Are you okay?" he stammered.

"Yes, but where are the others?"

There was no way to know. Where the two had stood moments before was engulfed in flames. The Dragon had arrived with a vengeance. Like an old west gunslinger arriving to the shootout with guns blazing, the Dragon was spitting forth fire in all directions.

Fortunately for Lee and Sam, Jonesy had taken no chances on this possible second encounter with the Dragon. He had carefully researched and enchanted amulets for each to wear around a necklace, or dog collar. The amulets would protect them from the effects of fire. The effect made the heat from the Dragon less of an inferno and more like a slow burn. Even with the added protection, they had little time to escape the flames before being overwhelmed.

"To da reever!" Screamed Jonesy, his Korean accent more pronounced in times of stress.

Lee knew that there was nothing more he could do here but die. Jonesy was right. They needed to retreat to safety and hope that Kirsasp would do what needed done. He and Sam followed Jonesy to the river bank to seek shelter from the fight. It was that or become collateral damage in a fight that had been brewing for three thousand years.

With the wizards gone, there was nothing to interfere with destiny. Azi Dahaka darted his right and left heads two and fro searching for hidden threats while his center head kept its eyes firmly focused on Kirsasp. Kirsasp's focus was singular. In his mind there was only one thing before him. His destiny.

"Who are you!" bellowed the voice of the Dragon in Kirsasp's mind.

Kirsasp puffed his chest out, struck a heroic pose, and spoke in a language long ago forgotten. "I'm the greatest warrior the world has ever known!"

The unapologetic boastfulness brought a wry smile to the Dragon's face, "Cocky, aren't you?"

"There is no arrogance in fact, wyrm."

Azi Dahaka began to chuckle. He held out the pearl that had entombed his sole for so many millennia, "So you plan to trap me again? This pearl is mine now! No one is going to put me back in it. The pearl is mine and so is this world!"

"I'm not going to trap you, demon; I'm going to kill you."

The Dragon began to chuckle loudly, then it began to laugh. Its heads swayed to the right and left and began to inhale preparing for the strike. Then Dahaka felt a sharp burning pain. He looked at his left shoulder and saw one of Kirsasp's spears buried deep in his flesh. The burning pain quickly turned to rage and rage turned to hate.

"Die, you filthy CURR!" he bellowed as he unleashed his fire.

Kisasp ducked behind his shield. No amount of flame or acid could penetrate the shield for it was made from the hides of other dragons, slain ages ago. Kirsasp the Dragon Slayer knew his trade well. Under the cover of his shield he inched his way forward through the flames.

Dahaka's rage had played into Kirsasp's plan. Spitting fire from all mouths at once meant that they all needed to breathe in unison as well. The moment the Dragon's flame let up, Kirsasp jumped from the cover of his shield and flung his second spear. The spear traveled true, impacting the jaw of the Dragon's left head and traveling through to the brain. The head immediately went limp and fell lifeless.

Panicked and out of breath, the Dragon spun its body around to attack Kirsasp with its enormous spiked tail. Most attacked by this monstrous tail either jumped to safety or died trying. Not so the mythical Dragon Slayer. With poise and agility Kirsasp leapt onto the tail like a puma leaping on a tree limb. Slowed by a lifeless head flopping around like a dislocated arm, Dahaka's remaining heads desperately tried to snap at the warrior and pluck him from the tail.

Knowing there was little time before heads and tail coordinated their efforts, Kirsasp leapt to the ground. The Dragon had made another critical mistake. He had brazenly displayed the root of his power. It was now time to get that pearl.

Shoving aside the lifeless head, the warrior darted under the belly of the beast and unsheathed his sword. As he prepared to pry the pearl from the mighty claw, gaping jaws and yellow eyes forced him to duck as the monster struck at him. Lying flat on the ground he looked up to see the legs of the beast intentionally buckling as Dahaka prepared to crush Kirsasp under his weight.

With lightening reflexes, Kirsasp rolled out from under the beast just as Dahaka belly flopped onto the ground. There was no more time to waste. Kirsasp sprung to his feet, gathered his posture and hacked with great force at the mighty claw guarding the pearl. There was a shrill cry as Azi Dahaka recoiled in pain, but before losing the initiative Kirsasp swung again, this time severing the claw from the once mighty demon.

Inside the Dragon awoke the Imoogi. Writhing in pain and haunted from the horrible dream that had been its recent life, the kind hearted soul became clearly aware of its surroundings once again. It could see the monstrous form it had become slowly shrinking in size and malevolence as it began to return to its previous form.

Kirsasp did not go for the kill quite yet. It was obvious from the shrill scream that the Dragon had lost more than just a claw. The pearl was its source of power. It had to be destroyed before the creature could be finished. He kicked the orb from the lifeless claw and it rolled to a stop not far away. It glowed in the darkness. The surface of the shiny pearl seemed to catch more than the flicker of light from the nearby fires, more that the reflection of the stars and the moon, it seemed to glow from within. As he approached, he took a stance of strength and prepared to strike the pearl with his sword. Only a force as great as his could crush such an object as strong as the pearl. With one swing he smashed the pearl to dust.

There was one last shrill cry from the monster and then silence. Kirsasp turned expecting to see a lifeless Dragon. Instead he saw something quite different. Lying on the ground was a creature of much smaller stature. It had only one head not three. Its body was serpentine and elegant, not an ugly amalgam of monstrous parts. It had a mane that seemed to shimmer in all the colors of the rainbow. Its eyes were a clear blue even in the dim orange firelight. The face wore a sad childlike expression. It seemed a beautiful creature made pathetic with its disheveled main, missing one paw, and bloodied ear that had been half torn off.

The Dragon Slayer's first thought was to spare this poor creature. It looked harmless and sad, not vicious at all, but it was this pitiable appearance that gave the creature away. The missing hand, the bloodied ear, and most of all Kirsasp's own spear still imbedded in its left shoulder. This had indeed been the same creature that had held the pearl. It was Azi Dahaka!

Kirsasp walked forward and picked up his spear that now lay on the ground. Not until this creature was dead could he claim his kingship of the world. Nothing would stand in the way of his destiny.

"Noooo!" cried Jonesy. With the orb gone, the spirit of Azi Dakaka had left the once possessed Imoogi. Now it was just a scared little creature missing an ear and a hand. The Imoogi knew it was going to die. Kirsasp's expression made that clear. He wanted more than to vanquish the beast. He wanted a trophy. And one claw was not enough to satisfy his quest for glory.

Jonesy did the only thing he could think of to prevent Kirsasp from killing the Imoogi. With his left hand he pulled out his whip and deftly snapped the spear away from Kirsasp's hand. With his right, he drew his revolver and fired into Kirsasp's flesh.

Jonesy had put too much faith in the protection glyph Lee had scarred on his body. Kirsasp was more than a zombie, more than a vampire. Kirsasp was the savior of the world and as such, mortal weapons were no more than an annoyance. The bullets made him wince slightly but did little more. With the second attack from the whip, Kirsasp grabbed the leather striker and pulled it from Jonesy's hand. He then unsheathed his sword from its scabbard and advanced towards Jonesy.

Disarmed, Jonesy mustered all the magical might he had left in his soul to throw a fireball in the hero's face. The impact was no more than a slap as Kirsasp continued his advance. Bravely, Jonesy knew he was soon to die but happily accepted this fate to protect one of his countries' historical treasures. Dahaka was gone, now the Imoogi must live.

Chapter 46

THE EXPLOSIONS OF fire by the riverbank had signaled to everyone at the Pegasus that there must have been an air strike. Most immediately assumed napalm but no one knew for sure. Taheri's Iranian friends had just finished loading the truck and weren't willing to wait around to see what happened. In their minds, the attack was meant for them and they had been lucky that the plane missed its target.

The exact same conclusions were bouncing around Erik's suddenly alerted mind. But he couldn't spool up his engines and fly off as quickly as the Iranians could drive off. The other difference was that the people he had delivered to this desolate wasteland were camped down by that river and he could not just leave them without at least trying to help.

"Hunter, let me borrow one of those jeeps!" he yelled.

"Sorry, buddy," the agent said coldly, "but we are out of here! Hop in and we will try to get you out of the country!"

It was a nice gesture but to Erik not good enough. If you grew up in a rural area you pulled over and helped anyone in need even if they were a complete stranger. And the people in need at that river bank were no strangers. There was no way he was going to drive off without at least trying to help. He had only one ace up his sleeve. Erik hopped in Hunter's jeep, reached into the cargo pocket of his shorts and pulled out a grenade. He had seen this trick in a movie once and thought it might come in handy. Luckily he had pulled the pin before he was shot dead.

"Alright," he said. "Everyone in favor of going down to the bank stay with me. Everyone opposed GET THE FUCK OUT OR I'LL BLOW US ALL TO HELL!!"

With that subtle cajoling, everyone except Hunter jumped from the jeep and into another vehicle. Hunter was stunned at Erik's display of loyalty to the crew at the river.

"Here you go," Erik said as he handed Hunter the grenade. The spy gingerly grasped the grenade being careful not to let the spoon go flying.

"Why don't we swap seats?" Erik said still holding on to the pin.With a live grenade a sneeze away from detonation, Hunter gingerly complied. The other vehicles were a dust trail by now and alone in the starlit darkness Erik said, "Toss it!" as he floored the gas and charged towards the river. Hunter threw the grenade far off into the brush as the jeep lurched forward.

Chapter 47

A S KIRSASP LEAPT forward immune from Jonesy's attack, Lee and Sam entered the fray. Lee touched an almost forgotten scar on Sammy's hind quarter and said, "Swarm."

Sam's individual mind immediately turned into a million as his seventy pounds of dog turned into seventy pounds of fire ants. The million ants immediately swarmed Kirsasp's legs in a desperate attempt to slow him down. The Sam swarm bit with every spicy pincher it could muster but to no avail. Kirsasp, immune from the painful bites shook off the Sam swarm and continued.

Lee then touched a scar on his own left arm and cried, "Shield!" He then leapt between Kirsasp and Jonesy and held out his left arm. Kirsasp pulled up sword and hacked at Lee cleaving a deep gash to the bone. Lee winced in pain and fell to the ground as Kirsasp continued his advance. Magic had no effect on him. In agony, Lee painfully looked up to see Kirsasp plunge his sword into Jonesy's shoulder.

With a sword in his shoulder, Jonesy reeled back and fell to the ground. It was obvious that no magic he or Lee possessed could stop this undead avenger. He scrambled back in fear until the trunk of a tree stopped him. Exhausted, he could go no further. He would have to wait for the final blow knowing that once he was dead, the hero of Zorastrian myth would kill the only Imoogi known to exist. In his eagerness to revive Korea's and perhaps the world's, great hope he had destroyed the only creature that could make that happen. Sam Do Soo had failed his life's destiny.

As Kirsasp grasped his sword and lifted it with both hands, Jonesy saw a light shine upon the hero, a light that made the ancient warrior even more frightening. Kirsasp was aglow with triumph. A mighty hero from old come to avenge the misdeeds of those who had hoped to make a better world. And just like that Kirsasp was hit by a jeep. The body was thrown a good twenty feet into the air and smashed into a tree. It was hard to tell if the cracking noise they heard was from bones or branches but when the body hit the ground, it did not move again.

Lee sat up clutching the wound on his left arm. Sam was Sam again panting in exhaustion. They looked over at the broken tree trunk and at the body lying at its base. Then Lee looked at Jonesy who was staring at the scene with his mouth open in shock.

"What the FUCK!" cried Erik as he jumped from the jeep.

"You hit somebody!" yelled Hunter

"Oh, shit! Is he okay?"

"Dude, I don't think so."

"Oh shitohshitohshit! I can't fuckin believe this!"

"Dude, chill out. This is Iran. Hit and runs aren't a big deal here." Hunter tried to sound casual.

"Well, it's a BIG DEAL TO ME!" screamed Erik.

"Dude! He looks like Tarzan!" Hunter exclaimed as he went over to look at the body.

"Oh, fucking thank you for that! I just killed the last known survivor of a long dead Iranian tribe! Now not only am I wanted by the law…I'm wanted by hippies employed by National Geographic! I can't fuckin believe this!"

Lee started laughing in relief knowing that the only person who could have solved their problem had shown up at the right place at the right time.

Epilogue

One month later

"LEE, YOU'VE ALWAYS been one for a good story," Ardi said as he finished his tiera miso. As promised, Jonesy and Lee had brought Ardi to Italy to treat him to an Italian meal but rather than Florence, Lee had suggested a place he knew in Cordona that served an elegant Italian meal fit for Caesar himself.

"Well, the sad part of all this is that it is true, Ardi." Jonesy said.

"Sure, sure," said Ardi. "and I'm really Prince Charles."

"Well, believe what you will, Ardi, but without your help, I'm not sure either of us would be here enjoying this meal with you." said Lee. He had tried to fill Ardi in on the truth of what had happened even though he knew his friend was a skeptic.

"Well, I'm glad to have been of help, even if I doubt that the situation was quite as dire as you've made it out. I'm just sorry you lost the orb through all this. I would have loved to have seen that. Still the parchment is exquisite. I shall be studying that for some time, I should think. Jolly good of you fellows to allow me to be the one to decipher it. It will most likely be the subject of a publication, but I promise to give you full credit for the find, Jonesy."

"I'm not sure I care at this point, Ardi, but I am most interested in reading what you write about it."

"No reason we can't collaborate on it you know, boys."

"Tell you what, Ardi. Keep us in the loop and when you have it worked out, let us know. Maybe we'll be more ready to join in on your efforts then. Right now, I think Jonesy and I need time to decompress. I'm thinking Sam and I will go to my place in Colorado to watch the aspen change colors."

"That sounds delightful, but I shall keep you up to date on my findings."

"That's good enough for me," said Lee. "Jonesy, you up for spending the fall in the Rocky Mountains? You are welcome you know."

"I'd love to, Lee, but I think I shall stay close to home and my new friend, Cho Joo-Eun." Jonesy had adopted his Imoogi friend and didn't want to stay away from her for long.

"Who?" Ardi asked then caught himself. "Oh, yes, the *Imoogi*!" He was clearly skeptical that such a creature ever existed but didn't want to argue with his friends. "Well, I shall be enjoying the fall in London as usual. But gentlemen, this was a fabulous dinner. My thanks to you both for such a special treat." he said as they all rose from the table to leave.

They took the train to Florence where they spent the night and in the morning, Lee escorted his friends to the airport for their respective flights home. Lee and Sam headed back to Manarola to begin packing for a trip to the States.

Hugh and Summer went back to their lives and **Truth Seekers**, wiser for their adventure but not fundamentally changed. They both secretly hoped Lee would include them in any other adventures he had in the future.

Erik finally got past his shock at having run over the tribal guy. He still felt bad that it had happened but everybody else kept congratulating him. He had come to like these folks but they were strange folk. Still, he had agreed to be on a retainer for Lee so that he would come when called. When he thought over the whole thing, he decided it was more fun than delivering Cheez-its.

Larissa was doing well on her antipsychotic medication. Her therapist believed that in time she would remember the attack as the terrorist attack that it really was rather than the "dragon" attack she believed it to have been. Her friend, Latham, was relieved and he and Larissa had decided they would no longer need the diversion of Furry conventions to seek excitement. They had decided to be married and that seemed to be a full time challenge in itself.

Lt. Gomez returned home and joined the priesthood. He knew he had been literally saved from the jaws of hell. Henceforth, his life would be devoted to his Savior.

Other survivors of the Dragon's vengeance were in the process of denial, some in therapy and many of them in physical rehabilitation as well. The nightmares would continue for a long time.

Cho Joo-Eun returned to her cave in the sea, but she wasn't going to be lonely anymore. She had lived a nightmare and hoped she would never endure it again but she had made a friend, Dr. Sam. She knew he would see her as often as he could and she thought she could help him too, so he wouldn't be so lonely. She even found that she liked Cheez-it's a lot!